The
WISDOM
of RAIN

To: Nadira

The
WISDOM
of RAIN

A bit of Guyanese wisdom!
Enjoy!
Eleanor P. Sam

ELEANOR P. SAM

IGUANA

Copyright © 2019 Eleanor P. Sam
Published by Iguana Books
720 Bathurst Street, Suite 303
Toronto, ON M5S 2R4

Publisher: Meghan Behse
Editor: Holly Warren
Front cover design: Daniella Postavsky

978-1-77180-319-9 (paperback)
978-1-77180-322-9 (hardcover)
978-1-77180-321-2 (epub)
978-1-77180-320-5 (Kindle)

This is an original print edition of *The Wisdom of Rain*.

To the ancestors whose incredible fortitude helped them survive the terrible journey across wretched seas to Demerary's soil; and to all those who came after them — my large, extended family.

PREFACE

This story takes place in another land, and in another time; a time that was more brutal and less humane than our own. However, it is also *my* land because I grew up on a sugar plantation in Demerara. I did not know or appreciate its history fully until writing *The Wisdom of Rain*. This book is rooted in my own experience of the echoes and legacies of slavery and the contemporary and more subtle forms of oppression, neglect, and diminution that continue to press on the lives of Black people. As the writing journey evolved, my struggles and pain were slowly given perspective and complemented by a deep respect, admiration, joy, and love for my previously unknown ancestors. The brave souls whose grit and resolve saw them through the Middle Passage and plantation life and death became like a new family to me. As I explored and learned their histories and suffering, which paved the way for my own better life, healing and gratitude began to replace bitterness and grievance. In their survival I have gained the choices and freedom they were denied.

Alice Walker said it best: "I think writing really helps you heal yourself. I think if you write long enough, you will be a healthy person. That is, if you write what you need to write, as opposed to what will make money, or what will make fame."

This book came together with the considerable help of many people, and I am sincerely grateful to all of them. Yashin Blake read a very early draft of the manuscript and provided me with sound, generous, and enormously helpful feedback. Wendy Blain read a draft and her feedback connected me with expert advice. As the ancestors spoke, Glynis Crawford helped me translate the Mende and Temne phrases. David Bester at StartWriting.ca got me started on this journey and Martin Townsend and Jennifer McIntyre edited early drafts. Meghan Behse and the team at Iguana Books took over and brought the manuscript to fruition.

I am blessed to have the most loving, supportive, and patient husband and partner, Walter Heinrichs. His ideas, contributions, and reading of the manuscript from early to final version made this novel possible. Thank you for your unceasing love and for being an unwavering champion of this endeavour.

I would also like to acknowledge the research done for this work, which was grounded in multiple sources, including the International Slavery Museum, Liverpool, England; Emilia Viotti da Costa's Crowns of Glory, Tears of Blood: The Demerara Slave Rebellion of 1823; and Trevor Burnard's Mastery, Tyranny, and Desire: Thomas Thistlewood and His Slaves in the Anglo-Jamaican World.

PROLOGUE

Mariama awoke to her favourite breakfast of hot cornmeal covered in creamy goat's milk, and steamed yams with fried egg stew. The porridge was smooth, just how she liked it — not a lump in sight. She savoured and swallowed every last bit, then she turned to the eggs, which were cooked in a buttery fat from the goat's milk and combined with sweet peppers and thyme from the village garden.

As Mariama took her last bite, young Braima appeared in the breakfast nook of the hut, rubbing his eyes, his face still rumpled from sleep.

"Go wash your face or no pap for you," Mariama teased her only sibling.

"And don't look at *YahYah* for help."

"You hear your sister … go wash, and then come and eat. Today is a happy day," Yenge grinned at both her children.

Braima ran out to the back of the hut, quickly splashed water from the earthen pot on his face and sprinted back inside. He rejoined his sister just in time to hear his mother's speech.

"You are almost a woman, my dear daughter. Soon you will go to Sande lessons, and we will celebrate *nda hiti* — your being made ready. And before you know it, we will have much merrymaking upon completion of your initiation into womanhood — *ti sande gbua*. For that occasion, I have another gift, but for now, I give you your own special lappa; a first symbol of womanhood." Yenge hugged her only daughter, smiled, and tied the blue and yellow cloth around her child's hips with much pride. "Step back. Let me see how beautiful you look. The colours suit you very well," she added. Mariama heard the tremor in her mother's voice and noticed the tears in her eyes. "It will go nicely with the cowrie shell necklace your father purchased at the market for you," she continued.

"You know, Mariama, when you came into this world, it was a very special time. It was the end of the sixth month of the year. The dry season was over in the savannah and the farmers were waiting for the wet season to begin — but the rains stayed away. You came to us after many, many moons of drought." She paused for a moment, wiped the tears from her eyes and then continued.

"You were the only baby born on the night of a very bright full moon. Just before the new day dawned, when my pain was most pressing, a reward arrived — you, my little baby girl. And so did the rain — it was like liquid silver that night, and every hut glowed in its light." Yenge's smile lit up her face, her eyes shining with the knowledge that something magical had taken place. "The village rejoiced that night for the gifts the gods had given us. Mariama, your name, which means 'gift of God,' became known to the elders as the 'rain baby.' Old Man Jaheem called you *Numui na ar waanjei* — the bringer of the rain. For this birthright you were held in high honour by everyone. And now, I am happy that my baby is turning into a woman." Yenge hugged her daughter one more time. She then picked up her woven raffia basket, left the hut, and walked over to the village garden to help the other women tend the crop.

PART I

CHAPTER 1

A GIFT OF THE GODS

June 1799

Mariama's heart felt light with joy. She was excited about this birthday and had woken up full of hope for all the good things the day would bring. After breakfast, she washed the dishes, took the palm leaf broom from the shelf on the kitchen wall and swept the entire hut. Braima finished his meal quietly, and he too began his daily task. He skipped down the short track of red dirt to the cattle pen, where he let out the six billy goats and four nanny goats. Then, passing through the clearing, he led them into the pasture to graze and joined the other young boys herding their sheep and goats, or pitching marbles in shady areas of the savannah.

Her chores complete, Mariama walked through the clearing and sat under her favourite tree — the baobab with the huge limbs and big, bushy leaves. She loved to sit in this place to think about important things. Today she thought about her upcoming Sande and initiation into womanhood.

It was her thirteenth birthday. Sande celebrations for her and the other four girls turning this magical age would begin soon. Like most Mende girls, Mariama had great expectations for this birthday

— the one that would complete her rite of passage to everything feminine and adult. She could only imagine all the secrets she would learn from the older women, such as how to be a good partner, wife, and mother, to how she might even become a female chief one day. In just a few days when the men came home from the marketplace, it would be time for the girls to leave the village to begin their secret lessons and then return for the celebrations: the drumming, the dancing, the feasting — lots of feasting. Her heart beat more rapidly in response to the pictures her imagination was painting and she shivered with the thrill of knowing that changes, big changes, were coming to her life, and soon.

There had been a buzz of activity as women prepared meals of corn and cassava and men repaired thatched roofs on some of the circular mud-daubed huts. Bursts of sunlight flooded the plain, and cumulus clouds dotted the blue sky as far as Mariama could see. The vegetation was lush and green from the recent rain. A temperate breeze was keeping the day relaxed and tolerable. Nature had joined in the preparations.

Leaning against the trunk of her beloved tree, Mariama closed her eyes and smiled as she daydreamed and listened to the excited voices nearby. Suddenly her reverie was shattered by rough grasping hands on her back and waist. A scream rose in her throat but was stifled immediately as one hand moved up to cover her mouth and nose.

She tried to break from the grip while struggling to breathe. Her attacker quickly lifted her slender body, kicking and squirming, into the nearby bush. Mariama's screams were muffled, and lost in the background noise of the village. Although other villagers were within earshot of this unfolding drama, no one could hear her. She could not see her captors or shake free of their iron hold.

In the concealment of the bush, he laid her down on her stomach. Straddling her slender body, he tied her hands behind her back and held her feet together. She could see a second man close by, securing the hands and feet of a young boy. It was Hindolo, from her village. He had a band wrapped around his mouth and tied in a knot at the back of his head.

Now a similar gag was being applied to her. By turning her head slightly, Mariama was able to see the faces of both captors. She recognized the eyes, now steely and heartless, of one of the men from a village about two miles away. He had come there many times to help her father and other villagers mend the damaged thatch on their roofs. She looked at him pleadingly; he looked back with empty eyes. The other man leaned in and carefully untied her hands and then Hindolo's, quickly linked Mariama's right hand to Hindolo's left and pulled both children to their feet. Their journey began.

CHAPTER 2

YOURS FOR THE TAKING

June 1799

"Wild animals, that's what they is mate," Edward Grimes had told him, jerking a thumb at the captives. "Use yer jolly nob; got to control them and beat them hard for the least insubordination. It's what will keep us safe. Don't be a clump, and let your guard down for even a second, or they'll rebel and take over the ship. Usually the blackamoors don't know or like each other, and most of 'em don't even speak the same tongue, so they can't gab to one another. It's what makes 'em easier to control. Back in their villages with their tribal wars, they'd sell each other to our mates to settle a score. It's how the merchants do their business — and that's how we get paid."

Not long after his introduction to the duties and privileges of slavery, they had docked on Gorée Island off Dakar, and once again Grimes had given him instruction. Taking John aside with a lewd grin on his face, he had pointed at a group of captive women sleeping on the women's deck and whispered, "T.J., this you should know, lad — those African wenches are always out for some. The sun causes their notch to heat up. So go on and help yourself. You'll be doing 'em a favour if you shag 'em. Helps cool 'em down."

He sniggered and continued, "Since you're new to this, you should go for the younger ones. They'd be easier for you to control and are usually up for it. In your case, you get to train 'em up, gaining more control as you go along. Blimey, my boy, I know you'll enjoy it. It's the most pleasure you will have on this ship, and you can take all you want. I can show you the best positions to control their bucking. You gotta tame 'em into submission."

Sensing John's hesitation, he frowned and then pulled him closer.

"T.J., my lad, these wenches like to be taken. They like a rough shagging. If they holler and fight, even better; it's all a part of the chase. Trust me, lad, they like it." He threw his head back, patted his bulging stomach, and chuckled again.

"You see," he continued, "they're not at all like white women, who expect to be wooed and handled with care. These wenches are accustomed to their men being in control. You know that many of them cling to one man, so the men have many women and call them their wives. But, they don't marry 'em like the English do. They just breed 'em for young ones, that's how it works, mate. Kin to them is like money to us — the more they get, the richer they feel."

"But … what if you leave 'em with a belly-full?" John interrupted.

"That's part of the game. The pickney becomes the property of the lucky plantation owner. It's not your responsibility. So, you lucky fella, go ahead and have as much fun as you can handle. It's your chance to practise, practise, and practise. Let's see if you can handle two queans tonight."

John looked at Grimes curiously.

"Did you say two? You can't mean…"

"Why not two? You're young … your pego can handle it," he said with a grin. "It should be sweet, me lad. Go on, now," he continued and gave John a gentle push. "Don't be shy, give it a try and see if you can double your pleasure … Just remember not to compete with the skipper, or you might be clawed-off." He winked at John and then walked to his station on deck.

John stood stunned where Grimes had left him. Was the skipper really a part of this debauchery too? *No,* he thought staunchly, *not the skipper.* The skipper was a stern and straightforward man. He would never lower himself to take advantage of one of the captive wenches, would he?

John's experience of women at that point was limited to a brief encounter with a prostitute at the Tarleton Street pub in Liverpool. He had never had any proper sexual relations with women, and he wasn't sure he wanted to start now. On the slave ship the women looked sad and frightened, their heads bowed, never making eye contact. He hadn't experienced them throwing themselves at men.

"Aye aye, sailor, get your arse in gear!"

It was the captain. John sprung to his feet. Offering a quick salute to the skipper, he hurried off to find Grimes. For the rest of his shift, he found it difficult to keep his mind on his work as he anxiously awaited nightfall.

CHAPTER 3

LEAVING PORT

June 1799

The ship sailed out of the river port. The red ensign flapped in the dry trade winds, signalling British-owned cargo was on board. Through the open hatch above, Mariama watched the gently swaying treetops pass by. Then there was nothing to see but the stream of daylight pouring in and parts of the ship's sails fluttering in the wind. A flight of squabbling seagulls, mostly white with patches of black on their wings, briefly circled overhead before darting off in unison, as if on their way to someplace important. Mariama learned about these creatures only from stories. Jaleel, an elder in her village of Yele, had told the children that these mysterious birds could fly across big rivers, rivers so big you could stand where the land ends and not see where it begins again.

A sudden terror came upon the young girl and her eyes widened in fear. Could she, like these seagulls, be travelling to some distant place, to be forever apart from her family and community? Hot tears welled up in her eyes. She squeezed them shut but it was of no use. Her knees felt weak; her legs began to shake and then gave way. Mariama sank into a ball on the rough wooden planks and joined in the wailing that rose from the hundreds of frightened voices around her.

With her eyes still closed, Mariama attempted to shut out the noise, and she desperately tried to conjure up her mother. "*YahYah, YahYah, YahYah!* Help me, *YahYah!*" she whispered. But she had been forced to walk many days away from her *YahYah*, who could not help her now.

From overhead came the sails' flapping sounds, as well as whistles, clanks, and noises she thought might be ropes being pulled and tightened. The old timber groaned as the flexing planks rubbed against each other. Mariama could feel the whole wooden prison of the ship shift as if in protest at its continuing departure from the shore. Her heart pounded fiercely.

"*Allahu Akbar!*" A man behind her shouted as he tried to lift his hands to the skies, but his gesture was cut short. Shackled to another captive, he could raise his arms only a few inches above his hips. A young man a few feet away grunted and thrust his body forward in a mindless effort to break free. He too was bound tight to another captive by wrist and leg shackles.

Amidst all the confusion, no one paid much heed as three burly crew members came down from above. Suddenly the sound of cracking whips interrupted the mayhem. The captives tried to scuttle away in every direction towards cover, but the lower deck was so crowded that there was no room to move. Crouching down in place was the best they could do.

Near the crew members was a slim Temne man about five and a half feet tall. He yelled out, as though trying to announce his presence, "Me Sule! Me Sule!"

The shortest of the three white men, with brownish hair and glinting green eyes, turned around, and in one quick jab of his right elbow smacked Sule hard in the face. A piercing, anguished howl escaped Sule's mouth and a gush of bright red blood shot out of his nose. As the blood washed over his lips, it was impossible to tell whether the blow had also damaged his mouth. Mariama felt her insides twist into a knot of sick revulsion as he stood there shackled and unable to mop away the tears and dripping blood mixing on his chin. "Me Ed Grimes," the crewman mocked. "You can call me Mr. Edward. Now shut your bloody gob!" He turned and spied Mariama.

"This one's a wench," he yelled out to his shipmates. He grabbed Mariama by the right shoulder and jerked her around to face him. She peered squarely into his eyes, which resembled those of the river crocodiles that sun themselves in the savannah grasses near her village. Mariama's breath caught in her throat. Then she looked away, mostly in fear, as he ogled her chest, naked above the lappa wrapped around her hips. "Puny apple dumpling shop," he smirked. He turned her away from him for a view of the other side and then shoved her towards the companion stairs leading to the upper deck.

"Shift your bob," he growled.

Mariama stood paralyzed, having heard the words but not knowing what they meant. She stared at him. Her paralysis frustrated him and he began to shout. "Don't just stand there glaring at me, you bloody numbskull. Shift it. Shift it, I said." With still no response from the girl, he seemed to have a sudden stroke of insight, threw his hands into the air and said, "Blimey ... you animals are dim-witted; you don't know the King's English or even each other's palaver for that matter!" Grimes sighed and rolled his eyes in frustration.

The young girl looked around, her eyes wide with fear. She wanted desperately to follow the crocodile man's orders but didn't understand them. Realizing this, Grimes pushed her again and steered her towards the stairs. Mariama began to climb with the weight of the leg shackles digging painfully into her ankles. She could feel the handle of his whip in the small of her back, prodding her forward, and his foul, damp breath on her neck as he followed close behind.

When she arrived on the middle deck, she saw other women and girls hunched together in one corner, none of them familiar to her. She immediately searched for a place within this group, but before she could find one, Grimes jerked her close again. Reaching around to cup her buttocks with his left hand, he squeezed both cheeks as he ogled her, a twinkle in his eyes. Mariama glanced uneasily at the older women for direction. No one looked back. Most looked down, discreetly but pointedly. Could they be showing her some kind of code? Not knowing why, she looked down too. Grimes released his grip and pushed her towards the other women.

She stumbled forward and took her place next to a young woman who looked a few years older. "Mariama," she whispered to the woman. But the woman looked past her without acknowledging what she'd said.

Mariama sat quietly for a few moments, feeling some reassurance from the presence of other women — some older than her, a few younger. But she also felt uneasy, not knowing where she might fit within this group of strangers.

CHAPTER 4

TRANSFORMED

July 1799

In the dark, on the hard wooden deck, Mariama lay and listened to the waves. She felt the gentle rocking of the SS *Archery*, as she had heard the crew call the monster vessel taking her farther and farther away from home. The *Archery* was a three-masted ship-rigged vessel, originally built to carry cargo; her keel was laid down in Liverpool in 1756. She weighed in at three hundred tons, with two decks rebuilt to carry slaves and a lower deck or hold to carry provisions and a cargo that might include rum, cloth, and dry goods, all housed in watertight barrels. The clearance was barely five feet on the slave decks and the atmosphere was stifling with the constant smell of human ordure. This was made worse by the poor ventilation, despite small portholes that pierced the ship's sides to provide fresh air. The captain's quarters were relatively spacious and occupied the rear section of the ship, with windows facing the stern and giving a view of the sea. Most crewmen slept on deck or in the forecastle in the bow of the ship.

Mariama had been forced to walk for four days with little rest to get to the ship. She was more exhausted than she had ever been. The only break in the relentless trek was when her group was handed over by their captors to white men somewhere along the way.

"*Tsaya, tsaya* — stop, stop," the group leader had shouted, raising his arms as though herding goats. Everyone stopped and waited for his next command. Out of the nearby bushes, three white men and a group of Africans emerged. Whispers between the two group leaders followed, and an exchange of bright-coloured beads that sparkled as beams of sunlight broke through the mass of trees and collided with them. Bales of bright-coloured cloth, cowrie shells — lots of them — and two small muskets were traded. A transfer of leaders took place and the previous captors disappeared into the bush.

"*Tafi, tafi* — go, go," the new leader screamed, and the abductors ushered the group to move forward. Mariama flinched as she thought about the interchange. For a fleeting moment, she had gotten lost in a daydream of riding a beam of sunshine through the trees, into the clouds, and back to her parents' compound, but the dream shattered upon the word "*Tafi.*"

Now, as she lay among these strangers, her thoughts returned to the events that had thrown her life into sudden uncertainty. For so many years she had looked forward to the birthday that signified ascent into true womanhood, recognized and celebrated by her community. But then, in a cruel split second under the tree in her village, everything had changed. Yes, she had reached that special age, but without her Sande ceremony it held little meaning and she remained a child.

She held her head to contain the storm of pain and disappointment exploding within.

A cool pocket of sea air descended from the companionway soothing her agitation as it touched her swollen and bruised feet; its salty freshness caressed her face, exposed shoulders, and aching back.

The familiar feel of the lappa around her waist reminded Mariama of the smile on her mother's face when she had given it to her. She welcomed the comforting memory. At that moment the garment brought her village briefly back to life, distancing her from her hostile surroundings. But the gentle comfort competed with her immediate anguish and the flow of her tears.

She tried to tuck her knees together to preserve the warmth she felt from the tender image, but her knees went smack into Khadija's backside. Khadija was a few years older than her, and the distance between them was only a few inches. Mariama quickly straightened both of her legs, but something or someone was now in the way.

Unseen rough hands suddenly grabbed her ankles and covered her mouth, interrupting her breath as it left her mouth. Was she reliving the experience of a few days earlier? Mariama's bulging eyes darted from side to side, trying to get a glimpse of the person unleashing this attack on her.

In one quick motion, she was lifted up from the wooden floor, and carried further into the ship. It was so dark that she could not tell who was carrying her slim frame with such urgency, only that her abductors were two men. She struggled and kicked, trying to break free of the powerful hands that were clamped around her waist and over her mouth and nose.

Half-suffocated, she jerked her head up to free her nose from the palm that covered it. The back of her head collided with the intruder's face. There was a startled gasp and an angry retort.

"Bloody wench! Nobody butts me. Bloody hell, T.J., this one is hog-wild. I'll show you how to tame a draggle-tail like this."

Mariama strained to understand what was being said, but many words were strange and unfamiliar and she missed the flow and meaning of the exchange between the men. Stunned by fear, her body shook involuntarily and her teeth clattered loudly.

The dim light in the galley revealed the rugged face of the short stubby white man — eyes gleaming, a devilish grin on his shadowed expression. Mariama caught a glimpse and squirmed in an effort to escape his tight grip.

Suddenly, she was thrust over a wooden barrel, the one the crew used for storing drinking water. Cold, coarse hands shoved her forward, and a firm hand on the small of her back kept her pinned in this position. A second later, the lappa placed there by her mother was ripped from her hips. She felt her bare buttocks exposed.

The battering violence that followed eclipsed any experience Mariama had ever had in her thirteen years of life. Something thick and unwanted was pushed into her, sending waves of excruciating pain radiating through her pelvis.

For what seemed like an eternity, she felt her slight frame take a fierce pounding from behind. Her now breathless attackers exchanged places several times, each one trying to outdo the other in ferocity. Feeling as though her body would split at any minute, Mariama wept and moaned in agony — for the second time in twenty-four hours.

The pressure of the assault forced her into the wooden barrel on which she was splayed until she felt melded into it — until she and the barrel were one. Slowly numbness began to replace the pain and her legs became limp, followed by her chest and then her arms. Mariama's head bobbed up and down as she gasped for air; the violence had exhausted her. She could feel her body slump across the barrel as everything wentblack.

"Bloody hell! We killed her, mate," said John. "She's dead, ain't she? She ain't breathing, is she? What a bloody cock-up!"

"Quiet, bloke! She's just out," said Ed Grimes. He was silent for a moment. "Let me think."

"What are we gonna do, mate?"

John paced around the barrel and rubbed his hands together.

"You keep a lookout and I'll put her back," Ed whispered. "Throw me her rag."

John kicked the lappa in Edward's direction and moved closer to the bow.

"Get a move on, bloke. The coast is clear," he whispered.

Edward quickly hoisted Mariama's limp and bloodied body onto his shoulders. Closely followed by John, he scuttled back to the section of the women's deck from where they had taken her earlier.

He set her down a few feet from the original spot and dropped the lappa next to her. The two men then hurriedly escaped to their sleeping quarters.

Satisfied that no one had seen them re-enter, they toasted each other with Grimes's hidden stash of diddle. Grinning with triumph, they clambered into their hammocks and turned in for the night.

John lay awake for a while mulling over what had just taken place. He felt a surge of new energy and he quietly muttered to himself, "Bloody hell, I am like the rest of the men now. I've had a wench, and it was fine. I am no longer afraid, and I'll know what to do next time. I am a sailor now, and a man." He smiled as his eyelids closed and he drifted off to sleep.

***

Thunder echoed across the dark skies, sounding like a stampede of zebra breaking through an invisible savannah in the clouds. The deep rumbling was accompanied by high whistling winds as white lightning cut into the gloom.

The rain poured down in torrents as the storm raged on, its fury fuelled by howling winds and crashing waves. Mariama's body rocked slightly as though in rhythmic response to all the elemental forces of nature. In her dreamlike stupor, she had a vision of something floating at the ship's bow, a silhouette, emerging and disappearing from view as the ship rolled in the waves.

Visible against the dark backdrop, the figure appeared to move in tandem with the ship as it tossed back and forth in the wind and the waves. A streak of lightning illuminated its now clearly female form. Though she was distant, Mariama could make out the woman's curves, but she was too far away for Mariama to see her face.

She recognized the silhouette as a *Sowei,* clad in full regalia of a wooden helmet mask with striking coiffure, and a long black raffia robe. Another flash of lightning and she was gone. Even in her trance, Mariama felt her body recoil from fear.

There was another peal of thunder, and suddenly the *Sowei* reappeared, floating now above the terrified young girl. The image moved closer, and through her fear Mariama noticed that the *Sowei* emitted a strange warmth. She reached out and softly stroked Mariama's hand. The touch was so tender that it immediately calmed the young girl's fears, and her body relaxed.

Now the *Sowei* moved even closer and began to console her by gently stroking her arms and shoulders, like a mother soothing a frightened child. As she did, she softly repeated, "*Tilongor abiay —* you are loved ... *bi nyandengor tao bi gbepengor* — you are beautiful and you are good ... *kpalee agelelor* — the pain will ease."

There was a familiarity, a knowingness, to the *Sowei*'s voice. Mariama studied the figure, trying her best to see the eyes of her soother through the mask, but she couldn't. Then, just as she had come into view, the *Sowei* floated away to the bow of the ship and into the still-raging thunderstorm. Mariama tried to follow the silhouette, but it disappeared from sight.

Moments later Mariama opened her eyes and found that the pain, though still present, was beginning to lessen. Remembering the ordeal she had been through, she began to sob, quietly at first, and then her sobs became more audible. "*YahYah, YahYah...*" she cried. "Help me, *YahYah!*"

Khadija, who had seen Mariama being returned, lay quietly and observed her for a while. Then, she quietly reached over, picked up the lappa and placed it over the young girl's hips. Drawing her closer, she stroked her head. It didn't matter that Mariama was from a Mende tribe and didn't speak the same tongue — she was hurt and needed care.

Mariama looked up at Khadija, tears rolling down her cheeks. She rested her head on Khadija's lap and lay in that position until sunrise.

CHAPTER 5

LITTLE WISE ONE

July 1799

An ominous thundercloud lay directly above the village of Yele. At any moment it would release its heavy rain to pour down and soak the living world below.

"Braima," Yenge called out to her son, "hurry up and round up the goats! Try to get them in the pen before the rain comes. The cloud will open soon."

"Yes, *YahYah*," Braima replied as he scurried out the door of the hut.

He skipped down the short dirt track and, passing through the clearing, peered left and right across the pasture. All of the animals were there. He then glanced over his shoulders to see if his older sister, Mari, was coming up behind him to help.

Where could she be? he wondered. She should be out there helping him. He never had to ask for her help; she would just arrive out of nowhere. Together they would finish the job in half the time it would take him alone. Usually, when they were done, they would race each other back to the hut. One of them would burst through the door with the other just behind. Most of the time it would be

Mari who got there first. Never too triumphant in her victory, she would wander over to her mother's side to assist in the preparation of the evening meal, a smug smile on her face.

But Mari had been missing for over four days. Braima had started to invent scenarios to explain his sister's absence. Maybe she was being given special treatment in preparation for the Sande ceremony by the village *Sowei*. Maybe someone would tell him and his parents soon.

As a boy, Braima knew little about the Sande. Still, he couldn't really believe his own explanation of her disappearance. Everyone in the village had been searching for Mari and another child, a young boy named Hindolo. Both had been missing for the same period of time.

Braima thought about how his mother would describe his sister's birth to anyone who was willing to listen. Braima memorized the tale, having heard it over and over again. Now he replayed it in his head to will Mari back home to safety.

His chores finished, Braima ran back into the house. His mother looked up expectantly and then, seeing him alone, turned her face away.

"Remember, son," Yenge said, "keep your eyes open for your sister. Maybe Mari will come home today when the rains come, and we must be here to greet her. Maybe she will escape from those who stole her from us. I pray for this from *Salat al-Fajr* — at dawn, to *Salat al-Isha'* — at dusk.

My soul is sore with pain and my heart breaks for her." Braima heard the quiver in his mother's voice as she tried to hold back her tears. "And what will your father do if he comes home from his trip and she is still gone?"

Yenge bit down hard on her lips to stop them from trembling. She squeezed her eyes shut as the tears slid down her cheeks, leaned her weary body against the smooth clay wall, and whispered, "Mariama, our special gift, may Allah bring you home to us safely!"

Just then lightning flamed across the skies. Loud, rumbling thunder followed, echoing through the savannah. Yenge looked out and knew that a fierce thunderstorm was in the making. Then, a torrent of rain pounded the earth, accompanied by a volley of fireworks, which continued for several hours.

Yenge sat on the mat in her family's hut as her thoughts dwelt on her daughter and how different their personalities were. Yenge's father had called Yenge "my little jackalberry" when she was young. Her slim stature and big bushy head of hair reminded him of the tree that dotted the savannah. Like Yenge, Mariama at six years of age had been slender and short, but while Yenge's face had been oval-shaped, Mari's at that age had been round like a calabash. Yenge's eyes were dark and shiny, but Mari's were like her father's — deep brown like the soil of the African plains after a rain.

Yenge's mother had died in childbirth, so women in the village helped her father to take care of her. Neatness of hair was important to the women and girls of Yenge's people, and many hands were needed to care for the child's wiry mop. It took at least four village women to braid her hair — two to do the braiding, a third to supply palm oil to keep the hair in place, and a fourth to hold Yenge in a leg lock to stop her from thrashing about. She was known for her ability to squirm out of any grip and would never willingly sit still to have her hair styled.

Mariama was unlike like her mother. She was quiet, thoughtful and obedient, even as a child learning to speak, she had said very little, and only spoke when spoken to directly. For this reason, her grandmother — her maa, as Mariama knew her — called her Little Wise One.

Yenge recalled that her Mari had remained at around three and a half feet tall for quite a few of her early years. At ten years old, she was still tiny for her age, though her small frame had begun to fill out.

A few moments later, Yenge's thoughts drifted to a conversation she had had with her husband, Kamal, after his last trip to the market. He had brought back gifts for the children, including a colourful string of beads for Mariama.

"It's perfect for Mari," Yenge had said, her face alive with pleasure as she examined the beads. "You know they mean the promise of many children, and she loves cowrie shells. She can wear them for her Sande celebration and be the best dressed in the group," she added. "Thank you for this gift! Kamal, you are a good man."

"Our daughter has grown into a beautiful and caring young woman," she had added reflectively. "I can't believe she is now thirteen. I remember not so many moons ago, when Mari was just a little girl, how she liked to dress up with the necklaces the village women created for the older girls."

"Do you remember how she used to sit and watch the older girls learning their dance steps in preparation for village celebrations? Then at night, before she lay on her mat, she would practise them quietly, when she thought we couldn't see her. Even without the sounds of the drums, she tried."

Kamal nodded.

Yenge continued recalling Mariama's good deeds. "How about the time she took food to Old Man Jaheem, who never left his hut after he lost his leg? You must remember."

With raised eyebrows, Yenge had waited for Kamal's answer.

"I do, I do," he said, smiling as he reflected on his daughter's kind-heartedness. "It surprised everybody. Even though Jaheem could barely see, all the other children were scared of him, but not our little girl. Her small arms weren't strong enough to carry all the food, so she made two trips to his hut to take him maize and cassava. She had seen us take food to the old man time and time again and wanted to do the same. It pleased the elders."

"Mari is a good girl," Yenge had said emphatically. "It's time to find her a husband — she'll make a proper wife. She can cook now. Soon she will go to Sande and be even better. There are many boys in the village, but if none are suitable, we should go to the elders and get permission to find her a husband in another village."

Yenge suddenly snapped back to the reality that her daughter was missing.

A search party had been out looking for her and Hindolo for the past four days and had not found them. Rumours that slave catchers had been taking people from several nearby compounds were rampant in the village now. She hoped that her daughter had not been taken by them.

Quietly she uttered a heartfelt prayer: "Allah, I miss my Mari so much. Please bring her home!"

In the meantime, the ship that took her daughter away was stopping at different ports on the West African coast picking up Mandingos, Kpelle, Kru, Senufo, Baule, Ewe, Akan, Ga, Yorùbá and Ibo peoples. At every port, news of its sinister purpose reached far into the surrounding countryside, as the foreign slave traders joined with local agents to separate families and splinter communities in their quest for captive human cargo.

CHAPTER 6

TALL JOHN OF SEFTON

July 1799

Shards of golden mid-summer sun glowed on the walls and dark cabinetry of the Missionary Society offices. The light also touched the serious features of the two men seated on opposite sides of a large desk laden with ledgers and notebooks.

"Refresh my memory sir, about your circumstances and why you seek to undertake a dangerous journey to such a distant place. I gather it is not only to serve the purposes of the Society."

"Sir, my name is Thomas Leighton. I grew up in an old English farmhouse near Sefton, in Merseyside. My parents, Margaret and Barrington Leighton, managed the farm of a relatively wealthy landowner in a rural parish north of Liverpool. My younger brother John and I made many pleasant memories there.

For the most part the years of our childhood were an adventure for me, though they were a challenge for my parents, particularly when it came to my brother. I can hear our father cautioning him, 'John, throwing rocks at the chickens is not a game.' If it wasn't the chickens, then it was the livestock, which he bombarded with rotten tomatoes. This mischief stemmed from impulses that John found difficult to control. He not only took pleasure in such transgressions but thoroughly enjoyed the excitement they stirred up.

"Pray tell, are you hoping to escape John's mischievousness by going to Demerary? We have many parishes here that will welcome your service. There is no need to move that far afield," the Society's director counseled.

"On the contrary, John has left home, and I miss him dearly. May I tell you a bit about my family, and especially about my brother?" Thomas asked.

"Of course you may, Thomas."

"Well, John was a sensory type of lad, very aware of what he wanted, and proceeded to feed that want without ever stopping to think of the consequences. Some people called him uncaring; others called him selfish. At the time I simply thought he was adventurous. I loved his high spirits, but his deeds did sometimes strain my Christian charity. God bless you, dear brother!

"One of my earliest memories of John's impulsive pranks comes from the time he was around six years old. As a part of our chores, John was sent by our mother to the barn to collect freshly laid eggs every day right after the hens were let out for their morning run. His job was to carefully place the eggs in baskets and then walk them back to the farmhouse, one basket at a time. On this particular day, John delivered the first basket and returned to the barn for the next round of eggs. He had been gone for a while when Mother and I heard a piercing scream. So desperate was the cry that it sent our terrified mother, with me in hot pursuit, dashing madly across the field to find out what catastrophe had befallen him. Wide-eyed, with our hearts thumping in our chests, we burst into the barn.

"We went in different directions, hoping to be the first to reach and rescue him. My mother followed the now-controlled sobs to the back of the barn, and there he was, hunkered down on the floor in the muck, surrounded by broken eggshells and blobs of yellow egg yolks. I could hear her gasping his name breathlessly. 'John, John — are you all right, lad?' Then her tone changed. 'John, oh John, what have you done?' I dashed in the direction of her voice and found our mother staring, aghast, at the dozens of scattered eggshells and broken yolks on the ground before her. She was debating how best to respond.

"It turned out that John's inquisitive mind had formulated a need-to-know question, and he'd concocted a sure way to learn the answer. He had observed how eggs were served at breakfast time and noticed that while sometimes they appeared flat on the plate with yellow centres, at other times they resembled little ivory balls the men at the parish church used in their billiard game on Sundays after service. In the billiard-ball version, the yolk was solid and spherical when cut open, entirely unlike the flat version on the plate. He had been confused, and his confusion had led to questioning.

"John being John, he had chosen to determine for himself the egg's true nature and had proceeded to smash open well over two dozen of them to see whether their centres were round or flat. He had been methodically smashing one egg at a time, hoping with each new one that the answer would be revealed. But when he was halfway through the third dozen he'd slipped on some of the discarded eggs, which now saturated the floor of the barn, stumbled, and hit his head on a piece of timber. Startled and in pain, he'd let out the scream our mother and I had heard.

"Now, with sorrowful blue eyes and tear-stained cheeks, John observed our mother with a look of bewilderment. 'They're all the same colour inside, and they're all round too,' he said. 'Oh, John, what a waste, and what a mess!' It was the only response our poor mother could muster.

"Our lives, including John's, changed in 1795. As our family sat down to tea one afternoon, my father said to my mother, 'William is enquiring about the farm, and he has invited me to visit him in Liverpool.' He cleared his throat and added, 'He thinks I might like to move us there.' Uncle William had first worked as a bookkeeper for a mercantile company and then bought into the business after earning enough money.

"Then fourteen years old, I had never visited Liverpool before. The only trips away from the farm were across the River Alt by boat to attend church at St. Helen's parish. John, who was twelve, was naturally curious about this possible relocation. He immediately peppered our dad with questions about life in Liverpool and how it might compare with farm living. Father pushed his plate to one side, suddenly uneasy.

"'There are no farms in Liverpool, John. It's a big city,' was his only answer.

"Eight months later we arrived at the house of William Edgar Leighton, my father's older brother, with our meagre possessions. William's growing wealth was evident. His overstated attire consisted of fancy wool breeches and complementary stockings, a waistcoat over a crisp white linen shirt trimmed with lace and a timepiece attached to his waistcoat by a silver chain. A frock coat hung on a wooden peg behind the large mahogany door of his study.

"Uncle William's wife had died two years earlier. His older son, George, joined him in welcoming us, their unknown relations, to Liverpool. After minimal pleasantries, Uncle William escorted us to our new home in Danube Street. The four-room row house was much smaller than our home back in the village of Sefton. To us, its newly arrived inhabitants, it felt closed in. Gone were the fresh air and green open spaces of the farm, replaced by close quarters and squalor, masses of people and the stench of unwashed bodies. There were piles of garbage in the streets, and everything was crowded into tight spaces. The contrast with the country life we had known was striking and difficult to grasp.

"Mother and Father had come in the hopes of finding a better life with improved financial possibilities, but so had most of the other souls in Liverpool. We had to quickly find ways to adjust to our new surroundings.

"Our parents enrolled us at the local school. I settled in well there but still could not abide our noisy neighbourhood. I spent more and more time in my room reading, lost in scripture and other works, to drown the city sounds with my imagination. Like me,

John struggled to adjust to this new world of cramped living quarters and teeming crowds on gritty streets, with pubs on every corner — pubs filled with gin-soaked patrons. For the first year after we had moved, John spent many evening hours looking out his window at brawls started by drunken sailors or idle young men.

"At school in Liverpool John was seldom engaged, and when he was, it was usually in a bad way. My brother was constantly embroiled in fights with other children, and as a result spent many hours outside the headmaster's office awaiting the strap. One such altercation happened as he walked to school one morning. To test the strength and reach of his right arm, John threw a fist-sized rock with no regard for the other pupils nearby. The instant the rock left his grasp and went sailing through the air, Big Jack, one of the neighbourhood bullies, stepped into its path. John hated Big Jack, and a perverse twist of fortune guided the missile against the back of Jack's head.

"The force of the blow knocked him forward onto the walkway with a heavy thud, where to John's horror he lay still and silent. No one noticed John steal away, but he never came home that evening or any other after that.

"Our family sought the local constable's help, but his searching yielded only false sightings. This was hardly surprising as the constable assigned to the task spent most of his time in local pubs, either breaking up brawls or imbibing in beverages during half-hearted attempts to keep the peace. Overall, he devoted little time to the search for my missing brother.

"Our mother was heartbroken. Our father grieved silently and longed for my brother's return. I prayed. But no further news of John came. He became like a hole in the fabric of our family life and was never seen at school again.

"Going to Demerary, I believe, will help me to heal from the loss and emptiness I have felt since John's disappearance. It will also allow me to carry out the Society's work to spread God's grace among the heathen."

"I understand your request better, and see no reason why you shouldn't go. I approve your mission, and wish you Godspeed."

CHAPTER 7

WATER PRISON

July 1799

Among the many captives on the SS *Archery* were a Temne couple, Sule and Khadija, who were captured separately a few weeks after their wedding ceremony. Sule, the twenty-one-year-old son of Chief Mustapha Samba, was his parents' second son. Sule's father, like many of the local chiefs in the West African kingdoms, was in constant conflict with rival tribes. Each fought to hold on to land and their traditions. Chief Samba ultimately lost both of his sons to tribal conflicts. His older offspring, Ade, had died in one of these battles; Sule was captured by rival tribes, imprisoned and sold to slavers.

Khadija, Sule's new wife, was the sixteen-year-old daughter of the Temne Chief Sahamji. He was the leader of one of the largest neighbouring villages and had been childhood friends with Mustapha Samba. As was customary, the marriage between their children had been arranged when the girl was very young.

When Khadija was four years old and Sule was only nine years old, the two chief friends got together and discussed the forthcoming marriage of their son and daughter. "Samba, our ancestral land must be kept by our families. My princess daughter will need a courageous and strong prince to carry and protect this legacy and strengthen the fortress handed down from our ancestors. I pledge my daughter Khadija's hand to your fine son Sule to ensure that the Temne birthright is preserved."

"Sahamji, I agree and accept your Khadija for my Sule. The day after her sixteenth birthday, they will take each other as man and wife. Our bloodline will continue until time immemorial and our clan will be strengthened." Samba grinned, clasped his hands together and nodded. "Bring us drink to seal this promise," he waved his arm joyfully in the air. Servants brought goblets of palm wine to toast the momentous occasion.

"Khadi" was her father's favourite name for his little princess. Born to his first and senior wife, she had surprised her parents by coming into the world early, arriving by candlelight in the middle of the night. She was thirteen inches in length and had beautiful cocoa-brown skin. Perfectly formed, she had a flawlessly round head, a tiny button nose, and puckered lips ready for suckling. Khadi's mother loved to run her fingers through her daughter's tightly curled black hair while gently massaging her scalp. Whenever Khadi was upset, this ritual always transformed the little princess's sobbing into delighted coos, and she would fall asleep. Chief Sahamji had wanted a son, a male heir to his chieftaincy, but his daughter's arrival brought him such joy that he quickly forgot about his earlier preference.

Khadi was accustomed to a life of luxury and to being taken care of by servants in her father's compound. Because of the status of both her parents, the bride price for Khadija, which included gold pieces, cowrie shells, and fine silk cloth was relatively high compared with that of other village girls. Sule's family was easily able to pay the price, and after the ceremony, the couple moved away from Khadija's father's compound, to begin their lives together.

It was perhaps this arrangement that allowed the two newly-weds to be more easily kidnapped. Khadija had been captured along with her manservant, Jab, on their return from visiting her father, and Sule was taken while purchasing cattle in a neighbouring village.

The couple had not seen each other on the gruelling march to the ship and had been held in different locations prior to boarding.

Khadija had been surprised to see her husband and Jab being brought aboard. In spite of the horrific conditions and their unknown fate, she felt some relief in knowing the two men were on the same vessel.

For Khadi, her present situation seemed too terrible to be true, but she couldn't deny that it was. Being held prisoner and treated like cattle or worse was relentlessy demeaning — it brought constant tears to her eyes. This ship was no place for a princess.

Khadi's mind travelled back to the hot muggy day she married Sule under the large tent in her father's compound.

The sunrise rapidly warmed the sky and touched the landscape and village with gold, as if in harmony with the day's celebration. The bride was dressed in a blue and gold kaftan draped with clusters of beads and cowrie shells. The groom's attire was a full white robe layered with fine gold embroidery and jewellery, signifying the respect and elevated status he now commanded.

When Sule arrived early that morning, the first thing Khadija saw was his enormous smile and perfectly white teeth, contrasting with his smooth coffee-coloured skin. This lit a spark in her belly and a joyful flutter in her chest. *This man is handsome, and today I will marry him*, her thoughts whispered as she swallowed hard to control the feeling of euphoria that surged within her.

She had looked forward to this day for many moons. It was a day of sacred ceremonies to seal an earlier promise between two Temne chiefs, a day of merriment and food — an abundance of food: smoked butter catfish, spicy roasted slices of goat and calf meat cooked on the iron spit in the large courtyard, millet, crushed yellow yams, cassava balls, jugs of rich palm wine. The feasting, drinking, drumming, and dancing would go on for three days as the village exulted in the new union.

Now, she felt lost, alone, and removed from her family, community, and those who cared for her. But seeing Sule and Jab on the ship reduced some of the desolation she was experiencing.

***

Mariama had been up all night after the assault. At daybreak, she heard whispers around her and noticed that a few of the women had woken up and were taking care not to wake the sleeping children. None of them spoke Mende. On the *Archery* there were five very young children, about three to four years of age, and three others around six years old.

Khadija, who had comforted Mariama during the night, reached over and touched her now to see if she was awake. She noticed that Mariama's shoulders were trembling slightly, and her eyes were closed. Mariama was replaying the *Sowei*'s words in her mind and considering their truth. The excruciating pain she felt earlier had eased somewhat, but she was still unsure if her legs would be able to carry her weight.

As the ship's crew began their organized shuffling and thumping above them, Khadija tried again to get Mariama's attention, this time quietly offering her a small chewing stick called a miswak, which she removed from the waist of her lappa. Mariama propped herself up, grasped the stick and began to chew on it. This was a hygiene ritual she had practised for as long as she could remember. All the members of her family did it every morning and evening, though her mother had to prompt her brother most times. It was familiar and comforting. She glanced at Khadija and gave her a small smile of thanks.

The children were beginning to rise now, and most of the other women were awake. Mariama was uncertain how many of them had really slept and how many, like her, had just lain quietly for most of the night.

Moments later, three middle-aged sailors came into the women's area, whips in hand. They grunted commands and prodded and ushered the captives towards the companionway. One sailor climbed the stairs and waved, signalling for the women to follow him to the upper deck. The other two crew members steered the shuffling group from behind.

When they arrived on the windy, sunny deck above, they were corralled into a corner near the gun carriage. Meanwhile, an older sailor brought three buckets containing a pasty mixture of cornmeal and flour from the ship's kitchen and placed them on the deck in front of the women and children. The food was not meant to be appetizing; it simply had to keep the captives alive. The sailor tossed a small wooden spoon into each bucket and gestured for them to eat. Then he turned around and left.

Most of the women and children had had their last meal back on shore in the slave dungeons the previous day. They felt intense hunger. First the younger children were fed, then the older ones ate. When they were finished, the thirty adults, except Khadija, had what remained. Mariama noticed that when her turn came, Khadija dipped up some food with the spoon and fed it to a young boy who was without a parent.

After a time the old sailor came back carrying two other buckets, filled with water. He set them on the deck, dropped two ladles in and left again. As before, the children were allowed to drink first, and the women took what remained.

Once the sparse meal was done, the atmosphere on the ship became much more clamorous. The clink of chains and shuffling of feet could be heard as half a dozen sailors, whips in hand, led the male captives, most of whom were shackled together in pairs with leg irons, from the lower to the upper deck.

For the captain and crew it was critical to maintain order, especially when transporting the hundreds of adult male hostages around the ship. It took about forty-five minutes for the convoy of men, both young and old, to climb to the upper deck. Each man emerged from the hatch; his eyes squinting in the morning sunlight, mouth open, gulping the fresh sea breeze to fill starving lungs.

Khadija sat next to Mariama in the shadow of a gun carriage observing the sad procession of figures as they blinked and ducked in the harsh brightness. She waited anxiously for Sule or Jab to come into view. After a while, Sule appeared, shackled to a feeble older man who looked deathly sick. Overwhelmed with his own suffering, he didn't notice Khadija.

"Sule, Sule! *Mi ni, Khadi ... noryan noryan* — It is me, Khadi ... here here!"

At the sound of her voice, Sule whipped around, his head bobbing and shifting to find his wife on the crowded deck. He could see clearly from only one eye — the other had been severely damaged by Ed Grimes's elbow jab to his face.

In the confusion of moving bodies, clanking chains, heavy sighs, groans, and barking orders from the seamen, Khadi lost sight of Sule. Frantically she tried to move towards where she had seen him, but a sailor armed with a cat-o'-nine-tails stood in her path. He glared at her and growled something in that coarse and ugly language she didn't understand. Anguished, Khadi slumped down again on the deck. She pulled her knees up to her face and sobbed.

Mariama, seated beside Khadi, noticed that more white men had gathered around at different points on the deck. Each man carried a musket. At this sight her stomach grew queasy. *What new horrors are about to unfold?* Her palms became sweaty and her lips trembled from being forced together. Then unexpectedly, hot fluid slithered down her legs, and her entire body began to throb.

Out of the bustle of slaves and shouting seamen on the ship, Mariama heard a familiar sound — the beat of drums. She listened closely and heard it again. Turning in the direction of the sound, she saw a clutch of sailors huddled around four male captives who were rhythmically pounding their fists against animal-skin-covered drums. The urgency of the beat increased and the sailors began swishing their whips in time with the music. To Mariama, it looked like some kind of water dance. She could hear the sailors shouting strange words, but for the most part she couldn't understand. Nearby, other captives gawked wide-eyed, and confused.

The sailor closest to Mariama leapt frantically into the air while yelling, "Jump, Sambo, jump!" Other sailors followed his example. A few of the Africans began to imitate the sailors — a swell of pulsating movement rising up in the air. Several, however, simply stood by, frozen. The armed sailors became agitated, some visibly angry. The onlookers paid the price for their aloofness as crewmen rushed around and fiercely whipped them at random. An elderly man so badly beaten collapsed, hitting his head fatally on the breech of the cannon barrel that jutted into the deck space.

"Shark food! Shark food!" the sailors chanted as they tossed the journey's first fatality overboard. Mariama shuddered from the looks of contempt on their faces. The body disposed of, the sailors turned around and hosed down the deck where the bleeding captive had fallen. As the days and weeks unfolded, such scenes were repeated over and over again in the wooden jail as it sailed relentlessly towards a destination its prisoners could not imagine.

CHAPTER 8

ONE WITH THE SEA

August 1799

Under bright starlight the ship rocked from side to side, and the contents of Mariama's stomach began to slosh in concert with the ship's movement. She swallowed hard to avoid gagging and throwing up the slop she had eaten earlier. Through a wave of dizziness she crawled along the wet middle deck of the ship, heaving and retching. Then she felt a rush as the contents of her stomach exploded through her nostrils and throat.

Propped up on her hands and knees Mariama gasped for air. Her small body went limp and she collapsed onto the wooden planks. A sickly, pale yellow liquid escaped her partially opened mouth. Through the slits of half-closed lids, only the whites of her eyes showed. Her chest moved up and down rhythmically and her heart raced.

Khadija watched this scene unfold from her corner a few feet over. At first she just observed, expecting one of the other women to go to the girl's aid, but they were all lost in their own thoughts. It was about seven weeks into the voyage, and the ship had been still for about three days now. Earlier that afternoon after their second meal on the upper deck, she and Mariama had overheard Grimes taunting the captives.

"We ain't moving because the ship's too bloody heavy; the skipper will have to get rid of some of this lot so we can move on. I wonder who the sharks will eat tonight." Grimes had said in a slow, eerie, mocking voice as he scanned the deck. His sly tone and malicious expression had not escaped the captives' attention, but his words were not understood, and a tired Mariama just lowered her head.

Now Khadi crawled over to sit by Mariama's side. She noticed that the girl's breathing had become normal again. She lifted the prized lappa to Mariama's face and wiped the drool from her chin and her cheeks. Cradling her shoulders, she gently lifted the feeble girl's head and placed it against her thighs. Mariama moaned gently, opened her eyes, and looked up at Khadi.

"*Aw di*, Mariama?" Khadi asked her softly.

Mariama was too weak to answer. In fact, she didn't know how her health was. She knew, though, that to show any signs of illness could mean being thrown overboard like so many other sick captives. The thought of this paralyzed her with fear, and she began to sob uncontrollably.

Khadija patted Mariama on the shoulder. "*Tri ka ma dira* — Try to get some sleep."

But Mariama was already asleep and missed Khadi's words of comfort. The gentle shoulder patting had relaxed her.

Careful not to disturb Mariama, Khadija pulled her legs up now and tucked them beneath her buttocks. For the next five to six hours she remained in this position, only shifting occasionally. She had not been able to sleep lately despite her immense tiredness. Khadi was losing ground. As the daughter of a wealthy chief, she was accustomed to maintaining her dignity in difficult situations. But the constant worry and brutality, along with the meagre rations, were beginning to wear away at her.

Memories surged back of how frightening it had been to see her captors the first time — the strangeness of their burnt pink-skinned features, their hairiness, like warthogs, their constant movement. It was as if pointing and jabbing, dripping sweat, and shouting kept them alive. Khadi remembered thinking: *their eyes are dead like someone under a shaman's curse back in the village. They are a coarse, doglike race, always barking in our faces with foul hyena breath, spraying a dog language full of spit, panting tongue and bared teeth.*

Their ugliness made her cry because she could still remember beauty; their cruelty made her regret her own foregone acts of kindness. The evil they expressed made her doubt the truth of any goodness she had ever known. *This is what they have done to us*, she thought.

That night, when the ship was dark, Khadija listened to the many sounds around her — the keening wail of sorrow pervasive on the women's deck and the low, continuous moaning rising from the men's deck below. She joined in and quietly wept.

For the first six weeks of the voyage, just after her morning meal, Khadija had positioned herself as close as possible to the companionway leading down from the upper deck.

It was through this stairway that all the captives, including her beloved Sule, were brought up for meals and their daily exercise.

In recent days, however, he had been one of the last ones to emerge. He had not looked well and continuously gasped for breath well after emerging into the fresh sea air. Khadi had also noticed that he was limping excessively. He could no longer participate in any of the exercises on deck with the other captives, and instead mostly leaned against a post.

On that fateful morning, Dick, one of the more aloof crew members, had screamed something at the enslaved Africans and raised his whip. This had frightened Sule, who lunged forward and attempted to join in the dance routine with the others — his movements clearly out of sync. The effort was too much for him, and after just a few steps, he collapsed. With a scream of outrage, Dick pounced and proceeded to viciously whip the fallen African.

The cat-o'-nine-tails swished through the air, landing again and again across Sule's back and head. He lifted his arms in a futile effort to shield his face, but the beating continued, and the drumming and dancing didn't let up.

Khadija closed her eyes, unable to watch. Even with the intense sound of the drums, she could hear the hissing of the whip as it flew through the air.

And then it stopped. Khadija opened her eyes. Sule lay in a bloodied heap in the far corner of the deck.

The few minutes that followed felt like hours. Khadija had to get to Sule without calling attention to herself or letting her intentions be known by nearby guards. She quietly joined the dancing group as Mariama cautiously watched, her eyes darting around at members of the crew, her heart pounding out of concern for her friend.

With every controlled dance step, Khadi moved closer to where Sule was slumped over. Looking furtively in his direction, she hoped he would, just for one moment, look up and notice her. Carefully she edged closer to him, and could now hear him moaning, even over the rhythmic booming of the drums.

First scanning the deck to ensure she hadn't been spotted by one of the crew members, she sat down beside Sule and whispered his name.

"Sule, Sule! It's me, Khadija."

She touched his hands, still cupped around his battered face. Sule's moaning ceased. He slowly lifted his head and looked at his wife. Khadi's heart sank. His one eye was swollen shut and leaking puss. Dark blood oozed from his purple parched lips, and tears trickled down his cheeks.

Khadija bent close to him, stifling a sob, her body began to quiver. Her Sule was sicker than she had imagined. But before she could speak or comfort him, a whip seared her back, shoulders tightening instinctively, head jerking forward. Another whack followed, and she turned and looked up to face her attacker.

Ed Grimes's cold eyes pierced hers like a dagger. He was the crew member who had placed Mariama's limp body near her sleeping quarters on the first night of the voyage. Since that terrible night, Khadi had done her best to avoid him. Her breath caught in her throat. She stared defiantly back at Grimes and was surprised to see the anger in his eyes soften. His eyes trailed down to her naked, firm chest and then back to her face. She looked away, disgusted, as Grimes slowly licked his lips.

She looked over at Sule. His head was now back in his cupped hands and he had begun moaning again. Sule could not help her. He could not even help himself.

Grimes prodded her with the handle of his whip. "Get up!" he ordered.

Torn between her allegiance to her husband and her fear of Grimes, Khadi obeyed. She rose up, moved a few feet back and resumed her spot in the corner among the other women. She was relieved to be away from Grimes but terrified for Sule. Mariama, who was watching the exchange, immediately lowered her head to observe the deck floor. Khadija sat and watched, helpless, as the ship's skipper, lured by the commotion, arrived on the scene. Accompanied by four of his sailors, he strutted along the deck observing the captives. Two of his men were armed with muskets and two held whips. When they got to where Sule lay, the captain stopped and commanded, "Rouse him up smartly." One of the men jabbed the prone figure with the handle of a whip. Sule didn't respond.

Khadija and the rest of the captives watched intently, silently, as the skipper turned and said something to his men. A split second later, two of them swooped down and picked up Sule by his arms and legs. In unison they moved to the rail of the ship and swung Sule's emaciated body over their heads into the waiting sea. There was a distant splash as it hit the water, and the rest of the captives gasped.

Khadija clasped both her hands over her mouth. Eyes wide, she sat frozen and glared at the spot where the sailors had just thrown her husband overboard. The women around her waited for her to react, but she remained motionless. Mariama shifted her body closer to Khadi's and touched her right shoulder. Khadija didn't respond to this gesture either; instead, she closed her eyes and kept them closed until it was time to go back to the women's sleeping quarters. She rose mechanically and walked slowly away, looking straight ahead to avoid the ship's rails — the place she last set eyes on her beloved.

Mariama sat beside Khadija, holding and intermittently squeezing her hand. She was offering her friend the only comfort she could. Khadija's eyes remained fixed. Only the rise and fall of her chest belied her seeming lifelessness. After a few hours, Mariama lay back and fell asleep.

In the gloomy, dark corner of the women's deck, hot tears flowed down Khadija's cheeks. She wept for the beautiful new life with her husband, now brutally cut short. She wept for her cherished family and village, now so far away. But most of all, at that moment, she wept for the family with Sule that would never be.

During her days on the ship, Khadija wore five rows of cowrie shells and one row of colourful glass beads around her neck. Before her capture she had worn the beads across her hips and pelvis to adorn her lappa as a sign of impending fertility. As she lay listening to the sea wash against the ship's wooden planks at night, she would run her fingers along the necklace and reflect on the significance and the promise she had made to Sule on their wedding night.

"I will give you five boys and one girl — our children will be six, a nice round number," she had smiled, tucked snuggly in Sule's arms.

How could that dream ever materialize now? Her new husband had, just hours ago, become one with the sea.

**

When Ed Grimes arrived later that night and yanked Khadija from her corner of the deck, she was stoic and didn't resist; she was there in body only. He had expected a fight from this tall and willowy black princess, but he got none. He marched her off to the far end of the deck, shackles in place, threw her on the cold, wet timber and raped her repeatedly. He was going to teach her a lesson. She was nothing but a slave, and like the captain, he believed that for now, he owned every inch of her body.

At first Khadija felt the physical pain of Grimes's assault. Then her mind went blank and her body limp. Her thoughts escaped to a faraway place, and her eyes became hollow. For twenty minutes Grimes violated her body, thrusting punishingly. He pawed her breasts and ran his tongue over her nipples, hoping to arouse her, but Khadija lay unresponsively, like a dead animal. Frustrated, he slapped her, hoping she would cry and beg him to stop, but Khadija was stolid. Finally, he gave up, dressed hurriedly, and grunted, "I'll finish this another time. Get up and get dressed, bitch."

Khadi did as she was instructed. Her body felt weak at first, but she rose up, straightened her back, lifted her shoulders, and despite the shackles, with purposeful strides, returned to the far corner of the women's deck. Grimes followed closely behind, his short rough footsteps a jarring counterpoint to her control. She then sat down in her corner, and stared into the distance — her eyes showed nothing. Grimes watched her for another minute, confused; he shook his head and went back to his quarters.

Khadija didn't sleep that night. Neither did Grimes.

CHAPTER 9

HOME GOING

September 1799

At sunrise, shades of orange, pink, purple, and pale blue brushed the morning sky. Gently rising out of the east, orangey-pink hues kissed where the heavens met the waters. The warmer colours then melded into the purple and changed it to cobalt.

Khadija was transporting buckets of the morning meal to the upper deck and paused to watch the magnificent vision unfold. For a moment she forgot about the heaving wooden prison as it drifted farther and farther from the land she loved. And she also tried to blot out the tragic and terrifying experience she had lived through just hours before. The dawning of this day, with its warmth and colours, brought her an inner calm that matched her unruffled outward appearance. She drew in a deep breath as the crown of the golden yellow sun pierced the sky. A new day had begun.

On this day, the kitchen galley team comprised Kumba, a young woman around fifteen years old, Khadija, and Mariama. The women helped Jack, the ship's cook, prepare the morning meal. He was a short, plump, balding, and generally quiet older man, noticeably shorter than Khadija. In girth and bulk, however, he was easily four times her size and must have weighed three hundred pounds.

A roster of chores had been created shortly after the ship had sailed from the West African trading post of Bunce Island. On it, Jack had been assigned a set of captives as helpers to assist with preparation and clean-up after the two prescribed daily meals. Jack used mostly hand signals to get people working together. It was a technique that worked well for him as a cook on many slavers. The first time he attempted to undo the shackles from Khadija's ankles, she was caught off guard and became confused as this squat man got down on his knees and touched her feet. She retreated, convinced that he was up to no good.

Jack observed her misinterpretation of his action and slowly mimed the removal of the wretched instrument. He then did a little hop into the air to showcase his freedom from the chains. The other assigned women soon caught on and let him remove the cruel metal bindings they hated. But at the end of their work shifts, the shackles were replaced.

Jack liked his job, except that he detested having to pitch in with other crew members to pump bilge water from deep in the ship. That was back-breaking work, and the horrific stench and the constant bending made him dizzy. Cooking, on the other hand, brought him pleasure, despite the misery of the human cargo around him.

Preparing meals with Jack and the others lifted Mariama's spirits and reminded her of when she helped her mother prepare food back at their hut. She worked hard during meal preparation in the galley and learned a lot. Lately, however, she had not been feeling well, Khadija had noticed Mariama's low energy level, and without being directed pitched in extra to get the job done. The morning meal of corn and rice was usually completed in quiet motions, the clink of the cooking utensils providing the only sounds.

Today, something felt different to Khadija. As she moved over to the feeding area, dragging a heavy food bucket, she looked up at the tall poles with the big puffs of cloth that helped to push the ship across the water. They were more majestic than usual. A strong wind blew across the upper deck, causing the cloth to belly out and the poles to creak and strain. Streams of dazzling sunlight reflected off the undulating sea. There was something strangely beautiful about this day.

It was nearing the time when the female captives would be allowed on the upper deck for exercise and their morning meal. The crew on the early watch were already in place, as Khadi and Kumba toiled at their task and Mariama was occupied with clean-up duty in the galley. Suddenly there was a loud swishing sound followed by a series of thuds. Startled, Khadi and Kumba turned around to look. What they saw caused their eyes to widen in wonder. The air was filled with fish flying in from the sea and many had landed, flipping and flapping, on the deck. Some had become entangled in the security net on the ship's rails.

Terrified, Kumba scampered back down to the galley and hid, while Mariama climbed tentatively up the companionway to view the unusual events.

Khadi watched as the sailors tried to scoop up as many fish as they could. For a moment, she was back in her village watching the women doing a rain dance — only here it was a fish dance. She remembered how, after the villagers had asked the gods for relief from drought, they would come out to the clearing and dance euphorically at the sight and feel of the first rainfall.

Khadija clasped her right hand over her mouth and watched in amazement as sailors rushed in from every section of the ship, frantically jumping and trying to grab as many fish as they could. Some flailed at the fish flapping on the deck; others tried to nab the ones caught in the nets along the rails. Most failed. The net slackened and the fish flapped back into the sea.

Suddenly, Khadija heard a voice in her head say, "*E yema kuh ne* — Time to go." It was time to leave this place of horror that had imprisoned her over almost eight weeks. Slowly, deliberately, she scanned the deck, watching for a break in the disorder. She walked slowly at first but quickened her steps as she got close to her target. The escape net below the rail was still sagging, having been pulled down by the weight of the fish. Khadija glanced back to check that no one was immediately behind her. She slid her prized necklace from around her neck and dropped it onto the wet floor, then she yanked at the drooping net to create an opening. Someone called out her name. It was Mariama's voice, but she could not risk looking back. In a clear, steady voice she uttered the words, "*Lemne, Mariama* — Goodbye" and like a saddle-billed stork launching herself gracefully into the open sky from the branch of an acacia tree, Khadija flew up and over the ship's rail. She dove head first into an ocean that opened up and enveloped her into its watery fold. Like Sule, she had gone home, and was now one with the sea.

"*Nyamao, Khadija!* — Wait for me!" Mariama screamed as Khadija's body disappeared from sight. But it was already too late. Khadija could not wait. She had already left her behind. Mariama rushed over to the place where her friend had exited and saw the cowrie shell and glass bead necklace lying in a small puddle on the deck. She reached over, picked it up and tucked it into the waist of her lappa. Then she scanned the placid sea hoping to catch a glimpse of Khadi, and that's when she saw them — several large triangular fins cut the water a short distance from the ship. Mariama's mouth became dry, her stomach tied up in knots, and her feet felt heavy as though planted in place. She closed her eyes, as she sobbed uncontrollably and imagined her friend being gobbled up by many big fish.

The sailors, initially stunned into immobility by the suddenness of Khadija's leap, broke into movement as they realized what had happened. Two of them dropped their fish and dashed to the spot where Khadija had jumped. They examined the net and discovered that it had become partially detached during the commotion over the fish. Quickly, they restored it and then checked the entire line for any other breaches but found none. They did suddenly notice

Mariama who was transfixed by what had occurred. "Get back to your duty wench or have a whipping!"

The remainder of the day was somber. Meals were served hurriedly, and exercise curtailed. The captain was angry about his lost cargo but could not hold any of the crew responsible. Only Jack looked sad about the debacle. He prepared fish for the crew that afternoon and gave some to Mariama and Kumba. Mariama hardly ate any of it.

There was now a general uneasiness among the crew as the skipper tried to prevent any further losses and augmented security on the upper deck. As the mood on the ship changed, so did the weather. The gentle morning breezes shifted into strong blustery winds. An impending storm began to show its intentions and by early evening they felt the first effects of the gale. Waves now crashed against the sides of the ship, which began to heave and roll in the swell.

***

Mariama lay awake late into the night, overwhelmed by the day's tragedy. Khadi had been her only close connection on the ship. She had come to her aid and comforted her when she was hurt and sick. Deathly afraid of being alone again, Mariama felt her stomach tie itself in knots as nausea rose in her chest. How was she going to carry on without Khadi's friendship and support? She gently rubbed Khadi's necklace as she replayed the events that had transpired earlier.

To Mariama, cowrie shells were a sign of beauty and importance. Whenever her mother got dressed up for any significant village celebration, she wore her cowrie shells. It meant that something grand was about to take place. Mariama found some comfort in that memory. Surrounded by the roar of a raging storm lashing the ship and distressed by the painful wailing from the men's deck below, Mariama held on tightly to Kadhija's necklace and cried herself to sleep.

This time the *Sowei* came without fanfare, but as before, wore a face mask as she hovered above the young girl's body. The *Sowei* didn't linger as she had on her first visit but seemed to have another message to deliver.

"*Ndengesia tilubangor tao tiloko luabima*," she whispered, but Mariama was either too sick or too sad to immediately understand the *Sowei*'s message.

She scrutinized the *Sowei* and wondered at her words. She had heard them before but couldn't remember where. Suddenly the voice and the message came together in her mind. Her eyes now fixed on the *Sowei* — it was her grandmother. She had always used that saying to new mothers after a birth in the village: "Children are a blessing. You have been chosen."

"Maa? ... Maa?" Mariama called out softly. But the *Sowei* had left just as quickly as she had come.

Mariama woke up with a jolt. She heard the rain still beating against the ship, but the storm's ferocity had dissipated. Rubbing her eyes, she sat up and listened; everyone was either asleep or lying quietly in their places. Mariama found no evidence of her grandmother. She could not be here — back in the village her maa had gone home to be with the ancestors when Mariama was ten years old. And what she had just experienced must have been a dream. She sat with her legs drawn up and her arms wrapped around her shins, just like Khadi used to do. She thought of Maa and Khadi and knew that they were both with the ancestors.

***

Morning came and there was another shift in mood on the ship. The sailors were busier than ever, pumping bilge water, scrubbing down the deck planks with stones, and flogging it dry with rags all before the sun had fully risen in the sky. The ship had picked up speed. Tendrils of umber began to mottle the deep indigo of the ocean — the blue seawater had turned to a brownish colour.

At first Mariama thought that the pumped water from the ship had caused this colour change. Crew members stood at various sections of the ship's rails, hands shielding their eyes from the bright sunshine and peering into the distance, some pointing and talking excitedly. Mariama wasn't quite sure what most of it meant, but she heard the word "Demerary" over and over. It had to be significant, because the skipper joined the sailors at the rail, and he too used the term: "Nearing Demerary."

Mariama sat uneasily and looked on. Kumba joined her.

CHAPTER 10

DEMERARY

September 1799 – February 1800

A forest of masts filled the harbour, and the wharf behind them bustled with activity. The ship warped slowly in as the crew prepared the vessel for docking. Ropes and chains were pulled in different directions and then secured to large planks that plunged into the mudflats under the landing.

The crew began to bring the surviving male slaves up on deck. Each man was hosed down with murky brown water from the river. After the wash, sailors placed a bucket with oil and pieces of rag in the centre of the deck and showed male captives how to rub the oil into their skin and on their heads and faces to enhance their appearances. Next, women captives were ordered to do the same.

Crew members led the Africans off the ship as they had been led on in shackles and irons, in the seemingly endless weeks before. Now, though, here in Demerary, there were a lot fewer of them. Eighty souls did not survive the voyage. The sailors then herded the enslaved into a large wire cagelike structure at the far-right corner of the wharf called "the pen." The crew now corralled about fifty mostly naked Africans into the belly of the pen at a time. The operation reminded Mariama of the goats she and Braima had herded back in Yele.

White men were gathered at the dockside. Dressed in clothing excessive for the heavy heat, they strutted about, sweating profusely and checking timepieces hooked to chains on their waists. They circled the pen and observed the caged goods, scribbling notes and barking comments. Once each man had made his selection, his picks were prodded out of their holding area back onto the open dock for closer inspection and, usually, purchase. This sequence of events was repeated until the entire batch of new arrivals had been sold. A few Africans as well as other brown-skinned men with straight dark hair had accompanied some planters and observed the transactions. The white men called them Indians.

Stepping back on solid ground was disorienting for the recent arrivals. The earth seemed to shift as if they were still on board the *Archery*. A few men knelt and lowered their faces to the ground with their palms against the earth. There were shouts of "*Yabo godiya!*" and "*Chi otuto!*" and "*Mungu wa sifa!*" and "*Allahu Akbar!*" as they thanked God, in multiple languages, for sparing their lives on the long and treacherous journey.

***

"Quick sale — two strong young bucks. Only sixty-five quid."

"Young wench — twenty-five quid."

The auctioneer spoke rapidly. About two hundred and forty-five men, women, and children were sold that afternoon. Joseph Blumefield purchased six of the lot — three young males, one middle-aged male, and two young females.

"Line 'em up, Bart, line 'em up!" he called out.

Bart, the old blacksmith, pushed and probed the newly purchased Africans into a straight line with a sharpened tree branch. Then he turned to a large rusted iron pot filled with white-hot coals, pulled out a glowing red iron prong, and methodically passed along the queue, stamping the letter B into their exposed right shoulders.

"Hiss ... hiss," the sizzling sound erupted, and a sickly coppery smell permeated the torrid tropical air as the brand met human flesh.

Mariama choked on the smell. She held her nose and covered her mouth to prevent from gagging as shrill screams erupted from the recoiling captives in the lineup ahead of her. Eyes closed, she dug her heels into the damp red dirt and let out a shriek that startled but didn't deter Bart as he approached her. The searing pain that shot through her shoulder with the branding strike was crushing, and her scream mingled with the agony of the others around her.

Bart then corralled each burned and bruised captive onto the back of a waiting dray cart and drove off. Joseph Blumefield hopped into his horse-drawn carriage and Buck, the five-and-a-half-foot tall mule-man and occasional blacksmith, took the reins in the driver's seat.

"Go, boy!" Blumefield ordered.

Buck pulled on the reins and the mare began a slow trot, trailing the dray cart to the right, towards the parade ground and onto Vlissingen Road. So began the journey on Demerary soil.

***

The journey from port to plantation was lost in a haze of agony. The midday sun added an extra layer of heat to the burning, swollen wound in Mariama's right shoulder, making the pain almost unbearable.

Mariama only realized that the cart had stopped when she felt something touch her exposed knees. A dark blue garment lay across her legs. She looked ahead and could see a woman, close to the age of her own mother, walking alongside the stationary dray cart, distributing garments to the newly arrived, mostly naked captives.

For the first time since Mariama had received the iron imprint, she began to observe her surroundings.

The cart had stopped at an open wooden gate. Mariama looked up and saw the compound that would be her new home in Demerary. A large odd-shaped wooden house with different levels stood in the distance. The roof a dull reddish-brown, the exterior walls the colour of dried straw. The many shuttered windows around the house looked like the closed eyelids of sleeping children. Mariama gawked at this strange sight in astonishment.

Joseph Blumefield's voice interrupted her thoughts. She turned to follow the sound of the owner. He was standing outside the carriage, glasses resting on the bridge of his nose and his face was flat and without expression.

"This is where you will live from now on — your new home. You must never leave this compound without permission, which means you must ask and be granted leave by me, my wife, or an overseer. You will work six days every week, from six o'clock in the morning, or at daybreak until you are told to finish up for the day, usually eight o'clock in the evening, so after sunset. You will get two thirty-minute breaks for watering and food. On Sundays you will plant your vegetable plot, which you will share with your neighbours. This plot will help to feed you. I will provide salted codfish, sugar, some clothing, and sometimes a hat to keep the sun from your eyes.

"Don't try running away, because you will be caught and whipped — no fewer than one hundred lashes, and if you fight back, you will be shot dead."

Recognizing that most of the captives may not have fully understood the gravity of his direction, Blumefield lifted his musket and shot into the air. Six shocked captives scrambled around the dray cart ducking for shelter and screaming in fear for their lives.

Moments later, a shaken Mariama and the other captives were nudged along a dusty dry path that led away from the house towards a row of tiny huts. Mariama was ushered into the first one. The slave woman who had passed out the clothing earlier opened the door.

The hut was tidy and almost bare except for a few straw mats on a smooth earth floor. Two enamel cups and plates, an earthen goblet for holding water, a crude table fashioned from a tree stump, a half burnt candlestick, one small iron pot and a saucepan completed its contents. The woman pointed to one of the mats and Mariama walked over to it and sat down. Mariama then looked over at the woman and for the first time noticed that her left eye was severely damaged. The woman looked back and softly introduced herself.

"Me, Jameah. Who you?"

"Mariama," she replied.

"Dis you hut too. Dat you side, dis me side," Jameah added, pointing to the far corner, and then patting her chest. A few minutes later she walked away and sat outside the hut.

For the first time since being taken from her village, Mariama was alone. Like a dam releasing built-up pressure, she broke. The little hut could not contain her wailing, and slaves walking by outside paused for a few moments to listen.

"New one, new one," Jameah said, waving her hand to fend off the curious onlookers.

Mariama could no longer supress the sadness and fear that had consumed her throughout this journey. She thought about her family and how much she missed them. Her heart ached for them and for her home in Yele. She couldn't know what her life would be like from then on.

During the last part of her voyage to Demerary, she had felt extreme fatigue. Apart from the constant nausea, she had difficulty lying on her stomach at night.

At first she had thought it was because of the sea. But even when the seas were calm, the nausea and vomiting had continued. Gradually, it had dawned on her that there was a life growing inside her, and she had no one to tell. She wanted her mother, needed her. But deep down, she knew that she would never see her again.

And so in her new home in Demerary, she cried uncontrollably. Eventually, she fell asleep.

Sometime in the night she awoke to find the clothing she had received covering her body. Mariama lay quietly on her mat and listened in the dark. Someone else was in the hut. She could hear breathing. Her stomach grumbled in hungry protest at the lack of food in the hut. When the familiar sound of a cock crowing woke her at sunrise, she realized that she must have fallen asleep again.

The smell of hot sweet bush tea and steamed green plantains with cod greeted her. Jameah had prepared her breakfast, which Mariama devoured in a few minutes. Soon after, a short, heavy slave woman with round features and suspicious intrusive eyes came over from the hut next door.

"Driver say come get she," the woman announced.

"She field hand?" Jameah asked.

"She second gang," the woman answered.

The visitor waited outside while Jameah called Mariama. When the new girl stumbled through the doorway dressed in a baggy shift, too long to walk in properly, the woman looked her up and down.

"You got no rope fuh tie dat up? How you gon' wuk like dat?" She rolled her eyes. "Me bring you some. Wait heah."

The visitor hustled to her own hut and brought back a two-yard length of cord, promptly tied it around Mariama's waist and reefed up the garment, so the hem was now above her ankles.

"Me Josie. What dey call you?"

"Mariama. Me Mariama."

"Come wid me," said Josie, and motioned for Mariama to follow.

The two women walked down the lane together. They passed one pond where some older women were washing clothes and another where a few older men were bathing. "Dem third shift," she muttered, as Mariama eyed the bathers.

Over a small hill they met up with a second shift-work gang, comprising mostly women. The group then fanned out across the sugar cane fields owned by Joseph Blumefield. Mariama was assigned to Josie to learn her planting techniques.

***

Mariama continued to rise early every day and join the second gang in the fields. It was the planting season, and each day she inserted up to one hundred and fifty new cane shoots into pre-dug holes prepared by the first gang. At the end of the day, she cut bundles of grass from the nearby pasture and brought them to the horse barn to feed Dottie the mare and her Massa's two hogs. As her belly grew, she became slower, so she had to wake up at least an hour earlier to prepare. Being late for work was a recipe for being whipped. She had seen this happen to other women.

Fredric was born early — five months after she arrived on Plantation Victory. She had been experiencing sharp stomach pains two days prior, but had attributed it to her constant bending in the field. When she walked into the hut that night, Jameah looked over at her questioningly.

"You pee youself ... or de pickney come now?" She watched the trail of liquid flowing down Mariama's legs and pooling on the earthen floor of the hut.

Mariama followed Jameah's eyes to the small puddle beneath her swollen ankles and puffy feet. "Pickney. Now?" she looked at Jameah with bulging eyes and disbelief.

"Lay down, lay down. Me go to Josie fuh bring mo' light," Jameah said as she darted out of the dimly lit hut. Mariama did as she was told and struggled to curl her ninety-pound body on the mat, but the new life around her middle made it difficult. Her lips trembled with every jolt of pain as she fought to breathe. Gripped by fear and memories of the excruciating agony she experienced on the ship during the first assault, she anxiously awaited Jameah's return.

"She pickney comin'. Len' me you light." Jameah called out as she banged on Josie's door. Her neighbour greeted her with a small kerosene lantern.

"Okay, okay. Me come wid you. Maybe you need me help."

"Me got fuh hurry. You can fetch water come, but stay outside."

Josie looked at Jameah guardedly and kept her thoughts to herself. She waited outside the hut as Jameah hurried back to Mariama's side.

The young girl lay coiled like a green parrot water snake, writhing in pain. She groaned for her mother. "*YahYah, YahYah*, oh *YahYah*."

Jameah used the hem of Mariama's skirt to wipe the beads of sweat from her forehead. She then dunked the cloth into a saucepan of water and cleaned Mariama's entire face.

"Open and push, push mamie, push…"

Mariama obeyed, screaming throughout the anguish as the suffering intensified. Meanwhile, Josie paced outside the hut waiting to be summoned. She knew why Jameah wouldn't trust her to help, although the reason was never openly discussed.

The groans and squeals rode the night air, reaching the ears of slave women in neighbouring huts. Hessie came down from the main house to investigate and stood with Josie to keep her company.

The loud noises eased and a few minutes went by; then Jameah popped her head out of the door and took the additional saucepan of water from Josie.

"The boy pickney heah," she announced, and headed back into the hut.

When Mariama set eyes on the child who had finally entered the world, she was dumbfounded. What Jameah held up to her was frightening. She covered her face with trembling hands and peered through the small cracks of divided fingers. The baby boy was "yella" in complexion. His skin looked like the belly of an African lizard in the midday sun. His eyes were a strange bluish-green colour that reminded her of the big sea she had crossed. Mariama stared at him as tears pooled between her quivering fingers. She was horrified.

When her brother Braima was born, her father had rushed into the hut after he heard him cry. He danced with joy to have been given a son, held him up to the midday sun, and thanked Allah. As these memories flooded over her, an intense sadness engulfed her like a dark tide. She had a son, but not a husband to rejoice at his birth. Her body quavered as the loneliness crept in and she peered at this strange creature lying next to her. Maybe if she had her Sande, this would not be happening.

The enormity of her predicament hit. Unrelenting tears streamed from her swollen eyes as her isolation and the burden of this strange unwanted child weighed on her own fragile life. Mariama turned away from the newborn, and like a snail seeking comfort in its shell, she contracted her body and withdrew into a small hidden place inside herself.

The baby, as if aware of his mother's absence, also began to whimper.

Jameah retreated silently to her mat. Determined not to interfere, she let the crying duet go on for a while. But when Mariama's weeping continued rather than coming to a lull, Jameah got up, picked up the baby, and began to suckle him herself. The baby latched on to her breast and quietly nursed until he fell asleep. Out of the corner of her eye, she saw Mariama turn over and watch.

Jameah placed the sleeping child on the mat next to his mother and returned to her own mat and lay down. By this time Mariama had quieted, and only the odd shudder escaped her. Soon the trio were asleep encircled by the dim walls of the tiny slave hut.

A few minutes later, the soft sound of rain woke Mariama from her restful sleep. And then her maa was there leaning over and caressing the new born child. "*Ndui nyandengor* — The child is beautiful," she whispered. As Mariama tried to speak her maa waved her hand over the girl's face and quietly said, "*Tilongor abiay* — You are loved." Then she was gone.

***

One month to the day after Fredric was born, Maudie, the Blumefields' junior housekeeper, went to be with her ancestors after a bout with malaria.

Henrietta Blumefield requested a new girl who was young, quiet, and hardworking. Mariama fit the description and so was brought to work in the great house.

"Your baby will remain in the hut with Jameah," Henrietta told her. "She can take care of him and continue to nurse him. You can visit him when your work in the house is done."

"Yes, ma'am," Mariama said with some relief. Jameah had more experience mothering, though she had no children with her at present. Nursing Fredric had come as second nature to her. Mariama had found this puzzling and asked her why.

"Me old Massa sell me two pickney, Mariama," Jameah had told her. "He sell dem fuh pay fuh dem eggs me tek. Den he sell me to Massa Blumefield. So, me tek care o' de boy fuh you."

Jameah's voice was soft, and for the first time Mariama saw the sadness in her face. Jameah would take care of Fredric much better than she could.

The next day Mariama began her duties in the great house at Victory working from dawn until dusk, six days each week.

PART II

CHAPTER 11

LESSONS

March 1800 – August 1801

Mariama stared at the woman who greeted her at the side door of the great house. She had light-green eyes and light-coloured skin, so unusual in a black person, but similar to her own newly born son's appearance.

"You mus' be Mariama," she said, squinting in the early morning sunlight.

"Yes, me Mariama,"

"And me ... call me Hessie, come in, come in." she beckoned.

When Mariama entered the house, she was taken aback by the abundance and opulence of the rooms and their furnishings. She had never seen anything like it before.

A large dining table with ball and claw foot legs dominated the middle of the dining room. High back chairs covered in red and gold silk damask fabrics encircled it, and a slightly ajar tall chest of drawers took up one corner of the room. It contained cutlery, lace-edged linen napkins, and multiple white tablecloths. Queen Anne sofas in burgundy hues, framed by coffee and side tables with fluted cabriole legs, stood on colourful patterned rugs in the parlour and living room. Framed portraits of smug white men and women with lips pursed in disapproval looked down on the opulence. And here and there the portrait of a favourite horse added to the gallery.

A strong scent of linseed oil and fresh lemon engulfed Mariama as she stepped inside. Someone, most likely Hessie since Maudie's passing, had carefully attended to the cleaning and polishing chores. Where there were open windows, sheer ivory-coloured muslin curtains moved softly in the currents produced by outside breezes. The air was heavy, close, and damp, and everywhere the polished wood, imported fabric, metal, and glass seemed to breathe and sigh in the languid heat. There was a ceiling fan in each room — Demerary was scorching most of the year, even throughout the rainy season — but they awaited the manual labour of slaves to be effective.

"Dis Mariama, ma'am." Hessie said as Henrietta entered the room.

Mariama glanced over quizzically at the woman who had just joined them. *This can't be the Missus*, Mariama thought. *She's tall and skinny like a spindly newborn giraffe. If a strong wind blew in unexpectedly, she might bend and break.* She had expected a more robust and commanding physical presence in a mistress. However, this impression of weakness was belied by a sharp gaze and firm voice.

"I hope you work well girl," Henrietta said as she looked her new junior housemaid up and down. "I like a clean house. I will show you the rooms and Hessie will tell you the work that they require." She had already started walking, pointing to each room as she moved along. Hessie followed her closely and Mariama trotted along behind glancing at the areas to which Henrietta pointed.

A few minutes later, the tour complete, Hessie escorted a perplexed looking new house servant around showing her the cleaning utensils and how the mistress liked to have the job done.

"Missus fuss fuss, but me show you how she like it," she said as she brought Mariama to Henrietta's bedroom. "Missus got nuff fancy sheet wid lace and frill. Dem only fuh she and de Massa white skin." She said with a chuckle. "She got white one, blue and green one, and one wid nuff, nuff rose, just like in she garden. Me use to wonder how it feel 'pon me skin, so when me come fuh turn down de bed, me lock de door, climb in de bed, close me eye and pretend me own it. Fuh one lil moment me feel rich like she. All de sheet dem soft, but de blue silk one slippery and cool, feel nice 'pon you skin. If you do it, you mus' neva get ketch." Hessie grinned; a mischievous glint in her eyes. Mariama tittered as Hessie continued. "Dis how it wuk: you empty and wash de night pot, mek up de bed, den you wash and dry de dishes, sweep de floor and mop every day, den dust all de furniture. And you must polish de floor Saturday and Wednesday. And clean de window 'pon Saturday too. Me wash clothes Monday, Wednesday, and Friday. Tuesday and Thursday me iron and clean Massa and Missus shoes and me turn down de bed every night. Me help you sometime, and Millie help you too. She de cook and she bake and clean de kitchen. She wuk everyday. Me show you how fuh set de table fuh morning, midday and night."

Mariama felt a bit overwhelmed. There were so many rooms, at least ten over two floors, but with Hessie and Millie's help she was somewhat reassured that it would be okay.

A week after she had begun her job in the great house, the newly minted junior house slave had mastered all her chores. Hessie and Millie were delighted, and Hessie kept her promise and helped Mariama when she had completed her daily chores. Soon the three house slaves developed a rhythm to their work that vibrated throughout Victory's great house. Henrietta was pleased that Maudie's replacement had worked out well.

***

Eighteen months later, Mariama stood listening closely to the exchange of opinions around her, never lifting her gaze from the darkly stained wooden floor of the dining room. Joseph and Henrietta Blumefield, sat next to each other at the head of the mahogany table. William Gladstone, or Bill to his friends, sat across from James McDuff, who was seated to the right of Henrietta. An intricately woven white French lace cloth draped the table. Mariama had brought in warm buttered scones with English apricot jam and Henrietta's favourite silver pot with steeping tea and placed them on the table. She had withdrawn quietly to the relative darkness at the side awaiting dismissal by Mrs. Blumefield, but instead the conversation continued.

"King George should send those bloody missionaries over here so we can treat them to some of this blazing heat," said McDuff. "That'd shut 'em up."

"They should have to put up with this backward lot. That'd teach 'em how bloody hard it is to earn a shilling in these parts," echoed Gladstone between short puffs on his tortoiseshell pipe. Perfect ivory smoke rings rose towards the ceiling; a liquorice-flavoured aroma punctuated the air.

"Actually, I hear a new missionary is due in Demerary soon," Gladstone continued, addressing no one in particular. "The Missionary Society has planned a few deployments to the West Indies and Demerary, and we will be lucky recipients of one of those chaps."

"Yes, I hear he's a bachelor, so there'll be no family," said McDuff. "I presume it could spell trouble for us planters." Looking at Joseph Blumefield, he added, "We could easily fix that, though. Just throw him a dark wench to keep his bed warm — though in this heat, he might prefer to keep his bed as cool as possible." He chuckled and looked around at the other diners. No one commented.

Henrietta Blumefield sat admiring her favourite teacup — on it a garden scene with a young male slave serving sandwiches to his masters. She cleared her throat, intimating her intention to join in the conversation and said in a voice barely above a whisper, "It would be a sin for a missionary man to lie with a black slave. Furthermore, Mr. McDuff, that does not count as a relationship with a woman."

McDuff's face turned crimson. Looking squarely at Henrietta, he said, "Forgive me, madam. I apologize for being crass. I should have been more sensitive in the presence of a lady."

Henrietta smiled, acknowledging McDuff's apology. "Perhaps this missionary will be too busy doing God's work, and he might find female company a distraction," she continued, raising her eyebrows and looking around the room. "Or perhaps he will have the dedication of a Catholic priest and exclude women from his personal life altogether."

Gladstone and McDuff nodded in earnest agreement.

Joseph Blumefield, a man of few words, simply smiled and said, "Whatever his bent, gentlemen, we have to support each other for the sake of our business and our profit margin. Missionaries are usually our foes in this work."

Gladstone appeared reflective for a few moments. "Joseph," he said at length, "you are correct. It is about the business. I have poured a lot of energy and money into it. We will just have to deal with the new missionary when he arrives. We can't let him ruin it for us. Lyken played by the rules and this new chap should too."

McDuff looked at Gladstone and smiled in agreement.

Gladstone then rose from his seat and bowed to Henrietta.

"I must take my leave. Will you be going in my direction, Bill?"

Gladstone left the table, followed by William, Joseph, and Henrietta.

As they moved towards the dining room door, Joseph nudged his gold-rimmed glasses a notch higher on his sloping nose and announced, "Whatever we do, gentlemen, we must not let the missionaries win. The Negroes cannot be taught to read the Bible. If they do, they'll soon be able to read for themselves about the abolitionists and their push to get rid of the great trade upon which we depend. We could lose all our property and become paupers. Keeping them illiterate is a battle we must win." Joseph's words had an element of urgency that caught both men's attention.

When they reached the front door, Henrietta remained inside and Joseph stepped onto the porch. In a lowered voice he said, "There is one more pressing issue I need to discuss, gentlemen, but it was too delicate for a lady's ears. I am troubled by the fact that my slave stock is not reproducing. I continue to purchase more slaves for the plantation, but see no offspring from the wenches within. I wonder if the problem lies with the stock of females, or the lack of good seed in the bucks. They are certainly randy enough, but to no effect. I have tried to remedy this situation by allowing my drivers free reign with the wenches in case a bit of release is needed," he winked at his visitors. "I have cautioned them to take care and not render them unfit for work. Do you have any such frustrations?"

McDuff eagerly answered, "Joseph, yours is not an isolated challenge. It is something we have discussed at the Gentleman's Club. Except for Desmond Wilder, who still runs a cotton plantation, many of us planters are dealing with this very problem. Wilder's slaves work five days per week, farm their gardens on Saturdays, and he gives them Christian counsel on Sundays. Some are suggesting we give the slaves spirituous drink with their meals on Friday nights to help the mating situation. Others are suggesting that we give them more time to rest so their bodies can heal and have a chance to reproduce. This will however be taxing on our income."

"Wilder has three 'families' on his plantation. The slave families have produced thirteen offspring in six years. According to records, two have died, but eleven have survived. There is hope." Gladstone concluded.

"Okay, gentlemen, let's have an open discussion at the club next Saturday. It is imperative that we come up with a clear solution. A safe passage and good night to you both."

Joseph watched as his visitors rode out of the plantation's compound. *Forced mating is the only solution, and that Wilder needs a swift kick in the arse*, Joseph thought.

Henrietta had returned to the dining room and waved Mariama forward to clear the dinner dishes.

As she began to clear the table, Mariama mulled over the conversation she had overheard. She didn't understand all of it, but what she gathered was that a man was coming who might want to teach the slaves to read and write. Her owners and the other white men were determined to stop that from happening.

Mariama gathered the last of the dishes, glasses, teacups, and the silver teapot from the dining table and took them into the kitchen. She then returned to the dining room and waited to be dismissed for the night. Henrietta rang the dismissal bell, and Mariama moved quickly along the narrow hallway that led to the kitchen to assist Millie, the cook, with the clean-up duties. Millie washed the dishes while Mariama dried them. When she had finished her chores, Mariama walked slowly down to the servants' quarters at the lower level of the great house. This level housed rooms for the head housekeeper, the cook, and the junior housekeeper. Mariama retreated to the third room, where she threw her weary body across the sleeping mat to rest for the night.

Sleep would not come to her, however. She was agitated and could not stop thinking about the conversation between Massa Blumefield, his wife, and the two visitors. Not knowing what it all meant, she wondered if she would still be allowed to attend Sunday service at chapel. And could she still hope to meet newly arrived captives there from her homeland? Since there were no mosques in Demerary, she had sought solace in the only religious sanctuary available, the Christian church, with its suffering and nailed God. She had hoped that by attending, perhaps someday she might hear news of her village or her family, or one day meet a captured village elder who could help with her transition to womanhood.

Mariama tossed and turned on her mat, disturbed by the threat of yet another loss.

Despite her fears, however, she decided not to tell anyone about the conversation she had heard. *It might not be wise*, she thought, *to raise a fuss about something that might not even happen.* As Old Man Jaheem always said, "*Biglorbe kebiwindia* — Look before you leap."

Eventually she settled down and fell asleep, but too soon the rooster began its annoying early morning crowing. It was time to prepare to face the new day, though she had barely slept.

She closed her eyes again before rising from her toasty warm mat. Thanking both Allah and the Christian God for another day of life was a ritual she had begun every morning and evening just before her son was born. She was trying to hold on to her old religion, while slowly learning to incorporate the new one. Saying one prayer at dawn and one at night, instead of five each day, was a compromise that kept her connected to her faith. She prayed for health and strength to survive the coming day and to learn to accept her son more deeply. Finally, she prayed for a miracle to receive her Sande.

Twelve months later, Thomas R. G. Leighton, evangelical missionary with the Missionary Society, arrived in the colony of Demerary.

CHAPTER 12

FOOD, THE CLINCHER

June 1802

One Sunday afternoon Mariama sat near Jameah's hut and watched a whistling Buck weed the carrion crow bush outside his own hut. Something amusing caught her attention. She noticed that after every three or four swings of his three-inch-wide machete, Buck would glance over at Josie's dwelling. For a few minutes she followed his gaze, but couldn't see anything of interest. Then Josie emerged from her hut, and Buck's whistling grew louder as he immediately puffed up his chest, raised his shoulders and hopped from side to side, like a male bird of paradise in a courtship dance. Mariama felt the blood rush to her cheeks as she giggled, and she looked away. It had been a long time since she had seen humour in anything. As she walked back to the great house, she could still feel the rare warmth of amusement.

***

The first time Buck saw Josie was at Stabroek. Both of them were being auctioned off outside the wharf after their slave ship moored.

Josie's five-foot, six-inch frame was barely taller than his, yet she was defiant of the orders being shouted by the six-foot-tall backra. She refused to lift her arms above her head or turn around to be inspected as she had been told. Buck had admired her defiance but was also frightened for her. He feared that at any moment she would feel the wrath of the backra's whip, and it turned out that his concern was justified.

Josie had taken forty lashes across her back for resisting inspection. The welts left great criss-crossed ridges, longer and deeper than Buck had seen before, even on a tribesman during the harshest of tribal wars. In the little Ghanaian village outside Accra where he had grown up and lived all his life, Buck's eyes had been shielded from this level of brutality, especially towards a woman.

Josie had stood in the blistering midday sun, eyes focused straight ahead, and taken her beating silently. Only in response to the very last few blows had tears escaped her eyes. The blows stopped when she lost her balance and fell to the ground. Buck felt his upper body jerk forward but stopped his legs in time from leaping forward to defend her. He could see that Josie was a warrior and had felt an instant connection to her. She was rebellious and strongheaded, and his heart raced as he watched her stand up to the backra.

When they ended up on the same dray cart on the road to Victory later that day, Buck had sat as close to Josie as he could and tried to make eye contact with her. But this warrior woman sat stoically, blood still oozing from the fresh welts on her exposed back. She stared right past him and every other captured soul on the way to a life of bondage.

Josie was the daughter of an Akan medicine man. Her mother held the esteemed senior position of his three wives. As a child, Josie had watched her father brew various potions to heal villagers with numerous ailments. She became familiar with roots, flowers, and leaves and their different properties. She watched as her father treated snakebites and blood disorders.

"Me learn de potion, and de code when village women talk hush-hush wid me mama," Josie had told Millie and Hessie.

She had confided, "Me mama give potion fuh secret sickness only woman talk 'bout. Neva man talk 'bout."

"De man piaba and de gully root mek good woman tea" was the code that Josie's mother used when agreeing to terminate a difficult and troublesome pregnancy. Josie was proud of all the knowledge she had acquired and shared it freely in this new society.

Buck tried for three cane-planting seasons to get Josie's attention, employing every tactic he could think of. He weeded in the cane bed next to her, took care to leave the huts at the same time she did every morning, and sat under the same tree as she did at the midday break. He even walked back to the huts the same time she did. But Josie never acknowledged the attention he gave her. He wasn't sure that she even noticed him.

Then one Saturday evening Buck tried a new approach.

"Dis fuh you, Ms. Josie," Buck stood at the door of Josie's hut, a big toothless grin on his face.

Josie eyed him and the covered enamel plate suspiciously.

"Tek it nah, me see you watch me cook me fish, eddoe, and plantain. Me mek it special fuh you. Open and see de okra and peppa. It come from me plot, and de fish come from de creek."

A slow half smile crossed Josie's lips as she fanned her hand in mocking protest. "Me mek me own food Buck, me don' wan' you food."

"Come nuh … try it and see if you like it," Buck said as he moved his secret weapon closer to her face, to allow the rich aroma of coconut broth to drift into her waiting nostrils. Her smile widened. Finally, he had broken through.

"Ok Buck, me try it, but me nah gon' like it," she said, trying to hide her delight. Then she turned and walked back into her hut, sat on her mat, and devoured every morsel. Buck was a good cook indeed, and her days of ignoring him were over. She patted her belly and smiled.

Buck skipped back over to his hut across the lane, strutting like a jacana bird that had just impressed a mate in a deep forest pond. "Yas," he whispered as he waved his clenched fist into the air.

A few nights later, Buck was sitting outside his hut to escape the trapped tropical heat left over from the sweltering day. It was much cooler outside after dark, and he often sat for a while by himself under the stars before retiring inside. On this particular night Buck thought he heard movement to his left, close to the other huts. It was too dark to see, so he had to depend on his keen sense of hearing. Now he heard further movement in the distance. Whatever, or whoever, was out there was moving away from him. There was the faint crackling of dry grass. Someone was taking care to avoid the laneway, as though wary of being detected.

Curious, he squeezed his left eye shut and listened more carefully. Someone was definitely moving around nearby, in between the huts. He called out ever so softly, "Who dere?" His question was met by an eerie silence. Buck opened his eye and looked around him. Nothing. All he saw were the tiny lanterns of the fireflies, glowing and fading in the gloom, and all he heard was the sporadic chorus of chirping crickets in the thick blackness. The sounds of movement were gone.

Buck slowly eased himself up from where he sat on the tree stump. He crept slowly, noiselessly, down the laneway, peering between the mostly dark huts. Then he heard the grass rustling again, closer this time. He stopped and held his breath, listening. The footsteps were moving away from the huts now.

He followed, quickening his pace as he tried to catch up, though he was not even sure whether what he was trailing was human or animal. *Maybe it's one of the slaves trying to run*, he thought with alarm. Silently, he continued along the laneway preparing himself to talk this fellow slave out of a hopeless escape attempt.

 He felt compelled to try to help this unseen person avoid a thrashing. Slave owners were vicious with their whips, and Buck had once seen a young, pregnant slave girl called Betty beaten until she died. She had wanted freedom for her baby and had tried to escape in the night but had been recaptured in the woods and given over sixty lashes. Still alive, her bruised and bleeding body had been left strapped to a tree trunk. The blood had dried and caked on her shiny black skin before she eventually died of shock and blood loss. Buck knew he should at least try to save whoever this was from a similar fate.

Moving off the path, he ventured between the huts and then paused to observe his surroundings. For a moment the night was still again. Then he heard it — a faint scratching of soil mixed with the sound of something brushing dry shrubbery. He moved closer on tiptoe, in sync with the scratching sound.

Someone was quietly digging up the soil at the back of a hut — Josie's hut. Buck gasped. Who could it be? Was Josie all right? He inched closer, peering into the dark.

"Who dere? You running?" Buck whispered. He waited, but there was no answer. "You betta come out or me call Massa Joseph, you hear?" he hissed.

"Buck? Dat you?" Josie whispered back now.

"Josie? Dat you? You running?"

"None o' you concern."

"Why you digging?"

"Go 'way. Leave me 'lone. Go 'way, Buck!"

"Why you digging in de dark?"

"None o' you concern," Josie repeated.

Buck moved closer to where Josie had been digging, but Josie moved forward to intercept him.

"Why you don' go, Buck? Go!"

Her voice had grown hard. Buck's eyes were becoming accustomed to the dark, and now he could see the outline of something on the ground.

"What you got dere, Josie? You hiding sumthin'?"

Suddenly Josie pounced on him. Lurching to the side, he lost his balance and fell to the ground. They scuffled for a few moments as Buck tried to grab whatever it was that Josie was hiding, which Josie tried with all her might to keep from him. She was the stronger of the two, however, and almost effortlessly she flipped him onto his back and pinned him with her body. Her full breasts fell against his face, and Buck stopped struggling. Josie took her time now, wriggling her body ever so slowly down across Buck's until her face was above his. Buck felt himself harden. He had waited years for this closeness with her.

But as he reached his hands downward to caress her buttocks, she shot up onto her knees, and Buck realized she was now holding the package she had been concealing.

"Let go, Buck! Let go!" Josie whispered, panting.

Buck took no heed. He held on to her even more firmly, kneading his strong fingers into her buttocks and kissing her breasts. Josie began to twist away from him, pushing at his arms with her free hand while still trying to keep a grip on the package.

Suddenly Buck felt something land on his left leg. Josie froze as he reached down to grasp it. He recoiled as his fingers cupped a tiny, damp head and glided across the emaciated face of a baby, still warm to the touch.

"Oh, *Nyame!*" Buck whispered, calling on the creator. "What ... who?"

He struggled to sit up.

"Josie, what you done did?"

"Me done nutten, me just send dem to de ancestors. Dey keep dem till me come."

"Oh, *Nsamanfo!*" Buck called to his ancestors. "Forgive ... forgive!" Then something she said struck him. "Dem? You got mo'?"

Horrified, Buck pulled himself up onto his hands and knees and began to grope around on the dark damp earth.

"Me don' got mo' now, me send dem befo' ... Buck, no mama want dis life fuh she pickney — so, me help de mamas, and me help dem pickney too."

Buck stared at Josie. His eyes began to fill with tears. The baby's body lay on the ground between them, as Josie sat with her arms hugging her knees. As she spoke, her voice cracked, and she rocked her body gently backward and forward.

"See, Buck, when all dis trouble done — when Massa done with teking me; when me no wuk from dark to dark no mo'; when no mo' whip go 'cross me back and head and foot; and no slap and spit go 'cross me face ... when all dis trouble done, me gon see dem all again. Fuh now, de ancestors tek care o' dem."

Chapter 13

Paradise Lost

August 1802

"So this is Demerary. Another paradise lost."

Thomas Leighton stood at the bow of the arriving ship and scanned the rain-soaked wharf as if searching the surrounding alleys and gullies for Lucifer. If the poet Milton was correct, then Thomas Leighton had his apostolic work cut out to regain God's paradise, at least this part of it. Thomas fell on his knees in quiet prayer.

"Oh, God of majesty and of grace, be my shepherd in this forsaken place. Let me walk daily in your light in this new land to which you have brought me. Dear Lord, let me spread your word to the heathen and to the downtrodden, so that I might regain this part of your paradise for your glory. In your holy name I pray. Amen."

Thomas opened his eyes and raised them towards the overcast sky. A lone white seagull flapped by in the humid air. He followed the bird's flight and watched it land on a wooden pole high above the sodden docks. It observed the approaching ship from its vantage point.

Before him, Thomas could see little other than a misty foggy grey. Only small patches of light were visible amid the dull scene.

Those bright spots emanated from the joyful faces of the white planters and their families who had come to the wharf to greet passengers on the arriving vessel.

As the ship was warped into the berth, Thomas watched sailors bustle around the deck. They lowered huge coils of twisted rope to the jetty to secure the barque in place. Overseers with young slave boys in tow boarded the vessel and began commandeering the lifting and transporting of trunks and cases. These young boys dragged multiple containers filled with cartons of Bohea or black teas, English jams, spools of lace, cotton yarn, osnaburg fabric, and the like to dray carts waiting in nearby alleys and avenues. Merchants checked bills of lading and small trading took place on the jetty below. English and Dutch postholders accompanied by their Amerindian slave catchers from the hinterland also bargained and traded annatto dye and indigo with the arriving crew.

Thomas clutched the handle of his small wooden trunk, tilted it on its side and began pulling it towards the ship's gangway.

"Ahoy there!" someone called out.

Thomas turned and looked in the direction of the voice. A tall, lanky fellow with a slight stoop, a big grin and dancing brown eyes was advancing. A short, stocky African was attending him.

"The Reverend Leighton, I presume," said the man.

"Yes, yes, I am Thomas Leighton. You must be..."

"Robert Lyken, and this is Quashee," the man interjected, still grinning.

Quashee smiled and nodded.

"I trust your journey was a good one?" the Reverend Lyken continued.

"It was for the most part, except for some tumultuous weather the ship encountered a few days ago. I can truly say that I am glad to see the journey over," Thomas Leighton intoned.

Quashee reached over and motioned to relieve Thomas of his trunk. Thomas hesitated, maintaining a firm grasp on the handle. He flashed a look at Lyken, not being quite certain of the protocol between missionary and slave.

"Quashee wants to help, Thomas. Please let him," Lyken explained.

"Quashee's owner, Mr. Sanders Janssen, has returned to the Netherlands due to illness and has allowed him to help Nell and me around the parsonage. As you can see, Quashee is an older chap and cannot do laborious field work. Janssen's other slaves are working on nearby plantations to earn him money and keep his business afloat. Quashee has become like a member of our household. He likes to be useful."

Thomas released his grip and let Quashee take the trunk, ornamented with brass tacks down the sides and cowhide trim. It had been a farewell gift from his parents and his Uncle William back in Liverpool. Holding the iron handles firmly, Quashee slid the trunk along the gangway and off the ship.

Together the three walked over to a waiting horse-drawn carriage. Quashee loaded the trunk onto the empty seat in the front, and Robert and Thomas sat down in the back of the carriage. Soon they were headed towards the parsonage, which was twelve miles to the east, past Plantation Gentleman's Paradise. As they travelled, Thomas observed how the red dirt road cut a gash through the green walls of vegetation.

"So what's your reason for wanting to give up your post here? Are you returning to England?" Thomas asked Robert Lyken.

"No, no, my dear man. There is much, much work to be done here. I am taking up a position in Berbice."

Thomas glanced over at Robert. "Berbice?"

"Yes, it's a county to the east. There are many enslaved Africans there. Missionaries are sorely needed."

Thomas said nothing.

"I leave in two days," Robert added.

"I gather this will be a fast transition for me, then," Thomas offered with a nervous half-smile.

"Don't you worry, my dear brother. Quashee and the other Christian slaves will help you adjust. The planters will not, however.

Just stick to God's plan, though, and it will become easier each day." Robert paused, looked over at Thomas, and continued.

"Most plantations are owned by British or Dutch planters, and many of the owners are absentee — you know, they live in Britain or the Netherlands. Usually, they employ managers, and in a few cases, overseers, to administer their properties. The slaves are customarily at the mercy of these hard-hearted chaps. There are some owners though, who live here and run the operations. Typically, they are more empathetic — at least, that's the belief."

Thomas listened intently, trying his best to absorb all the new information.

Quashee turned the carriage into the driveway of the parsonage. It was now dusk, and the glow of the candles in the front windows of the home offered the weary traveller a warm welcome.

Robert's wife Nell and their young son Jonas greeted them at the front door.

"Welcome to our home, which will be yours soon," she said with a smile, as she held the large wooden door open for everyone to enter.

The aroma of fresh baking filled the air. Thomas paused and took a deep, appreciative breath. The familiar smell of buttery, rich goodness transported him back to Liverpool and his mother's tiny kitchen in the Danube Street row house, a place where puff pastries, fruit pies, and other heavenly creations were prepared every Saturday afternoon to celebrate the end of a work week. He missed his home.

Robert escorted the new missionary to his temporary quarters in a bedroom at the back of the house.

"Here is where you can wash up and rest until supper," he said. "We eat at six o'clock. Come back in when you're ready." Quashee had already deposited Thomas's trunk beside the coconut-husk-filled mattress in the bedroom. After a quick face-wash over the enamel basin on the small mahogany stand, Thomas joined Robert and his family in the small dining room for a meal of pumpkin soup and freshly baked bread. Quashee ate in the kitchen. Later, Nell served mince pies and tea for dessert in celebration of Thomas's safe arrival.

Dinner conversation was mostly about the latest happenings in 1802 London and Liverpool. Robert Lyken and his family had moved to Demerary almost three years before and had never returned to England since coming to South America. They yearned for news about the mother country and welcomed the opportunity to hear Thomas's stories.

One particular topic they spoke about was the explored merger of the Society of Friends, a Christian denomination, and the Missionary Society. Thomas suggested that the merger could help reinforce William Wilberforce's fight to end slavery in the Americas. Both men admired this deeply religious and wealthy English merchant who was leading the charge for the abolition of the slave trade, and ultimately of slavery itself, in the British Empire.

"A tide of rising support would be good for the cause. It would help us to achieve more in these parts," Robert said.

"The work is happening, and the championing of abolition is growing. One can feel it in the air," Thomas reassured his host.

The new missionary retired to bed at around eight o'clock. Despite the strange surroundings and feel of unfamiliar bedding against his skin, he slept soundly until four thirty, when the boisterous crowing of the neighbouring plantation's rooster woke him. For a moment Thomas thought he was back in the old English farmhouse near Sefton in Merseyside.

CHAPTER 14

A MIGHTY FORTRESS

August 1802

Mariama rose early that Sunday morning. The Reverend Lyken was going to preach his last sermon before leaving for Berbice with his family. She would miss him. He had promised that a new missionary would come, but no one knew when this would happen. It was a two-hour walk from Plantation Victory to the chapel, a time Mariama looked forward to, when she could meet other slaves from neighbouring plantations. She found the banter and teasing among the crowd entertaining, though sometimes the stories people shared about new forms of abuse and other horrors brought tears to her eyes. Today she expected a full turnout.

As she prepared, Hessie's stirring in the room next door caught her attention. *Why is she up so early? Is she going to chapel? Hessie mostly goes to town on Sundays.* Mariama was baffled.

"Chapel is fuh praying people. I ain't a praying woman," Hessie had once told Mariama. "Why you pray, Mari?"

Mariama had looked away in the distance and slowly replied, "Prayin' bring me to home and Allah ... and God. That is why me pray."

"Bring you? Where prayer bring you? You still heah," Hessie had said with a giggle.

Mariama had thought hard and long. Then, clumsily placing her right fist in the middle of her chest, she had closed her eyes and said softly, "Keep home heah."

Hessie shot her a quizzical glance. "Home? Wha' home? Dis you home."

"No, me home, far away wid *YahYah*, *KeKe*, and Braima..." Seeing the puzzled look on Hessie's face, she had cut the conversation short.

Mariama now listened more closely to the sounds from the next room. *What could it be that Hessie is saying?* Though the words were muffled, she heard numbers. With a start, she realized that Hessie was doing something forbidden: learning to count. Smiling, she continued to get dressed.

Mariama arrived at the meeting place at the top of the dam just as the rooster started to crow. Here she joined the quiet chatter of field slaves from the huts on the edge of the estate. After the initial exchange of greetings, small groups strolled east along the dusty road towards Plantation Gentleman's Paradise. They had to get there by sunrise. As they walked, slivers of indigo and pink light grew on the eastern horizon, increasingly followed by tinges of yellow-gold. It was a beautiful sunrise, which reminded Mariama of the morning sky on the day Khadi went home to the ancestors. A wave of sadness engulfed Mariama. She paused for a moment but then composed herself and moved on.

Small groups joined the procession, converging on the road that led behind Gentleman's Paradise. The road did not have an official name, but slaves called it Chapel Dam.

A carriage with Robert Lyken and another white man arrived at the small unpainted wooden chapel just around seven thirty. The white visitor was unexpected. A sudden hush came over the chattering slaves as the Reverend Lyken and the stranger climbed down and walked along the path to the chapel door.

"Hello and good morning to you all!" Robert called out. "This is the Reverend Leighton, your new pastor," he said, smiling at the group.

Mariama, sitting on the side of the dirt road across from the chapel, lowered her feet into the shallow water-filled trench to wash off the dust and mud from the five-mile walk. Studying the new man cautiously from a distance, she decided he must be the missionary she had overheard her owners discussing during dinner sometime back. She slowly rose up, wiped the soles of her feet on the parched edge of the grass, and crossed the dusty road to get a closer look at the Reverend Leighton.

He was young and about Hessie's height. His brownish hair lay in limp curls plastered on his head; a few wisps had escaped onto his pale, shiny forehead. His eyes, she thought, were very warm.

Her thoughts were interrupted by Quashee's voice, as he rounded up all the slaves to enter the chapel. The Reverend Lyken and the new missionary walked ahead of everyone else. Mariama followed.

Church service began at eight o'clock with a hymn:

> *A mighty fortress is our God*
> *A bulwark never failing:*
> *Our helper He, amid the flood*
> *Of mortal ills prevailing.*

Mariama had heard this hymn a few times. It was one of the Reverend Lyken's favourites. She had always wanted to know what the word "bulwark" meant but could barely even pronounce it. Since God was a bulwark, she assumed it must be something important. Beyond the words, though, she liked the sound of the music and admired how the Reverend Lyken closed his eyes and lifted both his arms in a swaying motion when he sang the words.

As the hymn ended, the Reverend Lyken stepped aside to let the new missionary preach.

"The Bible tells us about Job..." the young man began, and Mariama settled back to listen.

Thomas Leighton was thrilled to give his first sermon to his new congregants. They seemed mostly fascinated to hear their first sermon from him. The experience was so unlike his first in his Liverpool church, where he had felt ill at ease, his every word judged by the congregation.

"Job was an innocent, good man who loved God and avoided evil," he continued. "Yet thieves stole everything he owned, fire destroyed his cattle, and a mighty wind destroyed his house and killed his children. After all that suffering, Job was struck down with a horrible, painful disease. But Job never lost faith. He loved God and trusted that one day everything would be made right for him."

Glancing across the crowd, he saw that the slaves were listening intently.

"In your trials and difficulties, I ask you to be like Job. Trust the same God that Job trusted, and he will see you through your troubles."

There was a final hymn, and then the service ended.

After their goodbyes to one another, the slaves streamed out along Chapel Dam and walked back to their respective plantations. Quashee and a few of the other male slaves remained behind to lock up. Robert and Thomas headed to the parsonage for lunch and to give Robert time to prepare for his journey to New Amsterdam, Berbice.

On her way home, Mariama pondered the missionary's teachings. There was something familiar about the story of Job. Old Man Jaheem had told a similar tale to the village children about a patient man who loved Allah but lost his family and everything he owned because the devil wanted him to give up on Allah. Jaheem had cautioned the children to look out for the devil, who would promise them good things if they followed him. He had told them that taking the shortcut to what might appear good usually turned out to be bad. "Trust Allah. He is always right, even when it does not seem like he is." The junior housekeeper's lips widened into a smile, even as hot tears well up in her eyes. How she longed to hear Jaheem again! How she longed for home!

Mariama became lost in her private thoughts and hardly heard the conversations of the other slaves. She thought about what she might have done to bring so much evil into her life. Stolen from her family, forced into slavery and then becoming a mother before her Sande. For many nights she had lain awake and wondered about the cruel and twisted pathways of her fate. She had tried to find answers as to what she might have done to cause so much suffering at the hands of evil people. She thought long and hard, but found no explanations. Yet, she continued to pray to the only source of comfort and support that she knew. She wondered when Allah or the Christian God would answer her prayers.

The two-hour walk back to Plantation Victory passed quickly. When she arrived, she saw Jameah sitting outside her hut, watching Fredric and another young boy playing in the lane. Fredric continued chasing the other boy, oblivious to Mariama's approach.

"Come, Fred, you mama heah!" Jameah called out.

Fredric paused, grabbed a handful of dirt and tossed it at the other child to slow him down.

"Fredric, you come now," Jameah said sternly.

Fredric lurched over to Jameah, still giggling from his triumph over the other child. Mariama smiled at Jameah. Tired from her long walk in the blazing sun, she picked up the calabash and scooped it into the nearby bucket filled with cool rainwater. She tilted her hot, sweaty head back and drank most of its contents without pausing to take a breath and then poured the rest over her head and face.

"Praise to Allah, praise to God," Mariama said as she raised the ragged hem of her long indigo skirt and lowered herself onto the tree stump outside the hut. "Jameah, de boy a' right?" she asked.

"Dis pickney good, but he don' eat. He magga and he move quick like lightning in de sky. Chapel good today?"

Mariama looked over at Fredric's thin build. "Yes, he boney," she said with a smile. "New precha come today and he talk 'bout Job, who suffer nuff but still love God."

She closed her eyes and reflected on the Reverend Leighton's sermon once again. Then, as though she had had a sudden epiphany, she placed her hands on her hips and raised herself up off her wooden perch.

"Going to we patch now. Mus' weed befo' Massa bring out he whip. Ain't bin there in a while. Jameah, you rest now."

"Come Fredric, come wid me," she called to the boy, who was digging a small hole at the side of the hut. As he leapt to his feet and raced towards her, Mariama realized Jameah was right — he did move like lightning.

Together, mother and son bustled down the lane and over the small mound of earth, or the little hill, as the slaves called it, to the fields below. The scent of fresh horse manure filled the air. The vegetable patches were lush with plantain, peas, okra, and pepper plants.

CHAPTER 15

DINGEY CHRISTIAN

May 1803

Hessie — young, wily, and beautiful — was the head house slave on Plantation Victory. She was also the personal servant to Henrietta Blumefield, mistress of the house. Hessie's one-hundred-eighty-pound body mass evenly balanced on her five-foot, ten-inch frame was complemented by brilliant sea green eyes set perfectly against sapodilla-brown skin. It was commonplace for strangers to Victory to react with surprise and not-so-subtle stares at Hessie's beauty and physical attributes.

It was rumoured that she had been fathered by the owner of Plantation Perseverance, a few miles from Victory, and that he had forced himself on Hessie's mother, a slave woman who died during the child's birth. The baby girl had been raised by slave women on Plantation Perseverance until she was sold to the Blumefields at age thirteen to pay off a debt.

Despite being a slave, Hessie had had a well-rounded upbringing on Perseverance. "Me live in de big house sometime, and den me live in de hut sometime," she once told Mariama. "Me learn difference wid slave food and Massa food. De Missus like me and feed me what lef' from she pickney — and she pickney is fuss, fuss. She neva finish nutten, and lil Hessie like that," she said, chuckling.

Old Nan, the washerwoman took a special liking to the motherless girl. To boost her owners' income, Hessie was sometimes hired out to neighbouring plantations to wash and darn clothing. Nan would warn, "What evva you do, Hessie, don' let dem rob you, or Massa gon whip you. Dem mus' give you two shilling — watch it good — it gat a Massa head wid leaf band wrap round he head. Mek sure only dat one you tek."

These experiences, coupled with her natural intelligence, moulded Hessie into a crafty and resourceful person who bartered and bargained to her own advantage — and to the advantage of her fellow slaves when the opportunity arose.

Once she had asked Henrietta to let Mariama off early when Jameah was ill and needed help to watch Fredric at night. "De boy still young, Missus. If you let she go and help Jameah, me stay here and help Millie in de kitchen tonight." For a full week this exchange of duties was allowed.

To maintain their trust, Hessie was loyal to the Blumefields. She made certain that the house was run well and that Henrietta and Joseph had everything they needed. She often walked a fine line, trying to please both the whites and the slaves. Mostly it worked in her favour.

By age fourteen she had gained Henrietta Blumefield's confidence and begun to oversee the day-to-day operations of the plantation household. "Hessie runs a tight ship with the household, so I have more time to keep an eye on the books, and Joseph can spend more time on the crops and exporting the molasses and rum," Henrietta once boasted to Penelope McDuff. Hessie also pleased Henrietta's husband in other ways, but no one ever spoke about that.

The male slaves on Plantation Victory often took notice of Hessie but knew she was clearly out of their league. "Me give me arm fuh lay wid she, but dat is like me wishing fuh sail back to Cameroon — it will neva happen," a young field slave had confided in Buck after he had caught a glimpse of Hessie and Buck driving Henrietta from town one Saturday. Hessie had the admiration of many of the young slave women on Plantation Victory as well, but some were envious of her position within the great house and gossiped behind her back. Hessie was indifferent to their envy. She worried only when she suspected that the wagging tongues would spur discord in the plantation house.

Male visitors to Plantation Victory could often be caught taking covert glances at Hessie. Some would even gawk, but everyone knew the unwritten code when it came to this particular slave woman: Look, but don't touch. Hessie could feel their eyes roving lustfully over her light-brown skin, though she never looked at any of them directly. It was the same feeling she had had when Massa Blumefield had first taken notice of her many years ago. Massa Blumefield's gawking had crossed the line to touching well before she was fourteen years old, and it had continued every Friday for many years now.

On Friday evenings around five o'clock, Henrietta Blumefield took her weekly bath, after which she would brush and style her hair and get dressed for dinner.

"It's a good time to check that our property remains in good repair," Joseph would tell Henrietta. "I'll just do a walkabout to ensure that all the slaves are accounted for and no runaways are hiding on our property." Sometimes he would comment on his need for more supervisory help. "One of these days I will find the appropriate overseer to replace Charles. It's hard to find good help."

Meanwhile, of course, Joseph had instructed Hessie to be in her room at five o'clock on Friday afternoons and used this time to visit her. Each week as regular as clockwork he would show up in her room on the lower floor at the back of the main house, to have his pleasure, ignoring her reluctance.

One Friday Hessie had tested Joseph by pretending to forget her promise to wait for him. She spent the time under a large breadfruit tree at the back of the main house. Joseph detested being disobeyed and gave Hessie thirty lashes the next day after she came back from town with his wife. To Henrietta and the other slaves who looked on, Joseph claimed, "This wench stole money from our bedroom. It was there when she entered and gone when she left. For this she will pay." This was a lie, of course, but Hessie kept quiet and took her punishment, fearing that anyone searching her room might find the coins she had stashed away. Blumefield had begun leaving small tokens of money for her after some of his visits to encourage her full participation on subsequent visits and instil in her devotion to him alone. "You belong to me and only me," he often said. "No one else can have you but me."

So Hessie took her beating. Afterwards she could barely move her body for a full week or lie on her back for a very long time. She never forgot it. The following Friday, she took her place on her mat and lay there waiting for Joseph to arrive.

Meanwhile, her cleaning chores done, Mariama headed up the stairs to prepare the dining room for the Friday evening meal. She walked smack into Massa Joseph, who was heading to the servants' quarters on the lower floor. She immediately bent her head and locked her eyes onto the dark varnished wooden stairs.

A sense of confusion enveloped her and momentarily her mind went back to her perilous and antagonizing journey to Demerary and the action of deflection she had learned. When the ship's crew were in the vicinity of the women's quarters, she and the other female captives mostly scoured the deck floors with anxious darting eyes to spot advancing predators and avoid their unwanted attention. She now reverted to this fail-safe action of avoiding eye-contact with backra men, especially her Massa. However, he merely grunted with annoyance, brushed her slight body out of the way, and continued on his determined path to Hessie's room.

Mariama swallowed hard and breathed out in relief. She felt empathy for Hessie but was happy not to have been chosen for Joseph's Friday afternoon escapade. She wondered if he knew that she knew.

After his Friday visits to Hessie, Blumefield would head over to the horse barn to wash up before returning to the main house to have dinner with his wife at six o'clock. Often after dinner he and Henrietta sat together in their spacious parlour. He would suck gently on his pipe, and exhale smoke rings of content while reading the Demerary Bulletin and any news clippings from London. She worked on her crocheting, a hobby acquired in Demerary.

At the same time, Mariama would clear the dinner dishes and Hessie would do evening duties, including closing the plantation great house shutters, laying out Henrietta's night clothes, and turning down the Blumefields' bed so husband and wife could retire for the night. Joseph studiously avoided acknowledging Hessie at such times, his eyes focused on the paper in front of him, through his round, gold-rimmed reading glasses.

On one of those Friday evenings Joseph's secret routine was almost discovered. Just after he arrived in her room, Hessie eased herself up off her mat onto her knees and dropped her skirt like a trained animal. She placed the palms of both her hands against her mat to support her weight and assumed the position that her Massa liked. These had been his instructions from the start, and she took care to follow them exactly. "When you assume this positon, I do not have to look at you or lie with you," he had told her once.

Joseph also had a ritual of his own. Dropping to his knees, he would lean forward and place his left hand at the nape of Hessie's neck to keep her in place. Then he would nudge her buttocks with his right hand to signal his readiness to mount her from behind. This time, though, her body didn't shift into position, and he recognized that something was different. With some surprise he noticed that Hessie had already moved her legs apart to provide him with the easy access he required to her now-exposed genitalia. This cooperation caught Joseph off guard. He had been expecting the usual resistance, but this time he would not have to force himself on her; she had willingly prepared herself for him.

In appreciation Joseph slackened his grip on the back of her neck and wrapped both arms around her torso. As he repeatedly thrust into her, Hessie relaxed, and Joseph, with a growing sense of wonder realized that she was responding to him in kind. He was taken aback for a moment. He had been with about ten other slave women but had always had to take his pleasure by force, although he owned them all. This was new.

That evening he mounted her three times with her full cooperation. After he reached his last climax, without speaking, he nudged her to the ground and used her body as a cushion to lie on. First he fell asleep, and then Hessie did. They lay on the mat together for well over an hour.

Hessie and Joseph awoke to a chorus of raised voices outside.

"Massa Joseph! Massa Joseph, you a' right sar? De Missus looking fuh you."

At first Joseph was confused — then reality set in. He had fallen asleep and missed the dinner hour. He had to devise a plan to leave Hessie's room without being seen. He dressed quickly and stood by the door, listening. He couldn't risk going to the horse barn to clean up, so he waited until the voices of the search party were well out of range. He then furtively left the room, silently mounted the stairs, slipped in the side door to the kitchen, tiptoed along the hall and ascended to the bedroom to clean up for dinner.

Millie and Mariama quietly watched him go by, both unsurprised by his appearance. Millie looked away and continued with her chores. For a few years she had had to endure the same fate as Hessie. On many occasions Joseph had accosted her and taken her against her will. He would enter and lock the kitchen door behind him and threaten to whip her if she tried to fight him off. But now she no longer had to fend off his advances, and that was fine with her.

Mariama could feel her shoulders relax and the breath slowly ease out of her nostrils. Her chest rose and fell again as she began to breathe normally and tension left her body. She had been worried the whole time Joseph was missing but feared to let on that she had seen him going to Hessie's room earlier. In fact, when asked by Henrietta if she had seen her Massa, she had shaken her head and said "No, ma'am," while her stomach rebelled and did double flips.

When Joseph entered the dining room, Henrietta was very relieved to see him. He offered the excuse that he had been chatting with one of the other planters and the time had gotten away from him.

"I would also like to share a bit of good news with you. I am delighted that Jemmoth Rhodes, a man known to keep the law and order, and a stalwart in the local plantation community will be my new overseer. He will begin work on Victory in a few months after he finishes up an assignment on Plantation Diamond. Rhodes comes highly recommended. I heard he keeps the slaves in check, his methods are ruthless and slaves fear him. We could use him around here."

Henrietta acknowledged Joseph's news with a polite nod. *Maybe with an overseer to look after the field work*, Henrietta thought, *he'll have more time for me.* They then ate their dinner in silence, Joseph reflecting on his close call, and Henrietta entertaining pleasant fantasies about how they might fill their additional time together.

Hessie was on her way up to prepare the Blumefields' bedroom for the night and heard Joseph's voice in conversation through the door. She paused in the hallway to listen closely and felt chills down her spine when she heard that Rhodes was coming to Victory as overseer. She had to get the word out.

***

It was earlier that same Friday evening, as she was waiting for her Massa's visit that Hessie had begun to ponder her own future. She thought of a place she one day hoped to be — anywhere except this place, and in this position.

"One day me get 'nough money fuh move to Stabroek and me own me. Dat day come soon, Hessie. Dat day come soon," she said to herself.

From then on, she quietly planned her purchase and her move. Every Friday evening after Joseph Blumefield left her room, Hessie counted her coins, adding to them whatever new amount he had left her.

CHAPTER 16

CROSSING PATHS

December 1803

It was a few weeks before Christmas and Henrietta was preparing to make the trip into Stabroek to shop for the annual makeover of the great house at Plantation Victory. It was her favourite time of year. She enjoyed trimming the artificial tree while the slave women lacquered the floors and mahogany furniture and hung new curtains. The tantalizing scent of Millie's rum pudding and spiced eggnog filled the thick tropical air. Henrietta and Joseph entertained other planter families including the McDuffs and the Gladstones during this season of celebration, food, and drink. She needed all hands on deck for the preparations.

"Mariama, you ride with Hessie and me into town today. But you must change your smock." Henrietta Blumefield ordered as she looked her young house slave up and down.

"Yes, ma'am," Mariama replied and scurried off to change into her only other indigo-coloured smock. She didn't get a chance to go to town often. It was exciting, and she liked the change of scene and travelling on the carriage between Hessie and Buck. Henrietta climbed into the carriage and began to give instructions.

"We have quite a few stops to make today, Hessie. The girl can help carry packages and speed things up. Buck, I need you to make a stop at the grocers on our way back. Let's go."

The carriage took its usual route into town. Today, however, Buck made his first stop on Camp Street at Johnson, Dyett, McGarel, and Co. of Stabroek to purchase lacquer and furniture polish. Hessie and Mariama accompanied their Missus into the general store and brought heavy jars and tins and polishing cloth back to the carriage. Next stop was at the clothing and fabric store, Messrs. Underwood, Johnson, & Co. This was Hessie's favourite, where she admired all the fine cloth and lace brought in on the big ships. She often imagined being able to purchase and wear some of these garments just like her Missus and the other planters' wives did.

Henrietta ordered new curtains made for the front room to showcase her Christmas decor. This year she bought ivory-coloured lace swags for the front and side windows and imagined the admiration and compliments of the other wives. Hessie and Mariama picked up bundles of ribbons and candles and lengths of decorative fabric and packed them into the back of the carriage. Buck waited for his Missus's directions.

"Drive to High Street," Henrietta called out to Buck. He did as he was told and Dottie clopped easily along the canal road and turned onto High Street. As the carriage rounded the corner, two young white men stumbled out of a public house hysterically laughing and, oblivious to the moving carriage, lurched into it. Buck abruptly pulled on the reins to bring the carriage to a halt, startling Dottie. The horse reared and raised her forelegs, tossing her head and neighing loudly.

Henrietta quickly climbed out of the carriage and put her training with horses into action.

"It's okay, girl. It's okay," she whispered into Dottie's ear while gently stroking her neck and back. This tactic calmed the frightened mare and she lowered her legs and assumed a more relaxed stance.

"Sorry, madam. We didn't mean to scare your horse," the taller of the two men said.

"Sailors, I presume," Henrietta admonished.

"You are correct. John Leighton at your service," the same man added. "We were ... he was trying to bamboozle me." The other sailor walked on, but John remained.

Hessie, Buck, and Mariama climbed down from the carriage and waited on a command from their Missus while observing the exchange with this stranger. Mariama stood between the two other slaves and listened.

"I'm Henrietta Blumefield, wife of Joseph Blumefield, sir, and you did scare Dottie."

"Let me help to get her settled by holding the reins until everyone is safely back in the carriage." John offered. Then he stood back and watched as Henrietta climbed into the carriage. She was followed by Hessie, Mariama, and Buck in their allotted positions. John thought there was something familiar about the younger slave girl, but he could not figure out what it was. He looked at her for several moments and felt the stirring of some lost memory, but it slipped away. He had seen her before, somewhere, sometime, but he couldn't remember. Maybe she had been one of the many slaves that came across the Atlantic on the *Archery* or *Gallantry.*

John watched and doffed his cap as Buck took back the reins and gave them a gentle tug. Dottie moved off, resuming her unhurried pace. She had calmed down nicely. The image of the slave girl stayed with John for a moment and then dissipated.

"One final stop at Mrs. Faulkner's shop and then we'll head back to the plantation so Dottie can have her rest." Henrietta called out to Buck.

"Why dat white man stare you, Mariama?" Hessie asked.

"Yes, me see dat too," Buck said with a slight grin. "He watch you, not de Missus," he continued. "You run away?" he whispered quietly.

"Me? No, Buck. Massa buy me from de ship. Me ain't run 'way. Don' know why he watch me." Mariama added curiously. She wished she had looked more closely at the stranger, but had become accustomed to avoiding the eyes of white men and as a result only obtained a fleeting impression, although it was enough to note his fixed gaze in her direction.

She joined Hessie and Henrietta in the grocery store and brought the parcels out to the carriage, but her mind wandered back to the mysterious stranger and his apparent interest in her. *Could he have been a member of the slave ship's crew that brought me over?*

CHAPTER 17

WANTING MORE

May 1804

Hessie had gone to the horse stalls to ensure that Buck was ready for the weekly trip with their mistress to town. It was a clear and sunny Saturday morning without a cloud in the sky. Hessie met Buck brushing Dottie as she chomped on a pile of fresh hay. Satisfied everything was in place, Hessie returned to the house in time to see Henrietta step out onto the front porch.

"De carriage ready, ma'am!" Hessie called to her, and no sooner had she uttered the words, had Buck rounded the corner in a clatter of harness and horse, coming to a halt in front of his mistress. Henrietta climbed into the back, and Hessie took her place in the front.

Buck drove the carriage down the driveway of the large estate house. Gently pulling the reins, he steered the dark-brown mare left onto the unpaved main road and headed west towards Stabroek. Her trot was gentle and precise, and this movement kicked up just enough dust to leave a small trail in the air.

The journey into town was uneventful until Henrietta's shrill voice abruptly punctuated the silence.

"The lily pond is approaching on your left. Pull the carriage over, Buck, and stop at the edge of the road."

Buck did as he was instructed. Just ahead was a small laneway that led to a clearing and a midsized pond. The surface of the pond was covered with enormous emerald-green lily pads that floated on the glossy, dark water. Palm-sized white lilies with yellow centres dotted most pads. Henrietta had always admired the lilies from afar, but today she had the urge to touch one.

The regal flowers reminded Henrietta of the beautiful English gardens she had grown up with. She felt a knot in her stomach and realized how much she longed for England, her true home.

Henrietta had married Joseph, a man ten years her senior who had possessed the promise of wealth, security, and upward mobility. As the son of an English aristocrat, he had land ownership and wealth in his bloodline, and dating him had brought her all the privileges of his social class.

Joseph's reputation as a womanizer, however, had preceded him. Many women in nearby villages and towns had gone out of their way to put themselves in Joseph's company. Henrietta was not one of them. She had turned down his invitations for tea on many occasions, preferring to don her riding habit and criss-cross the open fields on her favourite horses near her parents' home.

Joseph hated to be ignored. The experience prompted a pursuit of Henrietta that was encouraged by her father, a solicitor who oversaw legal aspects of the Blumefield family fortunes. She agreed, begrudgingly, to an outing with this persistent man.

The tea garden they had frequented during their courtship was well attended by the upper class. It was common to see lords clad in top hats, with frock coats over silken waistcoats, and ruffle-breasted linen shirts with barely visible breeches, and knitted stocking-covered legs ending in black, silver-buckled shoes. Ladies were usually dressed in ballooned frocks with petticoats of lace, their tiny waists strapped snuggly in, and wide-brimmed hats with flat crowns framed their graceful faces. Delicate hands at the end of elbow-length fingerless gloves held tiny teacups with their pinkie fingers raised. Cucumber sandwiches, scones, clotted cream, and marmalade or lemon curd were served on silver trays that glittered on tables throughout the chatter-filled seating area. Henrietta soon grew fond of the honours and graces that being with Joseph afforded. Eventually she began to like him too.

After six months of courtship, on a chilly November afternoon in 1794, Joseph dropped to one knee and said words to Henrietta that she had been hoping to hear: "I recognize that you like all the finer indulgences, my dear. I promise to continue to provide you with all the luxuries and outings you have become accustomed to during our courtship. Will you marry me?"

Henrietta didn't have to think about it. She simply said "Yes."

They were married the following month. It was not until after their wedding that Joseph told Henrietta about his plans to seek a quick fortune in Demerary. He told her about the money he could amass within three years. "The fortunes we could accumulate would be enough to own all of Liverpool and parts of Manchester," he had boasted. "It would increase by tenfold the number of lace items and silks in your wardrobe. It would buy you the best pearls and other fine jewellery."

Henrietta loved the sound of the wealth that Joseph promised, but the idea of moving thousands of miles across the sea to obtain it made her uneasy. However, three years was not that long a time, she had to admit, and eventually she agreed to the adventure of Demerary. She had no idea how much of an adventure it would turn out to be, and how quickly three years could become six and then nine.

Henrietta climbed out of the carriage, crossed the road, and began walking along the path that led to the pond.

"Come, Hessie. Come with me," she called out, glancing over her right shoulder. "Go into the pond and fetch me a lily," she said, as Hessie came trotting up beside her.

"You wan' me go in fuh flower, ma'am?" Hessie sounded hesitant, as though unsure she had heard her mistress clearly.

"Yes, go in and get me one. Hurry or we'll be late for town."

Hessie did as she was told and stepped to the edge of the pond, lifting her blue cotton skirt above her knees.

Henrietta could not help but admire the long, shapely legs of her woman servant as they disappeared into the cool water. She found herself wondering how Hessie looked unclothed and was surprised at the sensations that this thought stirred — strange and new but not unpleasant feelings. She watched and wondered as Hessie waded in to retrieve the beautiful white bloom, floating on its large green pad, ten feet beyond the water's edge. Could Joseph have experienced these feelings for Hessie too? She pictured herself lying in bed next to Joseph and reflected on their perfunctory and infrequent lovemaking.

"Ma'am? Ma'am!" Hessie said, breaking into Henrietta's thoughts.

"Yes, Hessie, what is it?"

"Heah de flower, ma'am, de one from de big leaf."

The flower was cradled in a fold of Hessie's wet skirt.

"Thank you, Hessie. Let me have it."

Henrietta leaned forward and cupped her palms to take the delicate white lily. Hardly daring to breathe, she looked down at it. She had always admired the water lilies from afar, in awe of how they changed colours overnight from a stunning white to a soft pink hue the next morning. But now it was more than just a pretty sight. It lay in her hands, soft, warm, and fragile like a sleeping kiss.

In spite of the natural beauty before her, Henrietta could not ignore the proximity of Hessie's shining wet body, curvaceous limbs, and firm buttocks, now clearly visible under the thin, sodden fabric of her skirt as she turned to move away.

Once Henrietta had caught Joseph observing Hessie from afar and wondered if he had ever been tempted, but she had immediately dismissed her suspicion. Joseph was high-born and would never give in to animal lust to lie with a slave. Yet there was something undeniably attractive about Hessie.

Henrietta wrenched her thoughts back to the beauty of the flower in her hands. She bore it carefully as she walked back to the carriage, with Hessie following close behind.

For the rest of the trip to Stabroek, Henrietta stroked the lily in quiet contemplation. Her thoughts returned to Joseph and how she might mend what was ailing in their marriage.

CHAPTER 18

GETTING IN ON THE ACTION

August 1805

Ed Grimes had arrived in Demerary to try his hand at the business of slave ownership. He had searched the marketplace at Stabroek for a deal and found one in what looked like an emaciated black buck, still in his shackles.

"Don't trust the scrawny look," the auctioneer had warned, jerking a thumb at the captive who lay curled in a fetal position below the auction stage in the town square. "This one is rambunctious. He will knock you off your feet if you're not paying attention."

"Clearly he has been beaten nearly senseless," Grimes interjected, eying the shrunken chap.

"Reportedly, he had struggled and resisted on the voyage from St. Kitts to Demerary and been whipped almost every day and then force-fed to keep him alive." The auctioneer responded. "Nothing that a good wash and some grub can't fix," he encouraged.

Most of the planters, not wanting a troublemaker in their midst, had selected equally strong bucks who were more submissive and left this one for the next buyer.

Ed Grimes, however, loved a challenge and had seen a deal to be had. He negotiated a low price of twenty-five pounds sterling and bought the buck, who was named Braima. He had also purchased Mahaad, a more docile male, at a considerable sum of sixty pounds Sterling, and thus was delighted to supplement this with a cheaper purchase. The two young men were the first of Grimes's slave holdings.

Together they had journeyed by dray cart from Stabroek to Blygezight, the home of their new owner. For the first two months, the rebellious one had been kept chained in the small shack they shared, as Grimes felt that he would only remain on the premises if restrained. The other male did as he was told and was allowed to move around the property without restriction.

For the first few weeks Grimes fed them only scraps from his table. Often they received no food at all, especially when Grimes had been out on a drunken binge the night before.

Mahaad, the unshackled slave, was a practical lad, and he quickly figured out how to fend for himself. He learned that food was not a certainty, but a chance. He scavenged for fruit and water for him and his shack mate, Braima. For the most part he found this easy; wild fruit trees were readily available.

At first the two young slaves didn't speak to each other. But one day Mahaad, returning from a food hunt, stumbled upon Braima prostrate on the ground, pointed in the direction of the morning sun. Surprised, Mahaad had greeted him with "*Salat!*" Braima looked at him and a smile slowly crossed his face. "*Salat,*" he repeated. From then on, apart from bondage, prayer was the thing that connected the two young men. They prayed together five times a day.

One morning during Grimes's check of the shack to ensure his property was still there, he threw some dried cassava bread onto the floor.

"Here's a nibble to keep you blokes till I'm back. Maybe today I'll find some work for you on one of the plantations, so you can start to earn your keep."

Braima sat silent on his mat and stared straight ahead, refusing to acknowledge Grimes's presence. Mahaad, however, crawled to retrieve the food, then clasped his hands together and nodded his thanks to Grimes.

"Teach your friend manners, mate," Grimes muttered gruffly. "He's an ungrateful beggar." Then, he turned on his heel and headed down the path to his waiting horse and carriage.

Mahaad watched until the carriage was out of sight. Then, leaving half the bread for Braima, he crept around the hut and out into the pasture to look for more food. Braima, of course, stayed where he was. His chains allowed him to venture only far enough to relieve himself in the nearby bush.

***

Over their first weeks at Blygezight this check-in by Grimes became routine. He showed up, tossed morsels of food at them, and left to seek work for his newly acquired property. Hunger was a constant companion for Mahaad and Braima, and the fruit that Mahaad found was a welcome necessity that they both consumed eagerly. They discovered the area's seasonal fruit, including juicy sun-ripened mammee apples; sweet, sticky star apples; awarra, the colour of an orange sunset; kokerit; milky simmoto; and coconut. Mahaad also perfected the art of bringing water for Braima in a large lily pad he rolled up into a funnel.

One day at dusk Braima sat on his mat after he and Mahaad had completed their evening prayers. From the corner of his eyes he saw something slithering along the hay-strewn floor of the shack: a labaria, headed straight for Mahaad's outstretched leg. Braima leapt forward, grabbed the snake by its neck with one hand and flipped its head backward with the other. The reptile struggled for a few seconds and then ceased to move.

Mahaad realized with amazement that his taciturn shack mate had saved his life. Gratefully, he took the snake's limp body from

Braima and then stepped outside and started a small fire on which he carefully roasted it. Though prohibited in their beliefs, the men chose sustenance over death. "Dey call me Mahaad. Me from near Dar Banda. Dem teif me many moons ago. Me live 'pon Antigua, and me Massa go back over de wata, so he sell me to de ship captain. How 'bout you?"

"Dey call me Braima, and me from Yele. Dem tek me while me graze me goats. Me was 'pon St. Kitts for many moons. Me was boy den; now me is man," he said as he clenched his fists and pumped them in the air. They both chortled.

"Why dem send you to Demerary? You Massa go back to he country or back to he ancestors?"

"Nah. Me too much trouble, so me Massa get rid o' me."

Braima chuckled and Mahaad joined in the laughter. For the rest of the evening Mahaad and Braima relaxed together, sharing stories of their lives on the islands of St. Kitts and Antigua — the people they had met, the abuse they had endured, and their struggles to survive. They also spoke about their first voyage from the African continent.

"Me know wood from back home, but me neva see so much in one place like dat!" Braima raised and shook his arms as he spoke. "De floor was wood, de walls and de ceiling wood 'cept up top where de sacred sky looked down with pity 'pon we."

Mahaad enjoyed listening to his new friend's entertaining stories.

Later that night, Braima lay on his back with his eyes closed thinking back to his first voyage across the seas. As a boy he had marvelled at the ship's mysterious and intricate construction and the large wooden poles rising high out of its depths like perfect straight tree trunks without any branches. They must have been hard to work smooth by hand. And there were smaller pieces that ran sideways and ropes everywhere, tying this to that or coiled up on the wooden floor. But most striking to his young mind were the massive, thick white cloths that billowed out from crosspieces in arrangements that the white men were always changing. These cloths caught the wind and pushed the vessel over the sea on its sinister quest, a quest he could not know at the time. And he remembered his young boy's thoughts that the white men couldn't leave the ship alone, always running up and down ropes and yelling and pulling and heaving things around and then doing it all over again. But now his older mind knew it all had a purpose, this big, moving vessel of pain, groaning and screeching all day and night as its planks and timbers rubbed and twisted in agony. It had leaked water and a sticky black blood from between its ribs in hot weather as if it had wounds that reopened when the sun was fierce and pressing. He recalled wanting the wind that pushed their wooden hell across this world of water to pick him up and send him flying into freedom. Up high over the curve of the golden ocean and far, far away from the despair floating below. On some days he had felt the anger of the sea as it rose with great force from deep below while the poor captive souls in its belly trembled and shook and prayed to every God they ever knew.

Although his present life was not a real life, but a burden without joy or comfort, Braima was glad that torture of the journey from his homeland was over.

***

The next morning, when Ed Grimes arrived to throw his table scraps on the straw mat as he usually did, Braima acknowledged him. He crawled over and picked up the scraps of dried cassava bread and then nodded to Grimes.

Grimes's eyes bulged in astonishment.

"Bloody hell, you finally got it, bloke. You've come to your senses. I own you. You eat what I give you or you'll die from hunger. Keep it up and I will take your shackles off next time."

CHAPTER 19

MOVING ON UP

June 1806

An advertisement in the June 1806 *Essequebo and Demerary Gazette* had caught Edward Grimes's attention: "For sale, one lot of land, part of a concession with all buildings thereon and four Negroes by owner William McKee."

McKee was a coffee planter, and the rise in demand for sugar had reduced the profits from coffee. He had sold many of his slaves and reduced production to try to keep his business viable, but the British demand for sugar won out, and he finally chose to sell his holdings and return to Glasgow.

Edward Grimes leapt at the chance to boost his assets and purchased the estate and its subsidiaries. The four Negroes consisted of three males and one female, siblings who had been separated from their parents at point of sale in Demerary. Grimes moved into Plantation Liefde and now owned a total of six slaves — his own small crew. He only had to rent slaves when there was need for a large gang.

Sixteen-year-old Louisa was the eldest of the new slaves. She took to Braima immediately. Braima liked her too, especially her big smile and visible dimples. They often exchanged beguiling glances, which infuriated Grimes. He immediately moved Louisa to the main house to become his cook and bedmate. Although she had once been the lead field hand working the coffee fields, she was now kept in the house to clean, cook, and submit to Grimes's every sexual fantasy. This upset Louisa's brothers and Braima terribly. They could hear Louisa's cries at nights from Grimes's beatings when she resisted him. The whippings and crying continued for many months. Braima was abhorred; so were her brothers.

CHAPTER 20

WORKING FOR THE MAN

October 1806

Joseph Blumefield leaned his head out the window of his carriage and addressed a small group of men gathered at the corner of Lamaha and Main streets in Stabroek. It was the middle of a sunny Thursday morning. "Do you know of any proprietors needing work for their slaves?"

A man in brown breeches and a funny wool topcoat too hot for the tropics poked his head into the waiting coach. His bushy eyebrows splayed out over his beady, bloodshot eyes, and his alcohol-infused breath caused Joseph to retreat ever so slightly.

"I can provide about a dozen black slaves and maybe a few Indians," the man said enthusiastically. "Why, pray tell? Do I detect your need for some help, my good man?"

"Step away, please, sir. Your morning cocktail precedes you, and not with a pleasant path."

Joseph flicked his left wrist, and the man took a few steps back from the coach as he eagerly awaited a response.

"I do need some help with my harvest for the next two fortnights, and my preference is for about a dozen Negroes. The sugar cane is quite bountiful this year, and I need many more field hands and some in the boiler house too. I must tell you, though, I'll work them from daybreak till nine at night, with just an hour's rest. They'll get thirty minutes in the morning and thirty minutes in the afternoon, and that includes their break for the watering hole. Are your Negroes up to the task?"

"Of course they are," the man in the brown breeches said, tucking his thumbs under his suspenders and flicking them against his chest. "My rate is thirty-five pounds sterling per week. I can have them to your estate by six each morning. Do we have a deal, sir?"

Joseph hesitated.

"My dear man, my price is a good one," the man continued with a smile. "If you need to get back to me, the name is Edward Grimes, Esquire," he added, a smirk bisecting his grubby face.

"I will think on it and let you know as soon as I've arrived at a decision. Thank you, and good day to you, Mr. Grimes."

Joseph ordered Buck to drive the carriage on and sat back in his seat. Grimes's deal sounded unfavourable. He would ask some of the other planters instead. There was still time. It was at least three weeks before the sugar cane had to be harvested.

To his chagrin, however, no other planters, not even Gladstone or McDuff, had slaves available, and several days later Joseph was forced to return to Grimes. In the meantime, Grimes, who was no gentleman despite the title he affected, now had raised his fees to forty. Seething, Joseph argued and worked out an agreement to reduce the fee to twenty pounds per week for the labour of a dozen male Negroes under the age of twenty-five. He refused the complimentary wench that Grimes offered as an inducement to extend the contract beyond four weeks.

***

Grimes brought his hired crew to Plantation Victory as agreed every morning at six o'clock and handed them over to Jake, the tall, laconic slave driver, who led them to the fields and the boiler house. Grimes returned each night at nine o'clock to pick up the crew.

Every Saturday evening Ed Grimes approached the great house to receive his financial settlement from Joseph Blumefield. It was on his very first visit to the house that he saw her — all five feet, ten inches of her framed in the front door of Plantation Victory — her piercing green eyes, light-brown skin and full breasts. The sight of her left him speechless. He had never seen such a vision in slave attire before. When she opened the door to his knock, he did what most other men did when they saw Hessie for the first time: he ogled her. He was now staring right at her breasts, which greeted him smack in his now embarrassingly red face.

"I'm here to see um, um … Mr. Joseph, um…" Grimes mumbled, dumbstruck.

Hessie looked down at his feet and quietly said, "Me get Massa Blumefield, sar."

As she quickly moved back into the house and towards the study, Grimes tried to imagine what her legs might look like freed from her long, bulky skirt.

"Bloody 'ell," he muttered.

Joseph came out into the hallway and beckoned the still-baffled Grimes into his study.

"Your Negroes are working well," he said when they arrived. He peered closely at Grimes, his brow furrowing. "Are you all right, Mr. Grimes? You look quite flushed."

"Oh no, I'm fine. Must be the heat," Grimes said as he struggled to compose himself.

"I believe we agreed to twenty pounds sterling," Blumefield said, handing over a stack of notes. "I will see you and your gang again on Monday," he said, and turned and escorted Grimes back down the hallway that led to the side door. Grimes looked slyly about him as they walked, hoping to catch another glimpse of the slave woman, but there was no sign of her.

***

The second Saturday morning, after Edward Grimes had dropped off his gang of labourers, he hung around the plantation. He had learned that on Saturdays Blumefield went to the gentlemen's club for lunch and drinks, as did most of the other planters. He had also found out that Hessie accompanied Henrietta to town on Saturdays but was usually back shortly before lunch.

Grimes stayed mostly out of sight, sitting in shaded areas and watching the various scenes unfold. He saw Joseph leave on horseback and then watched Buck drive the carriage with Henrietta and Hessie out of the courtyard and along the country road towards Stabroek. And although he didn't recognize her from the ship, he spotted Mariama and her young lad head out along the laneway. Grimes hung around, watching and waiting, until eventually he nodded off.

***

Mariama had finished her Saturday morning chores, and with Henrietta's approval, she used the rest of the afternoon to tend the communal vegetable plot — the one she shared with Jameah. As she headed to the vegetable grounds that afternoon, Mariama saw only one other slave woman and a young boy at the top of the hill returning to the little brown huts.

"Hurry, boy, we late!" Mariama called out to Fredric, who was now lagging behind. "We got to hurry and finish soon. You hungry?"

"Yes," he said matter-of-factly.

"Okay, we hurry up here so we soon get back to de hut and you can eat," Mariama promised.

At the edge of a row of plantain trees, she knelt down and began pulling weeds from between the neat lines of freshly sprouted pigeon peas. Jameah had done a good job of sowing the seeds, despite her poor vision.

"You pull de dry plantain leaf off de tree," she urged Fredric, wanting to keep him busy.

A few minutes later Mariama heard footsteps coming quickly along the path. She pushed her floppy straw hat out of her face and looked around. The approaching visitor was still on the other side of the small hill and not yet in sight. Not knowing who was journeying to the plot, and afraid that the boy had wandered off, she called out to him, "Fredric, stay heah!" Her cautioning was met with silence.

Worried about where he was, she turned around and was surprised to see him curled up in the shade, under the hanging leaves of a plantain tree. He was sound asleep. *So what, or who, is now causing the tall grass to rustle so loudly?* Mariama gently moved the plantain leaves aside and peered into the distance. From the corner of her eye she could see movement in the lane. Turning in the direction of the sounds, no more than forty feet away, she saw Hessie struggling with a short, ugly man. Her blood ran cold as she realized that it was Ed Grimes. Now she could hear Hessie's voice: "Please, Massa Ed, please! Me sick, sar. Me not well, sar. Me body hurt, sar."

Mariama gasped. She quickly clasped her left hand over her mouth to keep any sound from escaping. *How does Hessie know this brute, and why is she pleading with him?* From behind the plantain leaves Mariama saw Ed push Hessie to the ground and then hold a whip over her.

"Hush now, be quiet," he said with a nasty smile. "I have the perfect medicine to heal you and make you feel better," Grimes growled and licked his lips as his eyes roamed across Hessie's slouched body beneath him.

"Nah, nah, Massa Ed," Hessie continued to plead.

"Hush," Ed repeated again. This time there was some annoyance in his voice.

Smack! The sound of a slap to her face rang out, and Hessie's pleas were replaced by tiny whimpers as she covered her face to shield it from further attack.

Mariama held her breath. Crouching beneath the plantain tree, she watched helplessly as Hessie succumbed to Grimes's attack. She glanced over to where her son lay fast asleep, praying the sounds would not awaken him. She remembered, ever so clearly, how it felt to be taken against her will by this brute.

"*Mambale* — Bad man," she uttered quietly. She wanted to help Hessie fight off this *mambale*, but she felt paralyzed. Mariama closed her eyes, barely breathing, wishing with all her might for Hessie's ordeal to be over. She winced with every grunt that came from Ed, cringed at every whimper from Hessie. The muscles in Mariama's face began to hurt from her flinching.

The assault played out like an endless nightmare. Finally, Ed's grunts became quicker and louder, and Hessie's whimpers became amplified. Mariama covered her ears, her eyes riveted on Fredric: her greatest fear was that the child would awaken and bring attention to her hiding place. Mercifully, the boy was still soundly asleep.

Then, at last, it stopped. Massa Ed rolled over, grabbed the hem of Hessie's skirt to wipe his leg and pulled his breeches up.

"There now, ain't that much better?" he sneered. Glancing over his shoulder, he chuckled and began to walk away. "That was good, wasn't it, you green-eyed temptress? I've got much more where that came from. I know you feel better now."

Then he was gone.

Hessie lay crumpled, weeping softly. With a glance in the direction to where Grimes had vanished, Mariama hurried over to her side. Hessie flinched in surprise as Mariama touched her shoulder but let Mariama help her to a sitting position, sobbing all the while. Mariama knelt and held Hessie's head to her chest. The two women sat huddled together wordlessly as a yellow kiskadee sang in the trees above them.

"Me hungry, ma, me hungry," Fredric flopped down on the grass beside them, a yawn covering his face. His entrance startled Hessie, who was unaware that the boy was in the vicinity.

"The boy sleep Hessie, he don' see nutten," Mariama whispered. Then she glanced over at Fredric.

"Okay, we go now so you can eat."

It was time for them to get back to the main house. Mariama got to her feet and offered a hand to Hessie, who cautiously stood, and along with young Fredric, they slowly sauntered back.

The women left the boy at Jameah's hut to be fed and re-entered the path to the estate house when they heard raised voices behind them.

"De cutlass too dull. Me can cut nuff mo' if de blade sharpa."

It was a man's voice, tight with frustration.

"Massa Ed betta get sharp tool or no pay fuh he," a second man answered him, his voice flat with defeat. "Me tired eat fruit."

Just then, a gaggle of slave men walked past them. The group headed towards the main house. Mariama and Hessie stepped aside to allow them to pass.

Something in the group caught Mariama's eyes. It caused her to sharply turn her head in the direction of the main house to the group that had just passed. The back of the head and the shoulders of one of the men held her attention. There was something familiar about him. As she continued to stare at the group, she noticed that the young man's gait was also familiar, though his slight limp was not.

Mariama paused and looked fixedly. Then she let out a gasp, her knees weakened, and suddenly her head felt ready to explode. She was dizzy and had to sit down. Hessie was still shaky from her earlier assault. She had no idea why Mariama was suddenly sitting down on the grass but took the opportunity to kneel beside her.

"Me de one dat Massa Ed tek, Mariama. Why you sit down? You sick?"

Mariama's mind was racing. She placed both hands on her head and shook it fiercely, as though trying to loosen something from it. She looked back towards the house, but the men were now out of sight.

Could it be her brother — but why would Braima be on Plantation Victory? He couldn't be. She must be overtired and imagining things. She tried to move on with the rest of her day, but the vision of the men stayed with her. For the rest of the week she recalled the incident many times, always without telling anyone. She couldn't.

CHAPTER 21

BLESSED CHILDREN

February 1807

One afternoon, while Henrietta was preparing to attend a local event with her women's group, the staff in the great house gathered in the kitchen to complete various tasks. A bit of banter began between them.

"Me so worried 'bout Massa Rhodes comin' fuh be overseer, it mek me stomach sick. When me tell Buck and Josie how he bad, Josie eyeball nearly fall out she head." Hessie cautioned.

"You say he bad Hessie, but you neva say why he bad." Millie, who was usually quiet, asked.

"When me was 'pon Perseverance, me see Massa Rhodes beat people fuh lil' tings. An' when dem skin break from de lashes, he rub salt, lime juice, and raw pepper in de cut and put dem in de hot sun fuh lie down. If dem move 'cause dem body burn, dem get mo' lashes and he tie dem to de tree so dem can't move."

Mariama and Millie listened intently and cringed as Hessie reflected further.

"One time, he beat lil' Aju, and he mama 'cause he say dem tief sugar. 'So you want more sugar, I'll give you sugar,' he say. He tie

120   THE WISDOM OF RAIN

dem hand behind dem back and strap dem to de tree. Den he go to de bush, drop he pants and bring back he caca and rub it cross dem face, and shove it in dem mouth, and den he tie up dem mouth wid cloth. Aju mama dead dat night tie-up 'pon de tree, and Aju end up in de sick house for looong time. Me tell you, Massa Rhodes is a killa. If he come to Victory, nuff a we gon dead."

Millie shook her head and slowly left the room. *Massa Joseph had to be stopped. He could not hire Rhodes. Maybe it was time for a discussion with Josie,* she thought.

Back in the kitchen, Hessie tried to change the conversation.

"You boy seven year old, Mariama. Is lil' mo' dan seven years since you come to Victory. Me know 'cause me be fifteen when he come out," Hessie said as she watched Fredric out the kitchen window. The boy was running around the pasture behind the house collecting a pyramid of dried horse manure for the garden and placing it under a tree. He moved briskly.

"How come you mek no pickney, Hessie?" Mariama asked casually.

Hessie looked away into the distance and whispered, "Me mek, but dem just neva stay. Me sen' four back and two go back 'pon dem own."

There, she thought, *it's out now.* She turned to look at Mariama.

Mariama searched her friend's face for any emotion behind her gaze but found nothing. Even Hessie's smooth, light-brown forehead held no clue.

"How you sen' dem back?" was all Mariama could muster.

"Josie sen' dem back," Hessie replied. "Me was 'bout … 'bout thirteen when the first one go back."

She stared blankly at the partially washed lunch dishes in the stone kitchen sink.

"De cane crop been good dat year. Everybody wuk seven days, from befo' sun come up till long pass sundown. Some people stack cane, some feed de cane mill and some clean de megass from de mill. Nuff people foot and hand get burn in de boiling house dat year. Massa Joseph mek me, Maudie, and Millie help wuk in de field every afternoon, and come back and wuk in de house. One day, just after me lif' two cane bundle, de pain come sharp, sharp, and de wata rush down me leg. De pain get worse, and de pickney drop out in de field."

Mariama gawked at Hessie, her mouth slightly agape.

Hessie continued: "Josie wuk right nex' to me. She see de pickney drop, and she come over and push me down 'pon de ground. She use she cutlass fuh cut de string. Then she cover up de pickney in she smock and carry it 'way — a girl pickney. She put it wid she six in de netha world. She sey dem gon look after it. So she cover up de blood wid cane stripping and me wuk dat day till sundown."

The dish towel fell from Marians's hands; she had become suddenly light-headed and the temperature in the kitchen had risen exponentially — only there was no fire on the stove. She caught the look of defeat on Hessie's face as she sat down on the wooden stool in the kitchen. Hessie leaned her head to the right and dropped her shoulders forward. Mariama could see Hessie's eyes begin to soften, and her lips begin to quiver. Then Hessie took a deep breath and continued in a hushed voice, casting her eyes about to ensure Mariama was her only audience.

"Now all we pickney playin' in de netha world, spared of dis sad, sad life and cruel pain. Mariama, it hard fuh kill you pickney, yet not so hard, 'cause dis life is no life. Massa fadda all me pickney and some o' Josie pickney too," she whispered.

Mariama looked around the room, just as Hessie had done, and then quietly asked, "De Missus know?"

"'Bout de pickney or 'bout Massa?" Hessie raised her eyebrows and then continued, "Me don' know dat, and you be quiet now."

Mariama didn't need to be told; it was a secret that had to be kept.

Millie entered the room, bringing a sudden halt to their private exchange. Mariama quickly finished washing up the dishes, and then she exited the kitchen in silence. Without missing a beat, Hessie began chatting with Millie about food rations for the week.

"Is dere gon be plenty buyins dis week, Millie? De Missus buy so lil las' week."

"Missus ain't seem in a good buyin' mood lately. Seem she sad an' buyin' less," answered Millie. "Tea … get tea, milk an' de fish. Only got fish fuh dis week, and food run out."

"A' right, Millie. Me tell de Missus."

Mariama needed air. She forced herself through the back door and into the small sunlit flower garden. She felt sick but needed to keep her meal in her stomach. She opened her mouth and swallowed gulps of fresh air.

Her head was spinning. She made it to the breadfruit tree where Fredric was still stacking patties of horse dung. Mariama leaned against it and slithered down to the ground. She stared at Fredric as he innocently continued his chore, unaware of the thoughts exploding in her head.

Her maa had said that children are a blessing. Dizzying thoughts ran through her head: *If the boy is a blessing, Maa, why don't I feel love for him and joy that he is mine?* As his mother she wanted to, but she simply didn't have any of these feelings. She knew that she and her brother brought their parents joy and she felt their love. Why didn't she feel the same love and joy for her son? She hadn't thought to spare him this life of slavery and have Josie send him back to the ancestors. That would have been an act of love, but all she had felt was emptiness.

Mariama could feel her chest tighten and her face flush. She was ashamed of her thoughts, so as she had often done before, she prayed silently to find love for Fredric. What Hessie had revealed to her was baffling. Mariama wished she could talk with her maa again. She would have the answers.

Her thoughts were interrupted by the sound of footsteps. Joseph Blumefield was ambling down the path adjoining the main house.

"Don't you have work to do, girl? Get up and get going. Run along and get your chores done."

"Yes, Massa Joseph. Me be right 'long, sar."

Mariama bolted through the back door of the house. She grabbed her broom and mop from the cleaning cupboard and scuttled to the Blumefields' bedroom. Henrietta was dressed and ready for her trip to a Ladies of Demerary luncheon at Eve Leary.

"Put clean sheets on today, girl. I've laid these blue ones out," she said, barely glancing at Mariama. Then she walked to the front porch to find Hessie.

CHAPTER 22

PREACHER'S PROBE

May 1807

Thomas arrived at the chapel at seven o'clock on Sunday morning. Quashee and some of the congregants were milling around the compound, as was customary. After exchanging greetings, they wandered into their place of respite.

The Reverend Leighton opened the service with a prayer: "We give you thanks, Almighty God, for this past week, for the new week that has dawned this morning, for the faithful who have gathered in this place of release and for those who, because of rebuke, cannot be here with us today to worship you. We pray for the sick, the sad, and the lonely. We pray too for the planters and for their families. In closing I thank you, Heavenly Father, for the opportunity that you have given me to preach your word in this land of Demerary. Amen."

Then he announced the hymn:

Dear Lord and Father of mankind
Forgive our foolish ways!
Reclothe us in our rightful mind;
In purer lives your service find,
In deeper reverence praise.

The missionary loved this hymn and had chosen it carefully to introduce his sermon. He led the congregation in an uplifting rendition of it, swaying his arms and bobbing his head to keep the rhythm. But as he looked around the room, something caught his attention: a young boy about six or seven years old was rocking noisily in his seat a few benches to his left.

Thomas shifted his attention around the room to the other members of his congregation, but the boy continued his rocking movement while tapping on the bench. The young slave woman next to him leaned over and whispered to him. For a moment the lad sat still, then suddenly he got up and bolted from the woman's side and began to skip in circles around the room of worshippers. It was as though the song "Ring-a-ring o' roses, a pocket full of posies" had popped into his head and he felt compelled to act out the words. At first Thomas was merely amused, and then suddenly he narrowed his eyes and looked more closely at the child. There was something strangely familiar about him.

Mariama's eyes moved quickly from the preacher to Fredric and back again to the preacher. Why was the Reverend Leighton so interested in Fredric? Mariama began to grow uneasy, and now she realized that the preacher was no longer singing. One by one the other worshippers stopped singing as well, and thirty sets of eyes began to follow the preacher's gaze. Realizing that he had become the centre of attention, Fredric quickly retreated to Mariama's side and settled down.

Leighton and the rest of the congregation resumed singing, but periodically the missionary glanced over at Fredric. Mariama put an arm around the boy to settle him down, and he sat quietly for the rest of the service.

The sermon was taken from Luke 15:11–32. It was the story of the prodigal son. Thomas Leighton told his congregation about the father who had two sons, and how the younger son had rejected his father, taken his inheritance early and left home. He told them that the young man had then squandered all his money until he was left penniless, forced to struggle to survive in the world without help. He told the congregation that the young man had eventually returned home ashamed and asked his father for forgiveness. Despite the son's bad behaviour, Leighton said, the father had welcomed him back. In closing, the Reverend Leighton asked the congregants to forgive those who had done them wrong.

Mariama liked this story with its theme of forgiveness. She wasn't sure how to forgive but thought it would be worthwhile trying. Maybe the Christian God had given the new preacher a message for her — an answer to her prayers. Mariama closed her eyes and felt silent words building from deep within, addressed to this unknown God. *Although I don't know how to begin, I want to try. I feel hurt and broken by what happened to me on my thirteenth birthday under the baobab in my village, and by what happened on the ship. I ask you Christian God to help me forgive Massa Ed Grimes and the other man who raped me. I don't know his name, and I'm not sure what he looks like, because it was dark. Then Grimes raped my only friend, Khadija. Here in Demerary he forced himself on my other friend and raped Hessie near the vegetable plot. All of our bodies have been shamed and made unclean by that brute. And his crimes occupy my thoughts and the hate is so strong — it fills my life. I guess I must ask you Christian God to forgive Massa Grimes for these wrongdoings and maybe then I can forgive him too, but it is hard.* Mariama whispered these thoughts in her head and wondered if her forgiveness seemed too half-hearted. But she could not lie to any God, and this was the best should could do.

After the service ended, the congregation began to file out of the chapel, and the Reverend Leighton walked over to Mariama and Fredric.

"Is this your boy?" Thomas asked.

Mariama nodded her head. "Yes, sar," she said.

"What's his name?"

"Fredric, sar. He call Fredric," she replied.

"How old is Fredric?"

"He seven, sar."

"Which plantation are you from?"

"Victory, sar."

"Where is the boy's father?"

"He don' got fadda, sar."

"Is his father deceased, or are you not together?"

"Disease, sar?" Mariama tilted her head and gave the missionary a puzzled look.

Thomas slowed his speech. "Not disease — dead. Did he die?"

"Me don' know, sar."

"What don't you know — who he is, if he is dead, or where he is?"

"No, me don' know."

Thomas realized his questioning was making the girl uncomfortable but pressed on. "Does he live in Demerary?"

Mariama thought for a while and replied, "Me tink so, sar."

Her response caught Thomas off guard. He looked at her intently.

"Does he? Tell me more."

"What mo', sar?"

Locking eyes with Mariama, he asked, "Where does he live in Demerary?"

"Me don' know, sar."

Mariama could see Fredric becoming restless again. The boy was walking slowly towards the chapel door.

"Me only see Massa Ed one time in Demerary. Me got to go, sar ... de boy..."

Mariama's conversation trailed off as she quickened her steps to catch up to Fredric, who had now exited the chapel door and was darting through the crowd of worshippers outside.

"Who is Master Ed?" Thomas Leighton asked, but Mariama was already at the door. He watched as she hurried out in pursuit of her light-skinned son.

***

Back at the missionary house, Thomas paced the slim hallway that led to the parlour, struggling with what he had seen. That child had so many of his brother's mannerisms. How could anyone else have fathered him? But what if the vision was just a coincidence? What if there was no connection? Who was this white man named Ed, and did he live in the area? Finding it difficult to reconcile his thoughts, he prayed for enlightemnent.

"Lord, if this is your divine intervention, show me a path out of my muddled thoughts. Let me find the answers to do your will. Help me to understand, Lord. Help me to understand."

**

After the service Mariama had walked back to Plantation Victory with Fredric. The intense heat of the morning sun sent salty beads of perspiration slithering down her temples. Fredric trotted along most of the way, picking wild plums and tossing rocks into the odd puddles that dotted the road.

"How chapel, Mari?" Jameah called out as they entered the hut.

"Chapel good, Jameah. Me fix de boy some plantain and fish now, and later me get some rest. You want some food? The sun real hot today."

"No, me just back from de plot. Me gon lie down..."

Jameah's voice drifted off and Mariama realized she had fallen asleep. Her thoughts returned to the conversation after chapel. She had never seen the Reverend Leighton show so much interest in anyone before. Many questions ran through her head.

Why had the preacher glared at Fredric so curiously? Was the child a *ngafalui* — a devil child? Surely he couldn't be. But Mariama began to worry all over again. The Reverend Leighton was a godly man and might know a devil child when he saw one. Maybe that was why Mariama had never felt close to the child. She wondered if she should ask Millie and Josie. They were older and would know more about such things.

Shaking her head to clear these troubling thoughts away, Mariama turned her attention to preparing the meal on the small three-rock firepit behind the hut. Every so often she glanced over at Fredric, who was playing in the lane with an older boy from one of the other huts. When the food was ready, she called Fredric in to eat. Too anxious to have an appetite herself, she sat outside the hut and sipped a cup of cool water from the rain barrel down the laneway. After a time Jameah woke up and joined her.

"You sure you a' right, Mari? You don' look good." Jameah peered at Mariama, her brow furrowing.

"Me jus' tired," Mariama replied. "Me gon go back to de house. Me promise Millie fuh help she tonight. De boy eat a'ready."

"Uh-huh," Jameah said doubtfully as Mariama got to her feet.

Mariama began to walk down the lane, and after a few steps she turned and called out to the young boy: "Be good fuh Miz Jameah, Fredric."

Then she was gone.

CHAPTER 23

BLOOD RUNNETH DEEPER

May 1807

May 10, 1807
My dearest Mother and Father,
Today I saw a vision that shook me to my Christian core and plunged me back in time to my childhood at the farmhouse in Merseyside. I closed my eyes and saw the henhouse, the chickens darting from side to side to avoid the young rambunctious lad bent on overpowering them in his eagerness to outrun them.

Images of a frisky John Barrington O'Leary Leighton at the age of five, so full of life and mischief, came into my mind today as I preached God's word — a young boy blessed with the names of both his grandfathers, one whose curiosity caused chickens to scuttle away as far as they could in the open barnyard, the same one who threw variously sized rocks into small ponds to compare the size of the ripples. The force and precision of those throws killed ducks and their ducklings and drove the drakes to flutter off, yet that same child picked wild daisies and yellow daffodils to decorate the sanctuary for Sunday mass. Yellow was his favourite colour, an odd choice for a young boy, you thought, Father; but Mother, you said it matched his sunny personality.

Today, the vision was of another child, born to a slave woman but with many of John's mannerisms — his curiosity, his impatience, his restlessness. Mostly, though, he had John's eyes, his cheeks, his forehead, and his grin — definitely his toothy grin.

I could see his eyes dart around the sanctuary of the small chapel, as though searching for his next adventure to occupy his churning little mind...

Thomas set his pen down and left the room. His head was spinning. No, he could not yet tell his parents.

Later that day the English mail ship left Demerary. Thomas's letter remained at the missionary house. Thomas continued his enquiries about John, Mariama, Ed, and Fredric.

***

A few months later, on another Sunday after church service, the missionary began a lengthy entry in his personal diary:

October 5, 1807

I am still searching for courage but have not yet been brave enough to send to Mother and Father my letter about the young slave boy. I keep looking for the young woman each Sunday, but neither she nor the boy has returned to the chapel since my first sighting of the child.

Surely John could not have had a relationship with this woman? How could he? She is a slave and he a white British man of good and careful upbringing. I shudder to think that he could have transgressed in this fashion. This is something that only a rogue without proper upbringing would contemplate. I am ashamed to admit it: I am worried that he may have fallen into disreputable ways and lost his moral compass. I am even more determined to find him now.

My baby brother used to love the Lord and the church... Has the love in his heart lost its way? What state of degradation must he have reached, if he has indeed taken advantage of a helpless slave woman?

As long as I am in Demerary, I will seek his whereabouts. If there are more children like this boy, I must find them too, yet I am torn. I am fearful of what I might find but anxious to know the truth.

My prayers are more specific each morning and evening. The salvation of my dear brother John's soul leads my supplications each day. The needs of my own soul and those of the slaves come next.

CHAPTER 24

THE WALLS HAVE EARS

November 1807

"Lads, there's nowt sweeter than scoring a bit o' brown honey from Venus's honeypot when no one's watching you. Granted, it was quick, but still it was the best I've had in many a while. There was summat special about this one — its size and its feel was firm and healthy. If I was somewhere else, I'd have stayed with it much longer. You know … I may just have to go back for some more, mate. Yeah, it was that smacking good."

Ed Grimes leaned his head back, gulped the last bit of rum in his tumbler and swallowed hard.

Barney, the bartender, egged Grimes on. "This one must have been extra special, Ed. Tell us more," he said with a sparkle in his eyes.

Patting his bulging belly, Ed continued. "Maybe knowing that it belonged to someone else, someone who tried to cheat me out of me daily bread made it feel even better. To think he doesn't know and won't ever know … it's a good feeling, me lads, a real good feeling."

"So, then, it wasn't the shagging but the revenge that felt so good, my dear man," one of the regulars said as he pulled his bar stool closer to where Grimes was standing. The tavern was becoming louder as more patrons entered.

"It was both. Like I said, there's something special about this one. I'm just going to have to put me hand on it again to figure it out. This one's not like the others. This one is plump with big green eyes — and it's delicious." He snickered as his voice vibrated across the room.

James McDuff stood at the end of the bar observing Grimes. He had not been paying much attention to the man's conversation until he heard the words "plump with big green eyes."

"She belongs to Joseph Blumefield. She's called Hessie, and she is buxom, nicely padded," Grimes continued, carving out a female shape with his two hands.

"So what did you pay for her, my dear man?" said Barney, his curiosity piqued.

"She's a bloody wench, with a lick of the tar brush. I took her on his plantation, bloke. He gets the labour of my gang and doesn't pay full price, so I decided to get me own back." Grimes was enjoying his boastful account.

That evening McDuff met with his neighbour and friend Blumefield for a private conversation.

"My visit is one of importance, Joseph. I have uncovered an intrusion into your personal property. Today I overheard Edward Grimes boast of how he had imposed himself on your slave property and plans to do it again."

"Pray tell, what do you mean?" replied Joseph. "What was the form of imposition?" His eyes searched McDuff's face for a hint of what he was about to reveal.

"Well, Grimes bragged to Barney Walpole and the entire tavern that you had robbed him of the true price for the labour of his slave gang. As a result he claims to have taken his revenge by having his way with your slave — 'the green-eyed one,' he called her. Hessie. I felt it my duty as your friend and neighbour to let you know of this transgression."

Blumefield was astounded He looked fixedly at McDuff for a moment and then thanked him for his loyalty.

"I am disappointed and surprised at this news, James. I will take action tomorrow. Grimes's behaviour cannot be condoned. Thank you for letting me know."

***

Later that evening Joseph attended Hessie's room as was customary. Hessie took up her position, but Joseph stood by the door and observed her for a moment.

"Who else do you lay down with, Hessie?"

His question caught her off guard.

"Only you, Massa, only you," she answered timidly.

"Look at me. Let me see your eyes."

Blumefield's voice was stern and he remained in the spot he had taken up since he entered the room.

Hessie turned around to face him, and ever so slowly she lifted her head until their eyes met.

"Tell me again that you only lay with me. I want to see your eyes when you answer me. Go ahead, and don't forget to mention Edward Grimes," Joseph waited.

"Massa, me don' lay wid Massa Ed. He tek me, Massa, he tek me," Hessie blurted out.

Blumefield was seething, and Hessie saw the fierceness in his eyes.

"When did this happen?" he snapped as he began pacing around the confines of the small room.

"After me come back from Stabroek wid de Missus, me sit down under de breadfruit tree fuh cool off, and Massa Ed grab me. Me run, Massa, me run, but he catch me and tek me."

Hessie's body trembled as she recalled the incident.

"Why didn't you tell me?" Blumefield snapped.

"'Cause me 'fraid you whip me, Massa," a worried Hessie pleaded. "Massa Ed say dere be more where dat come from, me 'fraid he tek me again if me tell you, Massa, and you whip me. Please, Massa Joseph, don' whip me, sar!"

Blumefield observed Hessie for a moment and could tell she was afraid and told the truth.

"I will go and think about what your punishment will be. Don't you ever keep secrets from me — even if you think it will anger me. Do you hear me?"

Hessie's confession had enraged Joseph. She was special to him. He didn't like sharing her, and now this brute had violated his trust and her body. Just then, touching her felt wrong.

Joseph headed back to the main house. After dinner he told Henrietta that he would be retiring early and invited her to join him. She did. To her surprise, as soon as she climbed into bed, her husband reached for her.

"Whatever has brought on these amorous feelings, my dear Joseph? We made love only a few nights ago."

Henrietta was unprepared but happy. Of late, their spotty lovemaking had only happened once each month.

"Can't a man lay with his wife if he feels like it? Hush, let's just enjoy each other," Joseph whispered.

For the first time their lovemaking lasted for well over an hour. Henrietta was elated.

CHAPTER 25

COVET NOT THY NEIGHBOUR'S PROPERTY

December 1807

Joseph Blumefield paced the dark walnut floor of his study. Edward Grimes was due to arrive at five thirty that afternoon to receive the week's remuneration for his gang's work on Plantation Victory. Blumefield mulled over what he would say to Grimes. He thought he might say, "It has been brought to my attention that you have violated the gentleman's rule, sir." But Joseph was acutely aware that Grimes was no gentleman. He would have to be firm without letting this vulgar upstart see how personal the affront was. What he wanted to say was, "How dare you put your disgusting hands and mouth on my property and spoil my pleasure!" But he would have to choose his words more carefully.

A few minutes before Grimes was expected, Joseph walked to the front reception room of the plantation house and waited. Seeing Grimes coming up the path, he went to meet him at the door.

"A very good evening to you, Mr. Blumefield, sir," Grimes blurted out. He was surprised to see Blumefield at the door rather than a servant. "I didn't think I was late for our meeting."

"You are on time, Mr. Grimes. Take a walk with me. I have some other business to discuss with you."

Joseph's voice was steady and icy. Stepping outside, he began to walk towards the stables. Grimes kept pace with him. When they were almost at the stables, Joseph stopped, turned to Grimes and said, "It has been brought to my attention that you have violated my property."

This claim and tone surprised Grimes.

"I don't ... I don't know what you mean, my dear man," Grimes said, with hesitation.

"My information is solid, Mr. Grimes. I have good evidence that the incident took place right here on my plantation, and you have boasted about it. Violation of another man's property is an offence under the law. You, sir, have broken the law, and I intend to seek restitution."

"I take offence to this accusation, sir. I know of no violation of which you speak. This, I believe, is a dishonest attempt to discredit my good name."

Grimes's temples throbbed as the blood vessels in his head expanded.

"I will take my money and leave. I promise that I can forget this preposterous allegation for just a small apology on your part."

"There will not be any remuneration, Mr. Grimes. In fact, I am the party that should be compensated for the disgraceful abuse of my slave property. Neither Hessie — 'the green-eyed one' as you appear to know her — nor any of the slaves on this plantation will ever again be violated by you or members of your gang. I will now ask you to leave my property and never to return. You will be hearing from my solicitors and the Demerary Court of Policy. I bid you good night, Mr. Grimes."

Joseph turned around and headed back towards the great house.

Grimes was blindsided by Blumefield's awareness of his sexual encounter with Hessie. He realized that he had taken so many slave women that he had become careless of the legality of it. Now he had to face the consequences. He left Plantation Victory and headed home to consider how he might escape Blumefield's retribution.

***

The following day, Joseph rode out to meet with Fynn Vanderdijk, one of the sitting judges at the Court of Policy in Stabroek. They had become acquainted and still met occasionally on weekends at the Estate Club for Plantation Owners, a meeting place for members of Demerary's social elite.

"I come seeking wise counsel and recourse from you, my learned friend. I have been abused sorely by a business acquaintance and I require redress."

"In that case I am delighted you have come to me, Joseph. Will you have a drink with me?"

"Not only will I have a drink, I brought you something special to try that I think you will enjoy," Joseph replied, a twinkle in his eyes. He pulled a bottle of dark amber liquid from his black leather saddlebag and handed it over to Vanderdijk.

"Do I detect an element of fine sophistication in this gift, Mr. Blumefield, sir?" Vanderdijk smiled as he admired the bottle.

"As delectable as they come. There is nothing finer anywhere in Demerary or in the British Empire for that matter," Joseph boasted.

"To what do I owe this great gift, my dear man?"

Vanderdijk lit a short, bulging cigar and placed it in his mouth.

"I beseech you to send a warning to one Edward Grimes of Plantation Liefde. He has trespassed on my property and was heard boasting about a carnal impropriety carried out with one of my slaves. I want to send him a strong warning from the court. He is a scoundrel and must be stopped."

Joseph eyeballed the judge closely.

"That, my dear man, will not be a problem. Favours like those can be done easily for returns like the one in my hands. Consider it done. I will send a constable to deliver him a suitable reprimand so that the behaviour will never be repeated. He will no longer be a nuisance to you."

Joseph was delighted that Grimes would pay a price for his transgression. After exchanging news with some of the other planters, he rode back to Victory feeling restored to his former happiness. Now that he had attended to this matter, he could resume his visits to Hessie the following Friday.

***

When Grimes received his summons to appear at the Magistrate's Court to answer a charge of trespassing, or to pay a fine of fifty pounds sterling to the Court, he chose to pay the fine. He also promised to stay away from Plantation Victory. He kept his promise, at least for Blumefield's property. "Bloody Froglander," he muttered, when he saw that it was Vanderdijk who had signed the subpoena.

CHAPTER 26

ZAMBEZI REPOSE

September 1809

It was the morning of Sunday, September 17th, just before the Demerary harvest time. The fragrant aroma of Millie's blend of imported apricots, and prunes infused with essences of vanilla and almond wafted through the long hallway of the great house on Plantation Victory. She bustled about in her crisply starched cotton apron, focused squarely on making cinnamon and nutmeg-spiced rum pudding. It was to be Henrietta's contribution to the Ladies of Demerary Tea Party, which was to take place that afternoon.

In the Blumefields' bedroom, however, a different reality was unfolding. Henrietta was pacing to and fro as she anxiously awaited the arrival of Dr. Donald Drayton. Joseph had been ill most of the night and showed signs of getting worse. She had sent Buck to fetch the doctor, and Millie, who was the only house slave on duty that Sunday, let the doctor in and led him upstairs to the Blumefields' bedroom.

She could feel her heart pounding and appreciated the cotton apron that absorbed the sweat lining her clammy palms. As they drew closer, Millie could hear Massa Joseph coughing in a raspy tone as though gasping for air.

"Breathe, Joseph. You have to try to breathe. Breathe slowly," she heard Henrietta coaxing her husband.

Millie stood to one side as Dr. Drayton tapped on the closed door and then strode into the room and began to examine Joseph. Then she scuttled back along the hallway and down the stairs to Hessie's room.

"Is de Massa. He sick, and de docta come," she called out, as she pounded on Hessie's door. She waited for a response, and remembered something unusual that Mariama had said two nights before.

"Massa eat like a hog tonight," she'd said. "Neva lif' he head up from de plate at all."

Millie had been pleased. She had hoped this time would be the charm.

Hessie appeared in the doorway now, tying the last knot to the sash around her waist.

"Where de Missus? She wid he?"

"Yes, de docta and de Missus wid he. He ain't sound good tho'."

"We see wha' she say after de docta gone," Hessie said. "See if Mari lef' fuh chapel, case we need mo' help."

Millie nodded, tapped on Mariama's door, and then returned to the kitchen when there was no answer. Hessie walked into her room, closed the door and placed her head against it, listening for any movement outside or in the hallway upstairs. Not hearing any, she fastened the lids of the small preserve jars filled with her cache of coins and tucked them under the two loose floorboards. She folded her sleeping mat and carefully rested it over her hiding place. Then, straightening her skirt and blouse, she ran her hands over her braided curly hair and walked upstairs to where Millie was waiting.

"Mari done gone to chapel. Only we heah," Millie said.

"How long has he been struggling to breathe?" Dr. Drayton asked Henrietta.

"It started early yesterday, and he blamed it on the heat. I would say it became gradually worse after supper and has continued throughout the night."

The doctor moved the stethoscope around Joseph's chest and over his back. Then he glanced from his patient to Henrietta.

"I'm afraid he seems to have caught pneumonia," he said gravely. "I'll try to bring the fever down, and then we can go from there. He is very weak, madam."

Henrietta searched the doctor's face for any other answers but saw none.

"I am going back to my office but will return later. In the meantime you should stay with him."

Dr. Drayton picked up his bag and left the bedroom. He met Hessie at the bottom of the stairs and told her, "Fetch your master some tea. He needs liquid. Also take a wet towel to the room to bathe his face. The fever is very high," he added, almost to himself, as he let himself out the door.

"Yes, Massa Docta," Hessie replied and then hurried to the kitchen to find Millie. "Wet towel, wet towel fuh Massa face, and tea — get tea fuh him too, and…" her voice trailed off and she paced back and forth, twisting her hands.

Millie gazed at Hessie with apprehension. Hessie usually gave clear directions but now she sounded muddled and looked confused.

"A' right," Millie said.

Hessie began pacing around the kitchen floor.

"You a' right, Hessie?" Millie asked. Hessie seemed to know more than she was letting on.

"Just get de tea and de towel, Millie."

"Ain't no English tea gonna help he." Millie mumbled as she walked away, a smirk on her face.

Hessie was thinking about Joseph Blumefield. He had never been sick in the time she had lived on his estate. He had always been in control of everything and everyone. Having seen the worried look on the doctor's face, Hessie could not help but wonder what was happening with him.

Millie interrupted her thoughts. "Heah de tea, Hessie, and heah de towel too."

Hessie took the wet towel from Millie. "You come wid me and bring de tea," she said.

As the women began to climb the stairs, they could hear Joseph Blumefield's laboured breathing and his intermittent cough. At the top of the stairs Hessie paused and called out to Henrietta.

"Ma'am, we bring tea and towel. Can we come in, ma'am?"

For a moment there was no response, and then she heard Henrietta softly say, "Yes, come in."

Hessie gently pushed the bedroom door open, and the two women stepped quietly inside. Henrietta was distraught but paused to acknowledge them. She reached out and took the wet towel from Hessie and began to wipe Joseph's face. Motioning Hessie closer, she said, "Help me lift his head, so he can swallow the tea." Hessie did as she was told. Millie leaned in and moved the teacup to Joseph's lips. His efforts to drink were feeble. His head bobbed from side to side as he struggled to hold it erect. Drool seeped out of his open mouth and slid down his face, and his eyes rolled back into his head at times so that only the whites were visible. Henrietta, clearly overwhelmed, kept her eyes on Joseph.

When he had finished drinking, Millie stepped back from the bed and observed as Henrietta and Hessie fussed around Joseph for a few more minutes to improve his comfort. Henrietta elevated his head while Hessie fluffed his feather pillow. His coughing and wheezing eased.

"I think he will rest now," Henrietta whispered to Hessie.

"Yes, ma'am, he rest now," Hessie agreed, as she backed away from the bed. "We go now, ma'am?"

"Yes, go, but not too far. Stay close by," Henrietta instructed.

"Yes, ma'am, we stay outside de room," Hessie said obediently as she and Millie left the bedroom.

"Me gone back to de kitchen. Call if you need help," Millie offered.

As Millie quickened her pace along the hallway to the kitchen, she thought of Josie's words of caution, "Remember, stay quiet, cause bush gat ears and dirt gat tongue." This was their secret to keep.

Millie felt a quiet sense of accomplishment that Joseph was going to rest for a very long while. The Zambezi tail was the charm. Josie would be very pleased.

CHAPTER 27

FORBIDDEN FRUIT

September 1809

Henrietta gazed out of her bedroom window. It was dawn and she had not slept all night, not even a wink. She felt numb.

The soft white muslin curtain fluttered in the morning breeze. Henrietta sat at the edge of her empty bed, which now felt enormous, the soles of her feet sensing the cool of the greenheart floor beneath, as she struggled to comprehend what had transpired in the last four days. She inhaled the pungent mix of sweet and sour guava that wafted in from the garden. Just like life itself, the touch of tartness injected into the pervasive sweetness was an acknowledgement, a nod to nature's contrariness and variety. Her gaze moved over to the partially laden guava tree and the few dozen yellow, ripened, bird-pecked fruit scattered beneath it. Millie had not yet come outside to gather these gems up for her famous jellies.

Henrietta could feel the tightness in her stomach, chest, and shoulders and in her clenched jaw as she wavered between despair and panic. She had never felt this tense, at least not that she could remember. She quickly eased her shoulders, shook her arms free, and breathed in deeply to release the knots in her body and to think. Joseph had been buried three days before. He was gone and she was in charge.

It was close to the end of the rainy season in Demerary. Henrietta reflected that in Manchester it would be coming up to the end of the summer. She had thought about Manchester a lot these recent days, as she assessed her possible next steps in Demerary.

***

Joseph's funeral had been held at the small white-washed Moravian church just over a mile from the estate. The local minister was out of the county, and the Reverend Leighton had been asked to perform the service in his place. He had only met Joseph Blumefield once in the seven years he had been in Demerary. Henrietta sat in the front pew of the church. She wore a flowing black lace dress, and a thin black mesh veil covered her head and face. She was the perfect vision of a widow in mourning — patting at her eyes and cheeks with a white lace handkerchief during the service.

There were two hymns, one Bible verse reading, a two-minute eulogy by James McDuff, and the lowering of the greenheart box into the wet brown earth. The whole affair was over in thirty minutes.

Joseph had never attended church, so Henrietta was surprised at the turnout. Around thirty people attended, including some parishioners, managers, and other planters such as the McDuffs and the Gladstones. A judge from the Court of Policy had also been in attendance. *Joseph would be pleased*, Henrietta thought.

With his wife standing beside him, James McDuff said, "Penelope and I extend our sympathies to you, my dear madam," while offering her his hand.

"Thank you both. It happened so quickly," Henrietta whispered, trying her best to play her part.

Her thoughts meandered as she shook hands with and forced smiles for people she didn't really know or cared about. How had she ended up in this predicament?

Henrietta had become accustomed to being with Joseph but had never been in love with him. In fact, though she cared about him, she had never felt any passion for him at all. He was older and had usually taken on a caretaker role in the marriage. He had been a provider of fine things and had secured a good life for her. She had always felt that her main role was to keep him company and to do whatever he needed, whenever he needed it.

Intimacy between them had happened at times of Joseph's choosing. Henrietta had often wondered if she herself could ever bring passion to their bedroom. Her weekend baths, fine French perfumes from Oriza L. Legrand, jewellery, and new hairstyles didn't seem to do the trick. Though she felt no love for him, as a young woman, she had sensual urges and had longed for his embrace — or any embrace.

Henrietta had chosen one Friday evening after the harvesting season to try something exceptional. She had urged Millie to prepare a special dinner of Yorkshire pudding and roast beef, two of Joseph's favourite dishes. As she imagined, he was delighted and ate several servings and even had a snifter of his special rum afterwards, instead of his usual cup of tea. Reading his mood, Henrietta threw modesty to the wind and made her move. Masking her excitement, she excused herself from the dinner table early.

"I will turn in before you, my dear. I need to organize a few items before bed," she said to him with a gentle kiss on the cheek, lingering more than usual, and then exited the dining room. She retired to their bedroom, undressed, climbed into bed and lay in wait under the new cotton, lace-trimmed sheets. When at last he entered their bedroom, she shyly, slowly let her bare, slender right leg slither out from under the sheet, not looking at Joseph but rather waiting for his reaction, her heart raced. But as Joseph undressed, he muttered something about the exhausting day he had had and then simply rolled into bed with his back towards her. Within seconds he was asleep. Henrietta's heart sank; she had failed to release his masculine urges. Worse than that, the rejection spurred resentment in her. A quiet internal quest began that night, as she lay for hours without sleep.

"Henrietta, you may ride back to the estate with us in our carriage. There is no need for Buck to return to get you."

Penelope McDuff's wispy voice penetrated Henrietta's thoughts. Henrietta was happy for the black veil over her face, which hid her now bright crimson cheeks.

"Thank you, Penelope. I will," Henrietta replied.

"Madam, allow me to make your acquaintance. My name is Jemmoth Rhodes. Your husband hired me to be the new overseer at Plantation Victory beginning next week." A burly gruff man with gnarly stubby hands outstretched stepped in front of the McDuffs.

Surprised by the intrusion, Henrietta flatly replied, "Thank you for coming, Mr. Rhodes, but I will not need your services. I will be rethinking my approach to plantation life."

Rhodes was taken aback but managed to maintain control. "It is a terrible shock what happened to your husband, ma'am, but my services are still yours and I beg you to take a few days to consider the matter." Finding no encouragement in Henrietta's blank expression, he bobbed his head and lumbered away to gather his thoughts. He quickly left the church building muttering and grunting with dissatisfaction.

Henrietta bade farewell to other well-wishers in the churchyard. The Reverend Leighton offered to visit if she needed his help. She politely thanked him and then followed the McDuffs back to their waiting carriage. James McDuff's driver drove the carriage out of the churchyard and along the main road east to Plantation Victory.

Hessie, Millie, and Mariama waited inside the house, at the door, for Henrietta to return from the funeral. Buck, Josie,

Jameah, and some of the other slaves were gathered in the laneway behind the main house. A few of the children were oblivious to the solemnity of the day and played in the small field behind the garden.

"De carriage comin'. Must be de Missus," Millie said to the others as she bent forward and peered through the window.

"Yes, she wid de backra McDuff," Hessie agreed.

"Wonder wha' gon' come of we now," Millie said, echoing Hessie's thoughts.

In the laneway, Buck and Josie were having a similar conversation.

"You tink Missus gon' sell we?" Josie asked Buck.

"Don' know. Don' know how backra does tink," Buck answered, a tinge of puzzlement in his voice. "Not every big head got sense Josie ... just got fuh wait and see."

"Hope Missus don' separate we, Buck." Josie said, an edge of worry in her voice.

"We just got fuh wait 'pon she and live wid wha' happen. Maybe she sell we togetha." Buck added cautiously. An' if she sell we separate we done — dat's it. When coconut fall from tree it can't fasten back."

Moments later, Henrietta climbed out of the carriage and was escorted to the house by Penelope and James.

"Would you come in for some tea, please?" she asked, beckoning to them both. "I would like to seek your advice, Mr. McDuff. Do you have a moment?"

"Of course, of course. Anything you need," James replied, as he and Penelope followed Henrietta into the drawing room.

"Bring us some tea, Millie," Henrietta said. She turned to James. "Or would you prefer something firmer, Mr. McDuff?"

"I will have whatever you ladies are having. Tea would be fine," James said with a smile.

Millie and Mariama headed into the kitchen to fetch the tea. Meanwhile Hessie wandered back into her room. A sense of peace, coupled with loss, flooded over her. It was a confusing time. Despite the relief of taking her body back from Joseph's weekly grasp, she also recognized that this triumph meant the loss of the steady trickle of cash that her future depended on.

Retrieving her stash from beneath the floorboards, she counted close to one hundred and forty pounds sterling in those jars, amassed over ten years. Most of it had come from Blumefield, though some had been earned at Sunday markets. She had long dreamt about what the money might get her; now she had to wait for Henrietta's next move.

The McDuffs stayed and enjoyed a welcome pot of brewed English tea, warm buttered scones, and fresh guava jelly. Mariama took up her usual position by the door, but today Henrietta rang the bell and dismissed her as soon as the tea had been served.

"I am thinking about going home to Manchester," Henrietta began as soon as Mariama had gone.

The McDuffs took the announcement in stride, listening intently.

"I am thinking about seeing a solicitor," Henrietta continued. "Getting rid of the assets in Demerary would serve me well. I can rejoin my family and begin a new life in Manchester. I wanted to gauge your interest in purchasing the estate, Mr. McDuff. After all, ours is the property that adjoins yours. It might be worth your consideration."

She paused and looked at James and Penelope for their reaction.

"We will need some time to think on it, madam," James said, glancing at his wife.

"We do need a good gardener to help take care of my flowerbeds. I also mentioned to you last week that I need some more help in the house. Maybe we'll take Josie. She already does my ironing on Sundays, and a fine job too. I would love to have a good cook; ours is getting old and forgetting to add key ingredients to our meals — like salt." Penelope rolled her eyes, and then continued. "Could we take Millie as well? It'll save me the trouble of teaching new help to fit in?" Penelope implored.

"Yes, we can take them, but I have to consult our solicitors on the plantation." James replied.

"I can arrange for you to have Josie, Buck, and Millie the day I leave. Thank you for your consideration. I will await your response regarding the plantation, and I will also speak with our solicitor about other possible purchasers. I would really like a quick sale. I have sent word to our families of my wish to return. I hope everything will transition smoothly and I can have a safe passage home in the very near future."

"Let me know if you need anything in the meantime," Penelope said sorrowfully. I will miss having you as a neighbour, and I know that the Ladies of Demerary will miss your presence at our events," she added.

As soon as the McDuffs left, Henrietta retreated to her bedroom. She pulled the bolt across the door and secured herself in her quiet sanctuary. It felt good to shut out the world. Now she could think in peace, but not before she did something else first, something she had longed to do for a while.

Henrietta felt the full power over her life that she had recently been granted by Joseph's departure. She reached into the secret chest where Joseph had stored all his keys, and picked out a few of the unmarked single keys hanging on the wooden frame. She moved to Joseph's side of the bed, where there was a small wooden cabinet, and through trial and error, she discovered the correct key and turned it in the lock.

The cabinet opened, and about a dozen sealed bottles of dark amber-coloured high-proof rum greeted her probing eyes. Joseph and a local distiller had secretly undertaken to create the best rum in the British Empire. These bottles contained some of their finest efforts. Joseph had kept this covert activity from prying eyes, even hers. It was a part of his bribery chest, the one he used to get favours from high-ranking officials in both England and Demerary.

Henrietta had never tasted any of this gilded pleasure before. She had on occasion savoured infusions of prized alcoholic beverages, but none of this calibre. She had heard James McDuff and Bill Gladstone share with Joseph that there had been discussions among the planters to come up with a prized potion, a distilled spirit that would outperform all others in the region. They had often sung the praises of well-aged, smooth rum produced with English yeast in copper barrels.

Henrietta pondered over a conversation she had recently had with Joseph.

"Being ahead of the rest of the planters in producing the finest rum is very important to me. It is something I have worked at very diligently, and I think I might've achieved perfection." Joseph had nodded his head and smiled reflectively.

"Over the years I tried many methods, including adding regular yeast into copper barrels, but it had not worked very well. Then recently, I tested the fermented molasses distilled with special slow-acting yeast from the French Alps region and aged the mixture in oak barrels. I think I have come upon something extra special with this process. I have produced rum with a pleasant dark colouration, a full-bodied buttery smooth taste, and an appealing strong character. I will keep this finding a secret, and I implore you to do the same. This could be the gem that will set us above the rest — the qualities in a product that Gladstone and McDuff aspire to accomplish. We can produce the finest rums and fetch the best prices — I know people will want this and will pay for it. Henrietta, my dear, our dream of returning to Liverpool is in sight." Blumefield had suddenly jumped up from his chair, reached over, and hugged his wife.

Mariama had been summoned to clear the sherry glasses used by her owners a few minutes earlier, and she walked into the parlour at the same moment Joseph had embraced Henrietta. She had been taken aback and felt her cheeks flush from embarrassment. It was the first time she had seen any display of affection between her Massa and her Missus. She had retrieved the glasses and left the room flustered. Blumefield had lowered his voice and continued.

"I have used one of the bottles of this exceptional creation to gain favour from Judge Fynn Vanderdijk of the Court of Policy. He has offered to pay me up to fifteen pounds for each bottle I produce for him." Joseph had said as he sat in his favourite armchair with a smug look on his face.

Now Henrietta had inherited the secret stash.

Over the last few days, Henrietta had sorely needed calm and relaxation. Temptation surged as she caressed the bottle. She could do whatever she wanted with this prized spirit, and right now she wanted its dark, bold flavours to caress her parched tongue.

Henrietta placed her new treasure under a pillow, locked the cabinet and placed the key back in Joseph's secret chest, which was of course now hers. Smiling, she walked over to the French vanity table, which had been a wedding present from Joseph, and rang the bell for one of her helpers. A few moments later, she heard Mariama's familiar knock on the bedroom door.

"Bring me a pot of tea," she called out.

"Yes, ma'am," Mariama replied.

A few minutes later she opened the door and Mariama brought the tea tray into the bedroom and placed it on the vanity. Henrietta sat on the red velvet stool and watched her awkward attempt to pour the tea.

"I'll do that," she said with a wave of her right hand. "You can go now."

"Yes, ma'am," Mariama said. She left the room and closed the door behind her.

Henrietta got up and reached under the pillow for the hidden bottle of aged rum. She broke the seal with a quick twist of her wrist and poured a perfect shot into the empty teacup. The aroma was magnificent. She lifted the cup to her face and smelled the heady vapours that arose from the dark amber liquid. Then she tilted the teacup to her lips, and the spicy emulsion brushed past them and onto her waiting tongue. A beautiful blend of liquor, spice, caramel, and sugar filled her mouth. She tilted her head back once more and allowed the fullness of its flavours to fill every crevice of her mouth. Joseph had been correct. It was delectable.

Henrietta sipped until her first helping was finished, and then poured a second, more generous one. This time, she topped it with steaming hot tea, smiling as she swallowed every drop of the magnificent blend. Her body felt as light as a feather, and before long she was sound asleep.

Raindrops drumming on the windowpane woke her up.

"Where am I? What time is it? Who ... where?" she mumbled. And then it all came flooding back. She was in her bed, alone. Gripped by fear, she pulled her pillow to her chest and buried her head in it. She hated being in bed alone.

CHAPTER 28

SEARCHING FOR JOHN

October 1809

Ed Grimes sat across from Thomas Leighton at Barney's English Spirits, the local pub, on a hot afternoon.

"I have been told you know much about the slavers and their routes to Demerary, Mr. Grimes. I am looking for John Leighton and was told that you might know where I could find him."

"Last I heard, he was with the *Gallantry*, mate," Grimes replied. "It sails to Demerary three times a year. From the time of her arrival to her departure, she spends about three or four weeks in port. Usually she drops her cargo, gets any repairs needed, reloads, and pulls up anchor. You'll have plenty of time to find out if John is still with the crew."

"When was the last time you saw him in Demerary, pray tell?" Thomas asked.

"Can't say I've set eyes on that bloke in donkey's years — must be at least six now. After he and I had about three trips together on the *Archery*, I got a lucky stint and broke free. I signed on with a privateer out of Falmouth, in Cornwall. We were a small but mighty crew," Ed reminisced with a smile on his face. "We captured three

French merchant ships full of cargo, trying to avoid the British blockade. Were we ever in luck — the prize court bought the ships and, as is customary, each member of the crew got a good share. I took mine and moved to Demerary, where I bought a house and six slaves — five blokes, one wench. I've been here ever since, making me living on the backs of those darkies. T.J. should be so lucky," he said, grinning.

"T.J.?" Thomas gawped at Ed, mystified.

"John, I mean. See, because he was a lanky fellow we nicknamed him T.J. — Tall John." Ed grinned again.

Thomas nodded and smiled.

"How do you know him — T.J., I mean?" Ed asked.

"He is a relative. A close one, long separated from his family," Thomas replied politely.

"The next vessel arriving from Liverpool should be the *Gallantry*," Ed said. "I used to know the schedules, but I've lost track of those voyages these days. Ask the harbour master at Stabroek. He's a bit quisby, shirks his duties whenever he can, but he can tell you when the *Gallantry* is due in port. Depends on how fast they haul in a good load of them savages. Without enough cargo, the trip could be delayed for weeks. Weather can be a bloody spoiler as well. But there's always dark commodity on board to pass the time, I must say."

Ed winked his right eye and bit down on his bottom lip. Thomas gazed at him blankly. He had no intention of encouraging the direction of Ed's conversation.

"He was trained up well to do all his ship-bound duties," Ed continued, grinning. "I taught him myself. I made a man out of him, and those young savages on board the *Archery* benefited — the wenches, I mean. The first trip we took together was your John's first. It was on that trip that I broke him in. He did very well on his own after that, I'm sure. If you have time, I'll tell you some of what we got up to in those days. They're fine memories.

"You see, mate," he continued, "I know them seas well and I was on them Liverpool docks since I ran away at age eleven — just a lad — after me fayther got us kicked outta our cellar dwelling on Granby Street in Toxteth. I worked them docks for two years before getting on me first slaver owned by some wealthy blokes from Lancashire — the same kinds that me fayther worked for and complained about getting stiffed by — though deep down I knew that each bob went to the public ledger and bevvies.

"'Me lad,' I can hear me fayther inside me head saying 'dunno fear nobody lad. Beat 'em 'fore they beat you — be the beater not the beaten lad. Never the beaten. I'm spitting feathers here.' Then he would throw his head back and empty his flask of gin down his parched throat.

"So it was me who taught young John to take care of himself on that ship. I taught him what me fayther and the other men taught me — beat, don't get beaten by the slaves or the crew."

For the next hour Thomas sat and listened to Ed brag about his conquests, both human and material. After some time he was able to interject more questions.

"Do you have a name for the harbour master at Stabroek?" he asked. "I would like to check on the next expected arrival time."

"I don't know his name, but I know where his quarters are. I can take you if you would like me to — for a price, mate. What say you?"

"I will think about it and let you know. I need to be sure that it is the correct John Leighton we are pursuing."

Outside the pub the sun was beginning to set behind the large silk cotton tree.

"I must bid you farewell, Mr. Grimes," said Thomas, getting to his feet. "I do appreciate your most kind offer, and I will contact you should I need more direction. Good afternoon to you, sir."

"Aye aye, sailor," Ed teased, giving Thomas a mock-nautical salute.

The two men parted.

On his way back to the missionary house, Thomas could not help but feel excited. This was the first time in a very long while that he had received what seemed like credible information about his brother's whereabouts. All other clues over the years had proven fruitless — like the night long ago in Liverpool when the constable had stopped by his parents' home.

It had been past midnight when they heard the loud thumping of a tipstaff on the door of the flat.

"This is the parish, constable," a voice called out in the night. "There's been a sighting of the boy at the marine docks. I need you to come with me to identify him."

Thomas and his parents leapt out of bed and dressed quickly, ready to be escorted by the constable to the waterfront.

"You stay here, Thomas, in case he comes home, so you can let him in," his father said. "Your mum and I will go with the constable." And they were gone.

Thomas waited with anticipation. He tried reading but couldn't concentrate. So he rehearsed what he would say to his brother when he came home: "Do you know how much we've worried about you? Are you all right? Where did you go, and why didn't you send us word?"

About two hours later he heard the key turn in the lock. He bounded towards the door, excited to see his brother again. John was not with them.

"Where is he?" He asked his parents.

"It was another lad. The one they saw lives nearby."

His father was just as disappointed as Thomas.

"Maybe next time," his father encouraged. Then he turned and went into his bedroom, and Thomas's mother followed.

He wondered if Ed Grimes's lead would amount to anything.

PART III

CHAPTER 29

PEACE AND REST

November 1809

The auction began. Mariama and Fredric stood on the small platform in front of the magistrate court. Henrietta Blumefield's solicitor looked on from the shade as some of the human property of Plantation Victory was sold off.

"Young wench and lad for a small fee of one hundred and five pounds sterling — two for the price of one," the auctioneer called out.

Mrs. Jane Matilda Hoggsworth hoisted a stubby right arm above her curly dirty-blond hair, signalling intent to purchase. Glancing from left to right, she scanned the hot and airless room for any challengers to her bid. It was just past ten o'clock on a muggy Friday morning in the middle of November.

Sweat poured down Jane Matilda's face, a clear indication that the little wicker hand fan was not doing its job. She patted her forehead and her temples with a white lace-trimmed handkerchief as she waited for the auctioneer's confirmation of her winning bid. Jane Matilda needed new field hands for Plantation Mon Paix et Repos. The planting season would be upon them soon, and in the past twelve months she had lost family and four slaves to malaria and yellow fever.

Mr. John S. Rawlings, Esquire — or J.S. Rawlings, as he was known to the local planters — raised his hand to counter Jane Matilda's bid. He sat in the back a few rows over to the right, and Jane Matilda had missed his hand gesture. She only heard the auctioneer acknowledge a bid of one hundred and ten pounds. When she followed his gaze, it led to J.S. Rawlings, the proprietor of Plantation Ma Joie, which was a few miles from her own holdings.

Jane Matilda rose from her seat and turned around to face her competitor. Rawlings didn't acknowledge her or look in her direction but scanned the room for any other challengers. Finding none, he looked back directly at the auctioneer. Jane Matilda could feel the sweat trickling from her armpits and between her legs. She pulled at the sides of her flowing black cotton skirt to let in some air. It angered her to be publicly ignored by Rawlings. She wanted the Negro wench and the lad, and she was going to have them.

Suddenly Mariama's shoulders tightened and her knees began to wobble. She had a flashback. *Oh Lord*, she thought, *the boy can't handle the hot branding iron on his shoulder.* The image of what had transpired after she was bought by Joseph Blumefield was clear in her mind. *It will kill him.* The visceral smell of burning flesh was vivid and she worried for young Fredric.

As she observed the competition between the two planters, her eyes shifting from one to the next, she secretly hoped that the short heavy woman would win the bid.

The experience was as frightening as the first one. But now there was a child to think about — her child. A warmth came over her and she realized that her feelings for the boy had grown during his nine years of life, and now she wanted to protect him. She was relieved that Josie hadn't sent him to the ancestors.

The auction continued as the auctioneer called out a bid of one hundred and fifteen pounds. Jane Matilda raised her hand. She looked at the slave wench and small pickaniny standing on the raised platform in the front of the room. She thought that the wench must have been about twenty-one years old, the lad about nine, somewhat older than her Conrad would have been, had he survived the dreaded malaria. She wanted them.

"Do we have one hundred and twenty?" the auctioneer called out, but his suggestion was met with silence. "Going once at one hundred and fifteen," then, "Going twice…"

Jane Matilda looked Rawlings squarely in the eyes; he glared right back at her over his wire-rimmed reading glasses. He saw the determination in Jane Matilda's face and suddenly pity came over him as he remembered not only that she was now a widow, but also that she had lost her only child in the past year. Rawlings lowered his eyes, kept his hands in the pockets of his grey breeches, and gave up the competition.

The auctioneer banged his gavel. "Sold to Mrs. Jane Matilda Hoggsworth for the sum of one hundred and fifteen pounds sterling," he shouted, "the young Negro wench Marma and her lad."

And just like that, Mariama and Fredric had a new owner.

Jane Matilda walked up to the platform. "Come now," she said to Mariama, "and bring the lad with you."

"Yes, ma'am," replied Mariama, just as she had been taught on Plantation Victory.

"Henri, come on over here and take them to Tobias," Jane Matilda shouted. "I will settle some business with the auctioneer and the solicitor. Wait for me in the churchyard. I will join you soon."

Holding a fan in one hand and a handkerchief in the other, Jane Matilda scuttled over to sign the promissory note for four new slaves: three young women aged twenty, twenty-two, and twenty-five years, and a lad of nine years. Henri Rymes, the half-English, half-French overseer at Plantation Mon Paix et Repos, led Mariama and Fredric over to join the other two who were already waiting to be transported to their new home.

"What do they call you?" Henri said to his newest charge.

"Mariama, sar. They call me Mariama. And he Fredric." Mariama inclined her head at her son.

"Follow me, and bring the boy," said Henri.

Mariama held her bundle close to her and gently nudged Fredric along. They followed Henri along the narrow dusty lane to the small wooden chapel across from the market square and the magistrate court. As they walked, Mariama scanned the surrounding area for the branding iron. None was visible. They passed a chaise and then saw a horse and cart with three Africans. Two of them were in the dray cart, and one stood a few feet away from the back chassis holding a cat-o'-nine-tails. Mariama had seen enough of those whips to know that the person holding it was a driver. She stood next to Fredric and anxiously waited — not wanting to take anything for granted.

"Two more for you, Tobias. Pack them in."

"Yes, sar, Massa Henri, sar."

Mariama breathed a sigh of relief as Tobias motioned to her and Fredric to climb into the dray cart. They did so and clambered over bags of paddy, rice, and other provisions secured for the plantation. They moved to a corner of the cart where the other slaves made room for them. After they settled in, Tobias climbed into the front, picked up the reins and prepared the horse and cart for the trip back to Plantation Mon Paix et Repos.

Henri sat in the chaise awaiting Jane Matilda's return. He thought of her smooth, plump body, and wondered what it would feel like to touch and caress it. He thought about her simple and often subdued look and wondered how passion might alter it. What could she be thinking most of the time, especially at night? Did she miss having a man in her bed, one who would do the man's business on the plantation and deal with other men? She no longer had one in her life since the passing of her husband. With so few white women in the county, it was difficult for a white man to find a relationship with a woman, a respectable white woman. Henri considered the possibility of such a liaison with Jane Matilda.

He also thought about Grimes, the proprietor who travelled the coast with his work gang. When Grimes had found out that Jane Matilda was without a husband, his eyes had widened and his mouth had curled into a lewd smile. This was a man known for boasting to anyone who would listen about his many trysts with slave women. "Slave women are everywhere, and the ones I take are usually in my charge," he would brag. "The only challenge in lying with a slave woman is pursuing and taking down the ones that belong to someone else. That brings me satisfaction — just like stealing peppermint sticks from a candy jar."

Henri sensed that Grimes was after Jane Matilda not for a mate but for her money. Grimes was a scoundrel who would use whatever vulnerability he could find to get the upper hand, in this case a widow's loneliness. But Henri knew that Grimes was out of his league when it came to Jane Matilda. She was a simple and proper British woman, not a slave, and he too had to be careful about trying to get close to her. She was his employer, and he needed to keep his job. He could not afford to be too presumptuous. Again he found himself wondering why he was so drawn to her. She was a plain-looking woman, though buxom. At the best of times, she wore a solemn, almost severe look. Henri could not remember seeing her smile. He wondered what it was that had attracted her late husband to her but recognized the dangers of pressing for personal information. For the time being, he decided, he would keep his musings to himself.

"Henri, I am here." Jane Matilda's firm voice broke into his thoughts.

"Of course you are, Mrs. Hoggsworth, of course you are," Henri said as he rushed over to help Jane Matilda into the passenger's seat of the chaise.

"Move along, Tobias," Jane Matilda called. "We need to be back before the field hands take their midday break."

Tobias guided the long wooden dray cart into the street and headed away from Stabroek upriver along the bank and in the direction of Plantation Souvenirs Agréables. Jane Matilda's chaise followed closely, driven by Henri.

In the back of the dray cart, Mariama turned to the young woman sitting closest to her and Fredric. "Me Mariama; he Fredric. What dey call you?"

"Juma," the woman answered.

Mariama then looked to her left, but the other woman sitting there just gazed at her blankly. Mariama recognized that look. It was the look of a newly arrived captive who was traumatized and alone. She reached out and touched the woman's hand. The woman continued to stare blankly as Mariama squeezed her hand gently and smiled.

"We do dis togedda," Mariama said. But deep down inside, the smouldering mixture of anger and despair exploded in her head: *For the second time I'm being ripped away from a family I care about: Hessie, Millie, Jameah, Josie, and Buck. Allah, can you hear me? I am scared and confused. What did I do wrong? Fredric is the only one I know now. I don't hate the boy, but I'm confused about my feelings for him.* YahYah *said that Sande teaches girls how to become women — wives and mothers. I never learned how. I'm scared to make a mistake ... so scared —* then she opened her eyes and looked down at Fredric, whose body was now fully relaxed as he leaned against her. He had been rocked to sleep by the movement of the dray cart along the bumpy country road and the sharp, warm rays of the mid-morning sun.

As the dray cart trundled along the dry dusty road, Mariama's thoughts wandered back to Plantation Victory and the slave family she had left behind. Some of them had been sold to neighbouring plantations. She wondered if she would ever see any of them again. She would miss them all, especially Hessie. She wondered who her new family would be. Her stomach did small flips and she held her slight bundle close to suppress her internal murmurs.

CHAPTER 30

PLAIN JANE

December 1809

Jane Matilda was a quiet woman. People around her found it difficult to tell what her disposition was at any given time. After the passing of her husband, Ben, everyone had expected her to pack up and move home to London. But she had surprised them all and carried on with business as usual.

"Henri, you are indispensable on this plantation. I am hoping now that Ben is no longer here, you would consider staying and taking on some of the managerial duties Ben steered in addition to your overseer role. I promise to pay you handsomely." She twisted her ring and waited anxiously for his response.

"Madam, I am happy to hear that you find my service necessary. It will be my honour to continue to serve in whatever capacity you require." Henri hoped his facial expression masked his excitement of being asked to stay. He liked Jane Matilda, and more money and a manager's role would definitely help elevate him in a touchy Demerary society obsessed with position, wealth, and privilege. Jane Matilda was pleased with his response.

With Henri's help, Jane Matilda quickly adapted to running the other business aspects of the estate, including managing the finances. She didn't spend her time chatting and mingling with her class and so skipped the social teas put on by the Ladies of Demerary. As well, she only shopped for clothes or hats in Stabroek as was necessary unlike the other high society women.

Indeed, when she was not occupied with running the plantation, Jane Matilda liked to spend time in her garden, tending her flowers and shrubs. She and Ben had taken great pride in the grounds around the house and had planted Damask roses, primroses, and moss roses in addition to shrubs that flourished in the Demerary heat. Pale-skinned when she arrived in Demerary, like most of the British ladies, Jane Matilda's complexion after several seasons in the tropics was now a nut-brown colour.

She was the third of three siblings in her family. Jane had been sickly as a child, unlike her brother Cameron John and sister Gracie Anne, who had been healthy, happy-go-lucky children, excelling in every venture they undertook. Cameron John had become a solicitor at the age of twenty-one, and Gracie Anne had been married at nineteen to a young man named Philip Greaves, a captain in the Royal Navy. Both Cameron John and Gracie Anne had moved away from London to begin their new lives.

Jane Matilda had met Benjamin Hoggsworth in church and married him soon after, when she was just eighteen years old and he was twenty. As they settled into married life, an offer to manage a sugar plantation in the colonies for an absentee planter, Archibald McSweeney, was presented to Ben. McSweeney was a member of their church diocese.

"Managing the business for a few years would help us understand it, and then we could purchase our own plantation and run that for about five years. By then we should be able to see good profits from the venture. What do you think, my dear?" Ben looked over at Jane who was sitting in a shaded part of their garden sipping tea and eating homemade crumpets. Masses of blooming yellow roses filled the canopy in the walkway ahead of her. Jane paused for a moment and looked into the distance.

"Seems like a sound idea, Ben. I think our goal should be to move back to London as people of means, and then we should start our family," a warm smile filled her face.

"Wonderful then, I will let Mr. McSweeney know that I accept the job," Ben said, as he leaned over and gently hugged her from behind. At the end of their first year of marriage, they set off for Demerary.

However, as everyone knows, babies don't always wait for the right time, and Conrad Benjamin Hoggsworth was born to Ben and Jane Matilda exactly nine months after they arrived in Demerary. Surprised and delighted — and undeterred — the young couple carried on with their plans. For three years they managed the McSweeney Estate at Blankenburg. Then at the end of the third year, they purchased Plantation Mon Paix et Repos, along with ten slaves, and joined the planter class. Ben and Jane Matilda were an unconventional couple, being equally involved in the business, but it was perhaps because of this arrangement that they achieved financial success quickly.

Five years later, when both Ben and Conrad fell ill with malaria, Jane Matilda did her best to manage both home and business while trying to nurse them back to health. Her best was not enough, however, and within three days, Jane Matilda became a childless widow. Even in the depths of her grief, though, not once did she consider abandoning the dream she had with Ben. She was profoundly relieved and felt more secure now that Henri accepted her proposal and was fully on board.

Henri was a man of about Ben's age, who carried out his duties well and then kept to himself. Ben had trusted Henri, and she did too. For the next year, Jane Matilda and Henri ran Plantation Mon Paix et Repos with continued success. Jane took pride in describing this achievement in writing to her sister and brother in spite of her grief. One of her letters read:

December 28th, 1809
My dear Gracie Anne,

I write with deep pain still in my heart over losing my dear Ben and Conrad. I visit their resting place twice each week and deliver fresh English roses, just like the ones in mother's garden, and sometimes brightly coloured crotons and fresh green ferns.

I find reassurance in visiting with them. Their bodies rest just about six hundred yards away from my front garden. I feel they see me tending it and caring for our property. I take great comfort in this, knowing I am running things here in Demerary just as Ben would have expected. I now have full responsibility for the twenty-five slaves, and I have kept the overseer on to perform some of Ben's tasks. He is a good man and I can trust him with the day-to-day work of controlling the slaves and managing the livestock.

Plantation Mon Paix et Repos has, for the second year since their passing, had a very productive growing season. I am proud of what I have accomplished. I know that Ben is proud of our great harvest, too.

My health is good. Demerary's sunny coast has done wonders for me. Although I miss England, I do not miss the dampness and the cool weather.

God bless, until I receive your reply,
Jane Matilda

CHAPTER 31

CHAPTER AND VERSE

May 1810

"John Barrington O'Leary Leighton, a vision for my weary eyes!"

Thomas beamed as he gazed at his younger brother, who was perched on a wooden stool sipping rum from a mug.

John looked up, startled to see his brother, his eyes widened. He shook his head and stared at the smiling bloke in disbelief.

"Thomas … Thomas? Is that you? What in the … and why are you wearing a collar?"

"Of course it's me. I am a missionary here in Demerary. And don't I deserve an embrace?"

Thomas held his arms open and grinned. The two men clasped each other for an extended moment. Finally they stepped back and regarded one another.

"How did you find me?" John said as he ran his fingers through his scruffy beard.

"It was easier than I thought. My path to you began with a vision and some enquiry. I am so happy to have found you. May we spend some time together? There is much I want to talk with you about."

"Of course we can. In fact, I insist. My ship doesn't sail for forty-eight hours."

John sat down again and patted the chair beside him, but Thomas remained standing.

"Have you eaten, John? I would be honoured if you would join me at the little English teahouse for tea and sandwiches."

Although he would have preferred an offer of spirits, John agreed.

"That'd be grand," he said. As they began to walk, he asked, "Who do you preach to, and where is your church?"

"I preach to African slaves at a little chapel here in Demerary," Thomas replied.

Once they were seated and tucking into their meal, Thomas began to question his brother in earnest.

"When, pray tell, did you join that merchant ship from Liverpool?"

"I see you've done your homework, but I've not committed that date to memory, my dear brother," John said. "I do remember, though, that it was around the middle of summer that my first voyage from Liverpool began. That was well over ten years ago."

"Twelve years to be exact, John, since you left our home in Liverpool," Thomas said.

"I spent some time in hiding, and would have joined the ship the following year, so it would be eleven. But I have been back to jolly old England many times. I've been careful not to loiter in Liverpool, though, for fear of being found out."

"Found out? For what, might I ask?"

"For killing that bloody redhead on my way to school that day, that's what!"

"Killing? … What redhead?" Thomas was puzzled.

"Jack Howarth. How could you have forgotten that?"

"Is that why you ran away? You think you killed Jack Howarth? Well I can tell you that you didn't. You gave him a gash on his head, but he was very much alive well after you left, at least while I lived in Liverpool."

John could not believe what he was hearing.

"Are you sure about this?"

"I am sure. Very sure," Thomas said with a chuckle. He watched John cover his face and shake his head in disbelief.

"I remember staring in bewilderment at the bright red blood gushing from the gaping wound at the back of Jack's fuzzy red head, and as he lay there silent I realized that my shenanigans had caught up with me once and for all. A crowd began to gather, and fingers began to point at me. I fled the scene as fast as I could, walking briskly away from the school in the opposite direction to our home. As soon as I was out of sight, I ran as hard as I could.

"Believing myself a murderer, I hid in dark stairwells in the north end of the city during the days, and only at night would I go out in search of food.

"As time went on, I began to visit corner pubs similar to the ones near our home. I couldn't enter these premises because of my age, but I could do odd jobs for food or, occasionally, some gin. I soon found that there were other watering holes, dodgy places where drunken sailors visited and told tales of their travels on merchant ships to tropical lands. In such places my age was no barrier. There I listened with rapt attention as the men boasted of their sexual exploits with chocolate-coloured wenches with smooth, luxurious skin, women who came to them at their bidding and left when they were finished with them. 'Just like getting free candy from the candy maker,' said one of the sailors — his friends called him Ed.

"I heard first hand how these men enjoyed a life rich in alcohol, women, and travel. It also gave them money to buy some of the finer things in Liverpool, the sorts of things our Uncle William freely enjoyed. I liked what I saw and soon was determined to be a sailor myself, with help from my new-found seafaring friends. I went to the docks the very next day."

Thomas was captivated by his brother's story, and sat gaping at John.

"Well, this calls for a celebration," John said as he managed an awkward grin.

Thomas's questions continued.

"Now that we've cleared up that bit of misinformation, let's get back to the question of your leaving. How did you get on the ship?"

"I met some lads in the pubs. They brought me on. Told the skipper that I didn't have parents, and the rest is history," John said.

"We were all very sad when you disappeared, and the constable was of little help. I know our parents will welcome the joyful news that I have found you alive and well. May I implore you to do one thing for me? When next you get to Liverpool, could you please visit them?"

"Yes, yes, I will do that," said John. "I promise."

"They still live on Danube Street, and I know they will be overjoyed to see you," Thomas said with a smile.

Then his face grew solemn. "Now, I have a more serious question I need to ask you. Do you remember in which ports your first ship dropped anchor to pick up cargo?"

"Bloody hell, Thomas, how in the name of God do you expect me to remember that type of thing?" said John, exasperated. "I was so happy to leave Liverpool that I paid no attention to where we stopped, just as long as we were leaving England behind. You said yourself it was twelve … well, eleven years ago. I have taken many, many of those trips since then."

"Do you remember if that first ship picked up slaves at Bunce Island?" Thomas asked.

"It could have, but I am not sure that I remember clearly. Where are you going with this line of questioning?"

"I am asking because I am trying to corroborate a version of a story I heard," Thomas answered.

"What story, and where did you hear it?" John asked, puzzled.

"A story told to me by a Mr. Edward Grimes, Esquire. This gentleman professes that the two of you were shipmates on the *Archery*, which left Liverpool on Saturday, July 6th, in the year of our Lord, 1799. According to Mr. Grimes, on said voyage you had carnal knowledge of several slave women, including a young girl who boarded the ship at Bunce Island."

Thomas sounded like a solicitor, and not at all like a missionary. John was taken aback.

"Did you say Edward Grimes?" John asked.

"I did. Do you remember him?" Thomas leaned in, recognizing that he was getting somewhere.

"Yes, I do. I remember Grimes very well. He is the one I mentioned earlier. Where is that scoundrel, and how did he earn the title of Esquire?" John shook his head and continued. "We were shipmates on my early voyages to Demerary. How do you know Grimes?"

"I recently became acquainted with him during my search to find you. Could we continue our discussion about that first trip?" Thomas was eager to get to the details.

"Well," said John, "I won't deny that there was and still is a lot of shagging happening on those ships. Sailors get bored and those chimney chops are available. It's a game, really. It's normal — and besides, they like it."

"It is not normal, John. It is evil to force yourself on a female, even if it's a slave woman. And it's sinful to father children without being responsible for them. I am surprised you think that is acceptable."

"Don't make it sound so awful. It's only evil if you force yourself on white women. These are starkers — they run around without clothes! They're Athanasian wenches, and always ready to oblige."

"If you lived in their society, their customs would be your customs and you would dress like they do. Why is their attire or lack thereof a reason to judge them? The Bible says, 'Judge not, that ye be not judged. For with what judgement ye judge, ye shall be judged.' That's Matthew, chapter seven, verses one and two, in case you've forgotten."

Thomas paused and lowered his voice.

"Do you realize that your actions may be leaving a trail of children across this colony? More to the point, John, I may have met, however briefly, one of these children — a child that looks as you did when you were yourself a child."

John waved his hand dismissively.

"These wenches lie with so many blokes. It's not possible to tell who filled their bellies. And any children these molls have belong to the lucky planters who own them. These are children of slaves and as such, my dear brother, they are relegated to a life of servitude." He smiled smugly. "You know they are not like us, not really people, just animals. You know that we are superior to them just by the colour of our skin, don't you? It's in the Bible. You know ... light versus dark." He folded his arms.

"I don't recall superiority being based on colour of skin in the Bible. Pray tell me more," Thomas said mockingly.

"Well, man of God, I believe it is in the book of Genesis where it went something like, 'And God said let there be light, and there was light. And God saw the light that it was good, and God divided the light from the darkness.' See? Right there it says that light is good. God didn't say dark is good too, because it's not. In this business, Thomas, we must learn to exert that superiority to keep us safe." He sat back, pleased with himself.

"My dear brother, it gives me some joy to hear you cite scripture, even if you are doing so incorrectly. It shows me that you did listen and you did learn your Sunday school lessons."

John opened his mouth to interject, but Thomas cut him off, his voice caustic. "It surprises me, though, to find you here, and in the slave business. Slavery is unconscionable, and abuse of another human being is a very great sin. How could you have missed that lesson? The Holy Bible also says, 'Whoever says he is in the light and hates his brother is still in darkness. Whoever loves his brother abides in the light, and in him there is no cause for stumbling. But whoever hates his brother is in the darkness and walks in the darkness, and does not know where he is going, because the darkness has blinded his eyes.' First John, chapter two, verses nine to eleven.

"I encourage you to reflect on this scripture, my brother, and come back to the light. Think about how you may use your life to help, not hinder; and love, not hate; and know that when you judge, you open yourself equally to judgement. I hope you think on these things and come back to visit with me on your return trips to Demerary."

He stood.

"Have a safe journey back to 'jolly old England.'"

"God speed Thomas ... I mean the Reverend Leighton," he taunted.

***

John lay on his mattress and reflected on the events of the day. Seeing his big brother after so many years had turned out to be a mixed blessing. He had been happy to reconnect with Thomas, relieved to learn that he was not a killer and not wanted by the law, and delighted to hear that his parents were still alive. But the more he reflected, the more he felt a growing seed of resentment about Thomas's rebukes. Every other sailor on the ships had done the same things he had done — had, in fact, revelled in it — so why should he be any different?

He remembered his first voyage on the *Archery*. After they had sailed from Bunce Island, Grimes had encouraged him to force a ménage à trois on a young wench. She hadn't seduced them, but it was her first night on board ship, so maybe she was just timid, he reasoned. Grimes knew a lot about these women's sexual drive, and John had been nervous but excited. In fact, he had had fun that night.

Two days after this period of recollection and reflection, John was still brooding as he walked onto the gangway of the *Gallantry*. The ship would sail later that afternoon for Liverpool. For the first time John found himself thinking about his life on board the ship differently. The doubts provoked by his older brother had proved difficult to dismiss.

How many children had he fathered, he wondered? How many of them looked like him? Would he ever run into any of them, and what should he say or do? But could they really be his children? They were Africans and slaves. Any of his children would have to be white, wouldn't they? John's thoughts collided like angry waves crashing against the breakwaters on the sunny Demerary coastline. He struggled to reconcile them.

His only comfort came from his decision that this return trip to Liverpool would be his last. He was now desperate to escape any reminder of sinful encounters with slave women that may have resulted in dozens of children. The notion of this possibility would devastate his parents, especially his mother — her son, the father of slave children. He was finished with the sailor's life. England, with its meadows and towns, a land free of sugar cane fields and slaves, beckoned — a welcoming possibility. Or maybe Wales — he had heard so much about Wales. He could disappear in Wales, close to his old home in Liverpool but still far enough for comfort and escape. He would look into it when he arrived. His parents would have to wait.

John threw himself into his work, shifting barrels of molasses. When the ship sailed, just as on his first voyage, he didn't look back.

CHAPTER 32

FOUND

May 1810

May 18th, 1810

My dear mother and father,

*I have had success at last. I have found our family's prodigal son.
Our dear John is alive and in fine physical health. I do wonder,
though, about his spiritual health. He has spent the last eleven years
of his life sailing the high seas between Europe, the African continent,
the West Indies, and South America, shepherding slaves to feed the
trade on which some say Britain's prosperity greatly depends.*

*As I write to you, his ship, the SS Gallantry is on its return voyage
to Liverpool with multiple stops in between ports to pick up molasses,
sugar, and rum by-products. I cannot suggest a date when the
Gallantry will arrive, but I can tell you that your son John will be on
that ship. It sailed from Demerary two nights ago, on the sixteenth
day of May. I am hoping to catch the mail ship that sails for England
tomorrow, with only a stop or two in between. As such, this letter
should arrive in your hands well before John's ship docks in Liverpool.*

*Mum, I can envision your blue eyes lighting up as you read these
pages to Dad, and then your tears flowing as you reread the letter,*

pausing to ensure that you have understood all its details. Your eyes do not deceive you. I have found him, and he has promised that he is going home.

With a heavy heart I must admit, though, that my conversation with him has left me concerned for his soul. When you meet him again, be gentle and kind. By his own admission, he has not led a perfect life and his deeds cannot be regarded as the expression of a Christian upbringing.

I will let John tell you about his activities during those missing years, as his own words are the best testimony in such matters.

God bless you both!

Thomas

CHAPTER 33

NEW BEGINNINGS

August 1810

"John Alexander Smith is my name. I work in copper and coal mining, and I will need a quiet rental flat for the next year. Do you know of a place that is open?" John asked the bartender at the local pub on Orchard Street in Swansea, Wales.

"You're in luck, my lad, and I am happy to be acquainted. You look like a fine chap. I do know of a place on Mansel Street. I am the owner and it will cost you little, if you promise to do the upkeep of the property."

"That won't be a problem at all, Mister..."

"Owen. Morgan Owen. Do we have an agreement, then? I can take you there, Mr. Smith, after I lock up."

It was just that simple. John Barrington O'Leary Leighton had a new identity and a new place to live. He just needed to find a job to complete his transformation.

On his voyage back to England, John had plotted and planned on what he would tell his parents when he saw them. Despite their likely disappointment, he decided that he would tell them the truth, but in the interim, he needed time to find a new identity to avoid any connections to his old life and any blue-skinned children that could be linked to him. Swansea fit the bill.

CHAPTER 34

HOME BY CHRISTMAS

September 1810

September 17th, 1810
My dear parents,
I have come to a decision after much soul-searching. It is a decision I have not reached lightly.

I have called on my God on numerous occasions and he has heard me. His answers are sometimes not what I long to hear, but like a true disciple of his teachings, I have followed his word and waited for his direction.

He led me to Demerary in his service to bring lost souls to him. Until recently, I was satisfied that I was fulfilling his every command. If ever I felt conflicted, he always brought me clarity and showed me a path forward.

For many months, after reuniting with my long-lost brother, I called on this same God to help me understand my brother's choices, and I asked for courage not to judge him or his decisions. I have found that difficult, though, for my morals collide with the path he has chosen and the way he has lived his life. I must admit to you both, this situation has caused me to question the Christian values with which I was raised.

I lie at night tossing and turning, picturing all the children with dark skin that have my brother's white blood coursing through their veins. I think about those women who have no control over their very bodies because other people own them. I think about the slave men who also do not own their own bodies, and I stand by and watch as other men, always white men, take advantage of their power and privilege to unleash their cruelty. These owners of people abuse and often mutilate them. Men, women, or children, it doesn't matter; they are all human cattle. No, cattle are treated better, much better. How in the name of God can this evil be allowed to persist and grow in these beautiful lands we have claimed as colonies? How can I as a minister — a man of God — turn a blind eye to this terrible depravity?

I can only think that I have been brought to Demerary to be shown the evil ways of slavery. I can no longer preach to a people who are considered "the downtrodden." If they are downtrodden, it is only because we have put them in this position. The heathens I need to save are us, my own people. We are the ones who need salvation. In fact, I believe it is possible that these Africans are meant to teach us something about ourselves. They have at least taught me that I need to look within my own beliefs. I have been enlightened. I need to take action.

Wilberforce and the rest of the Christian abolitionists are correct. I have decided that I will return to London and join the fight to set these people free. I will send word to the Missionary Society immediately. There are missionaries waiting in the wings for these prized postings. I should be home by Christmas. God speed my journey!

Your loving son,
Thomas

CHAPTER 35

BLUE SKIN BOY

January 1811

"How come me neva see you heah befo?" Fredric questioned the young slave working the cane patch next to him. "You new?"

"Nah, me not new," responded the slender young man, who was about a foot taller than Fredric. "Sometime me wuk in de mill fuh 'move de megasse. Sometime me cut cane 'pon Letter A.

"Dem call me Watson, you can call me sar" he continued with a grin, "and you is Fredric — me 'ready know dat. Fredric de blue skin boy," he added with a smirk.

"Blue skin? Me not blue skin. Me jus' like you, black. Dat what me is."

"Well, you blue skin. Dat what me see and what everybady say. You blue skin, dat mean backra you fadda."

Watson picked up his cutlass and began to weed. Fredric was furious.

"Me not backra pickney. Backra beat slave, and me don' beat slave — me is a slave. And ... me don' tek woman. Backra tek slave woman all de time, even when dem don' want he. You wrong." Fredric protested. "Backra not me fadda ... me not like backra," he muttered as he picked up his cutlass and started to weed his patch.

"Just ask you mama. She know who you fadda be, blue skin boy," Watson shot back.

Fredric was seething. He had never been told by anyone, and certainly not his mother, that a white man had fathered him.

The two young men worked in silence for the rest of the day, Fredric in anger, Watson in glee. He had managed to annoy the light-skinned boy, and now he didn't feel the boy was superior to him. In fact, this encounter had drawn him closer to Fredric. The boy was one of them — a slave, nothing but a slave.

Later, Fredric sat in the corner of Mariama's hut and pleaded with her.

"How come you skin colour like psydium, dark and smooth, and me skin colour like sapodilla, and me hair colour like mamee fruit, and me eye colour like cat? Watson say, dem say, me gat backra blood. Tell me, Ma, you me mama or Hessie me mama? And who me fadda? Watson say ... dem say backra me fadda."

"Boy, me is you mama, and me is you fadda. Don't ask me no mo', Fredric."

Mariama's chest had tightened, and she looked at her son squarely in his tear-filled eyes. She dared not show him how flustered she was by this line of questioning.

Despite her outward composure, Fredric suspected that his mother was keeping secrets. Bowing his head, he stomped out of the hut. One day he would return to these questions. Maybe then he would get the answers.

The following day, Watson returned to the plot to work next to Fredric. This time, however, each simply observed the other. Although Watson mockingly smiled at Fredric, the gesture was not returned. The impasse continued every day for a week, until the morning that Fredric's cutlass missed the cane stalk and slashed his left foot.

"Awwwwh ... awwwwh!" Fredric yelped and threw himself into the muddy ditch lining the cane fields. "Me foot, me foot, me chop me foot! Awwwwh!"

Blood poured from the wound, turning the water a murky red. Watson ripped his shirt off, rushed over to young Fredric's side, and tied it around the boy's leg to stop the blood gushing from the two-inch wound that had barely missed his shinbone.

"Press 'pon it, press 'pon it!" Watson urged.

Tobias, who was standing a few feet away, hurried over.

"How you do dat, boy? Tek he to de sick house, Watson. Mek dem wrap de cut and bring he back. He can still tie bundle. Hurry, fetch he 'pon you back and come back quick."

Watson lowered himself to a crouching position, and Fredric hobbled onto his back. He was still whimpering, and the pain was excruciating.

Henri watched from his post under the breadnut tree. This was Tobias's responsibility, so he didn't have to intervene.

"Hol' on tight," Watson beckoned and he moved as quickly as he could across the field and back towards the great house. The sick house was about twenty yards behind Massa Henri's house, and the doctor was attending other slaves that day.

"He chop he foot in de field, and driver say bring he, sar," Watson said, lowering Fredric to the ground.

"Take the cloth off his leg and let me have a look."

In his first year of practising medicine in Demerary, Marcus Drayton, son of Dr. Donald Drayton, had treated nearly every possible ailment.

"Pour some clean water over it to get the dirt out before you bring him inside," he said to Watson. "Whoever applied this bandage did a good job to stop the bleeding."

"Me put it on, sar, me tie it tight," Watson said, pleased with this praise from the young doctor, who was just about his own age.

Watson took some clean water from the wooden barrel outside the sick house and washed Fredric's injured leg. He watched as the mud and tiny pebbles floated past his grimy ankle and into the rust-coloured earth.

He then lifted Fredric into the sick house.

"Bring him over here and lay him down on the floor, next to Wilmont." Marcus Drayton motioned.

Watson and Fredric watched as their fellow slaves lay head to foot on wooden beds in the sick house. At the foot of each bed was a board with circular holes, which opened to admit each slave's feet. The holes were then fastened and padlocked to keep the sick slaves from fleeing.

Dr. Drayton pulled out an enamel flask from his black medical bag. "Now hold him still while I disinfect it," he said, and with a flip of his wrist, he splashed alcohol on the wound. Fredric squealed, surprised by the sting of the liquid on his open flesh.

"Now put this clean bandage on it," the doctor ordered.

Watson complied. He was feeling good about being able to assist both Fredric and the doctor.

"He can go back to work now," the doctor said.

Tobias was pleased to see Watson and Fredric making their way back to the fields. He and Henri joined them, and this time Henri gave the orders.

"You," he said, addressing Watson, "place the boy over there and you drop your cane stalks near to him and let him tie your cane bundles. I expect the same amount of work at day's end from both of you." He nudged Tobias, and then together they walked away.

After the accident, conversations between Fredric and Watson slowly began to develop. By the second day the two were competing: Watson cutting cane as quickly as he could, and Fredric, in a sitting position, trying as fast as he could to tie bundles before Watson had stacked the next load. A friendly rivalry grew between them and persisted even after Fredric had gotten back on his feet and was able to resume cutting and stacking the cane in his assigned plot.

"Me wait fuh you," Fredric said one evening as they were leaving the plot.

Joining the stream of workers leaving the field around eight in the evening, they headed back to their huts. As usual, Watson eyed the young female slaves around him, and Fredric teased him about lacking the courage to speak to any of them.

Chapter 36

Grimes Takes Charge

March 1811

"Walk faster, boy! There are at least a hundred bundles of cane still to be taken to the factory from this lot," Henri shouted.

"Yes, Massa Henri, but me don' feel good today, sar. Me try, but me can't move faster, sar," Watson gasped in reply.

"You'd better speed up, or Tobias will help you do it," Henri growled.

"Me thirsty, sar, me jus' want lil' wata sar, jus lil' wata, me hot sar," Watson pleaded with Henri.

Fredric's ears perked up. He liked Watson and was happy to fetch water for his thirsty friend who always worked his patch well and helped others who needed it. But since Watson had returned from the sick house about a week before, right after an attack of yellow fever, he dragged himself around and worked much more slowly than usual. Fredric walked over to him and Henri.

"Me fetch wata and help Watson load cane, sar," he said.

"Get back to your patch now, boy. There is no time for a water break and Watson must do his own job," Henri said sternly.

"Is this snowball giving you trouble?"

Henri and Fredric turned to see Ed Grimes approaching. His gang had been hired to work on Plantation Mon Paix et Repos during harvesting. Grimes inserted himself into the exchange between Henri and his charge.

"You must know that you can't give 'em chances. You just gotta show 'em who's boss," Grimes said.

"I am fine, Mr. Grimes. I can handle the slaves, and it is not time for a water break. Watson knows that," Henri said, his voice sounding piqued.

Mariama looked up from her work bundling cane. She wondered what new cruel act Grimes would unleash, but figured that whatever it was would probably be restrained by Henri's presence.

"No need to get glimflashy, bloke. I was just observing the cheekiness in the lad. Let me show you what I mean."

"I was about to waste this water, but he can have it." As he spoke, Grimes began to unbutton his breeches. Henri watched him curiously.

"You," he pointed to Fredric with his whip, "hold his head and open his mouth." Fredric thought it was a strange order, but Grimes was standing over him and Watson was crouched over on the ground. Fredric did as he was told, as the frail Watson was now as light as a feather. As soon as Fredric was able to force Watson's mouth open, Grimes perfectly aimed a forceful spray of foamy hot urine directly into young Watson's mouth. His quick action caught Fredric, Watson, and Henri off guard. As soon as Fredric realized what was taking place, he tried desperately to shield his sick friend from this humiliating misadventure. As a result, most of Grimes's urine missed its intended target and splashed all over both Fredric and Watson's bodies, which angered Grimes.

Grimes grabbed Tobias's whip and, before Henri could stop him, began to whip Fredric.

"Don't ever waste water like that, do you hear me? Now git, git, boy! Git back to your patch like the man said!"

Mariama started to walk over to where Grimes was hitting her son, but Juma intercepted. She could not let her friend make such a horrible mistake.

"No, Mariama, stay, stay, or he beat you too," Juma whispered.

Mariama remained in place, but her tears didn't. They slid down her cheeks in a river of pain.

Yelping, Fredric turned and ran back to his assigned section of the cane plot. Grimes, still clutching the whip, turned his attention to Watson now. Watson's shoulders and back were slick with sweat and blood from hauling loads of cane since sunup. Now his head and upper chest also dripped with Grimes's liquid waste.

"Henri, see this slow blackamoor?" Grimes called, pointing at Watson with his whip. "This is how you do it, bloke."

Grimes's whip cut through the air and came cracking down across Watson's head and upper body, and he stumbled backward. Before he could recover, three more lashes hit him in rapid succession and knocked him off his feet. He lay in the mud, and the lashes kept coming, growing heavier and more ferocious as Grimes's anger fuelled itself. Finally, Watson crumpled face first onto the earth beneath him.

"Enough! You'll kill him!" Henri shouted, horrified.

"Good! Then he won't be able to be lazy anymore, bloody upstart," Grimes said, panting. He nudged Watson's leg with the tip of his boot. "It's just an act. I've seen this performance many, many times before. Snowballs are some of the best tricksters there are, bloke. You have to beat 'em at their game. Push 'em to the limit — that's what you have to do."

Grimes flexed his shoulders, then threw the whip on the ground and stalked off. When he was out of sight, Fredric ran over to Watson. Crouching, he shook his friend's shoulder. "Watson..." he said. "Watson!"

There was no response. The stillness of death had settled on his friend's body.

CHAPTER 37
MOVING UP

March 1811

Grimes was bent on shoring up his possessions at home while exploring other avenues of growth for his business. Jane Matilda Hoggsworth had been on his radar for a while, and with his purchase of Liefde, a respectable home and property, he had attained the legitimate status of a businessman and slave owner. Feeling sure of himself now, he called upon Jane Matilda at her home.

"Mrs. Hoggsworth, I have come to make you an offer," he said. "I see the great need for more field hands on your plantation, but I know that acquiring those hands will mean significant costs to your bottomline. I would like to provide free labour to you, madam, so that you can complete the harvesting of your crop and get it to market in Britain." Grimes fiddled with his waistcoat with one hand and rubbed the rim of his top hat with the other. "I might add, though, madam, that your only cost for this gift would be a few pots of fine English tea and your good company some late afternoons when the work has been accomplished." He tipped his hat to Jane Matilda and smiled broadly.

"What a kind offer, Mr. Grimes," said Jane Matilda, smiling coolly. "I will give it some consideration and let you know my answer after I have had a chance to review my books." Despite her outward calm, inwardly she was surprised by Grimes's offer and wondered why he was being so generous.

"As you wish, madam. I will call on you again tomorrow to see if you have come to a decision. I bid you good day, madam."

Grimes tipped his hat again and strutted down the front steps of the Hoggsworth plantation house. He was pleased with Jane Matilda's response. He had discomfited her, just as he had intended.

Jane Matilda closed the door and returned to her sitting room, puzzled. She had noticed Grimes's attentiveness towards her since she had hired his gang of workers a few weeks before. She had felt flattered and had begun to take extra care to brush her hair and pinch her cheeks before leaving her room each morning. But this offer had left her flustered. That night in the privacy of her bedroom, Jane Matilda sat on her bed, folded her hands, and sought guidance from a trusted source, as she often did.

"My dear Ben," she began, "I am flattered that this man, Edward Grimes, finds me attractive. He is kind and courteous with me and looks out for my welfare. He offers the support I need to maintain our successful business, a venture about which I can write home with pride. With his generous help I will have good profits to show and good tales to tell when I return to London, especially when I am invited to tea parties at my sister's house. I will be listened to and heard by the navy wives. I will be able to boast about our achievements. Free labour from close to half a dozen Negroes is worth its weight in gold to our plantation. I know you will understand my reasons for accepting his offer."

On the other side of the plantation, Fredric lay on his mat, sobbing quietly. Ed Grimes had murdered his closest friend.

Watson had been a good man and a hard worker. Often when the driver or the overseer was not around in the fields, he would offer help to other slaves. Now, because of this backra, Watson was lying in a shallow grave in the slave burial ground. Neither Missus

Jane Matilda nor Henri had done anything to help except tell the other slaves to go bury Watson and then hurry back to work.

As far as Missus Jane Matilda knew, Watson had simply died of yellow fever. Fredric and the others knew better. Clenching his teeth, he dried his tears and tried to will himself to sleep.

CHAPTER 38

NOT A FAÇADE

April 1811

Mariama was taking her mid-afternoon break at the edge of the cane field when she saw a familiar figure approaching. She shielded her eyes with her hand and then gasped in surprise.

"Braima?" she cried out. "Me eye see you, but me head don' believe." She peered at him again. "But me eye not wrong. Is you Braima? Is you?"

Mariama gazed in amazement at the figure limping towards her.

"Mari, Mari, is you? Is really, really you?"

Braima began to limp faster, and for a moment flashes of his childhood came into focus. It was as if he was back in their village and he was racing to the hut, only Mariama was not moving. He broke into a half-sprint now, covering the last few yards to where his sister sat frozen.

"Yes, yes, is me!"

Mariama raised her hands to her head. Her voice quivered. Her legs felt too weak to carry her to meet this advancing apparition. Her heart raced and her pounding temples felt like they would explode. It was him. He really was here. After so many years the thing she had wished for so often was happening right before her, and she was too astounded to respond.

"Finally, me finally find you!"

Braima knelt down and threw his arms around Mariama. She buried her head against his shoulder and sobbed.

"We've got to speak Mende so no one knows what we are saying. We'll only speak Creolese when we are with others. You agree?"

"Yes, yes," she nodded.

Fredric, who had been working a short distance away, straightened up and uneasily watched his mother and this strange man.

"How long have you been in Demerary?" Mariama asked.

"I have been here six years now," Braima replied. "And prior to that, I lived on the island of St. Kitts for about six years. I created so much mayhem there, the plantation owner sold me to his friend, the captain of a slaver. He sold me in Demerary."

"Who bought you?" Mariama asked cautiously.

"Ed … Edward Grimes," Braima replied.

Mariama's mouth fell open, but no words came from it. Her body flinched. Braima, feeling her stiffen, gently released his grip, moved her away from him and looked squarely at her.

"What's the matter, Mari? You know Edward Grimes?" he said quietly.

"Oh, Braima, Grimes is a terrible, terrible backra," Mariama whispered. She looked around and for the first time noticed Fredric. She beckoned him over, and Fredric began to walk across the rows towards them.

At the same time, Tobias, the driver, also began to walk towards them, his steps firm and his face set in anger.

"You dere, what business you got heah?" he said to Braima.

"Me wid Massa Ed gang," Braima replied.

"Wha' business you got wid she?" Tobias said, jerking a thumb at Mariama.

"Me tek she fuh me village kin — but me wrong," Braima replied, looking at the ground. "Sorry ... me sorry," he said to Mariama, then turned and walked briskly in the other direction.

"Stay wid you gang and don' meddle wid de rest," Tobias called out, but Braima was out of earshot. "Back to wuk, de two o' you," he said to Mariama and Fredric and then walked back to his post.

"Who dat man, ma? Why he hold you?" Fredric asked Mariama under his breath.

"He nobody. Go back to wuk," Mariama whispered. She gathered up her skirt, wiped the sweat from her forehead, and returned to stacking bundles.

Fredric walked over to his section, but from time to time he glanced over at his mother. The stranger kept his distance.

***

At the end of the day, the field slaves trudged wearily back to their huts. Mariama walked ahead with Juma.

"Miz Mariama a secret keepa," Juma said to her, grinning and a bit more upbeat than the rest of the crew.

"Me got no secret, Juma." Mariama blushed and looked down at her feet.

"You got man secret, Miz Mariama. Juma and everybady else see today," Juma said, giggling.

"Everybady wrong." Mariama shot back. She then paused and gently kicked the red dirt in the laneway.

"He not me man. Me got no man. He Braima from me village. He got news 'bout me *YahYah* and *KeKe*."

Astounded, Juma stared at Mariama for a moment. Her mischievousness turned to serious questioning. "He from ... he gat ... Oh Mariama, wha' he say?"

Covering her mouth with her left hand, Mariama muttered to Juma: "He tell me later — me no wan' feel Tobias whip 'cross me back. Me tink 'bout nutten else since me see Braima. Me pray fuh dis day long, long time, Juma."

Juma reached over and touched Mariama on her shoulder. "Me happy fuh you, Miz Mari," she said with a smile.

They reached the huts and the women parted ways. Fredric joined his mother in her hut. At eleven years old, he was considered a man and now lived in another part of the compound with the other male slaves.

"Tell me who dat man, Ma," he said.

"He not…" she began, and then seemed to change her mind in the middle of her sentence. "He you uncle, dat man is you uncle," she smiled, her eyes twinkling.

"Me uncle? How dat, ma?" Fredric said, puzzled. He had never seen his mother this happy in his entire life. The smile on her face was as big as the full moon.

"He you uncle, Fredric. He me brudda, Braima. He family," she said in an excited whisper. "But you mus' keep it secret."

"Why me keep secret, Ma?" Fredric whispered back.

"So Missus don' know — so she don' find out and separate we again."

"Uncle. Me uncle," Fredric said, a smile spreading across his face. He hugged his mother and then quickly left the hut.

For the first time since she had been captured, Mariama felt joy. Braima was in Demerary. She had seen him, touched him, and was assured that it was not her imagination. But … Grimes, Ed Grimes was his master. That vile brute owned her brother.

She lay wide awake that night, thinking of how to secretly meet up with Braima again. *Sunday market*, she thought. She could meet him there and still keep her secret. It would mean walking for three hours, and with any luck, Braima would be there too.

Smiling, she rolled over and fell asleep.

CHAPTER 39

SUNDAY MARKET

April 1811

Mariama tossed and turned in bed that night. The crowing of the rooster at four o'clock was a welcome sound. Despite the poor sleep, her body felt inflated with a drunken kind of adrenaline as she leapt up from her mat. She had longed for this moment for so many years. As she prepared for her trip to Stabroek, she quietly hummed the tune of a familiar hymn as its words brushed her consciousness.

As dawn broke over Plantation Mon Paix et Repos and early light began to stream across the morning skies, Mariama left her hut carrying a small lunch of cassava bread with steamed callaloo and salt fish. She brought enough to share with Braima if she were to meet up with him. On the main road that led to Stabroek, her strides were quicker and wider than usual. She needed to see him alone, to be with him and ask all the questions that had swirled around in her head for so many years.

About an hour along the road, as if they were children again, Braima showed up seemingly out of thin air. He was sitting at the back of a dray cart with about ten other slaves, part of Grimes's gang. They were headed to Stabroek to sell the ground provision and vegetables they farmed on Plantation Liefde. The cart stopped.

"Climb up," he yelled, a big sunny grin on his oval face, his eyes dancing with joy. "You off to Sunday market?"

"Yes," she answered, grinning back at him as she climbed in to join the rest of the travellers.

In a matter of minutes, the dray cart arrived at the market amongst the excited chatter of its passengers. They scattered into the square and Mariama and Braima discreetly wandered off along a small path leading to the river. As soon as they were out of earshot of the crowd, Mariama spoke up.

"We're alone now, Braima. Tell me, tell me everything."

"Where would you like me to begin?" he replied. "Let's sit down, I think we should sit down first." Braima reached out and touched Mariama's left elbow gently. "We'll go over there under that tree, and I'll tell you what you want to know."

They walked over and sat in the shade of a cashew tree about fifteen feet tall.

"*YahYah* and *KeKe*, the village … tell me how you left them?" she asked excitedly.

Braima closed his eyes for a moment and then opened them again to look directly into hers.

"Well, after you were kidnapped, enemy tribes attacked the village. They killed some of the men guarding the clearing. They separated the male and female villagers; women and girls to one side and men and boys and to the other. *KeKe* tried to protect *YahYah*, but one of the enemy warriors stabbed him in the chest, right there in front of me, *YahYah*, and the other villagers too. The chief tried valiantly to save *KeKe*, but the blood poured out his chest like water bubbling up from the ground in a volcanic spring. He fluttered like a fowl, and died right in front of us."

Braima paused as he was burdened with the horrible scene all over again. He took a couple of deep breaths and then continued.

"They marched us away and handed us over to one group of backra, then later to another. We walked day and night, till we got to the ship, then they split us up; I never saw any of our villagers again. I have no idea where they took *YahYah* and the other females. I assume they were sold to other backra. I have no idea."

Braima paused and looked at his sister, who had been eerily quiet as he spoke.

"Mari," he continued, his voice trembling. "I know it's sad, but you asked me."

"Oh, *KeKe, Keke,* now you're with the ancestors. *YahYah,* I wonder if you're with them too," Mariama moaned to herself.

Tears streamed down her cheeks as she propped her head up with shaky hands. She had hoped that her parents hadn't suffered the fate that she and Braima had.

Braima held his sister close.

In return, Mariama told Braima about the horrors she had experienced in the weeks after her abduction, the people she had met along the way, including Khadija, and the visitations from their maa. Then she told him about her life on Plantation Victory and the death of Joseph Blumefield and how she and Fredric had been sold to Jane Matilda.

"The only good in all this is that we've found each other again, Braima. We're family and we must find a way to stay together without backra knowing we're related; we mustn't let them separate us again." Mariama concluded, her tear-stained face slowly breaking into a beaming smile. They ate an early lunch, which became a celebration and reunion away from prying eyes.

CHAPTER 40

THE TIES THAT BIND

June 1812

Edward Grimes had been lending his field gang to Plantation Mon Paix et Repos on a regular basis, Mondays through Fridays. This arrangement allowed Mariama to see her brother more often and for her son to get acquainted with his uncle, Braima.

Many times Mariama had watched from a distance as the two bonded with each other. She experienced relief that they were getting along well and spent time working together. It had happened more since she had told Braima about Fredric. She felt a sense of family developing again. She recalled the awkward exchange between them.

"The boy is my son. He's called Fredric."

She had waited for Braima's response.

"Son? You said son? Who's his father?"

"His father … Massa Grimes is his father…" Mariama's voice trailed off, her face recoiled into a painful grimace.

Braima looked at his sister with surprise and then looked at the boy, standing about thirty yards away.

"You and Massa Grimes?" Braima stared at her open-mouthed, disgust in his eyes.

"No, no, no!" she pleaded. "We're not ... no, he took me on the ship. Oh Braima, it was awful..."

Mariama hung her head as she struggled to tell her brother what had happened. He didn't need to know all the details, but he had to know she was not a willing part of the event that led to Fredric's birth.

"The boy doesn't know, he doesn't know..." Her voice trailed off again.

Braima reached out and held her hand.

"I am sorry Mari. I'll keep your secret," he whispered.

**

Fredric sat with Braima under the breadfruit tree on the hill, a few yards from the cane fields. They were cooling off in the shade before going back into the afternoon sun. Tobias was busy and Henri was away with Jane Matilda in Stabroek.

"Why you hop when you walk?" Fredric asked Braima.

"'Cause..."

"'Cause what?" the boy pestered.

"'Cause dat is how me walk, boy," Braima snapped.

"Why you foot like dat?" Fredric insisted.

"Like what?"

"You only got toe 'pon one foot."

"'Cause..." Braima answered, beginning to show his frustration.

"'Cause what?"

"Go back in de field and don' ask questions," Braima said, scowling.

"Me done me wuk."

"You neva done backra wuk. When me was a boy, me and you mama finish we wuk an' have lots o' time fuh play. We play wid palm nuts, play catch togedda wid pickney in de village. Sometimes we play wid de goats, 'specially de black and white billy goats."

Braima smiled at the memories, and then his face became sombre again.

"Dis no way fuh grow up, boy," he said, waving his hand at the fields. "Dis place got no pickney and backra evil. He move you from one place to de next. If you move 'pon you own, he crush you like dirt."

He looked at Fredric, who was listening intently.

"Nuff time backra try fuh crush me," Braima went on. "One night in grinding season, me try fuh run, backra bring out de dog and he track me down. Dat time me get one hundred lashes and lock up fuh days wid no food. Next time me run and when backra ketch me, me get fifty lashes, he cut off me right ear and lock me up. Last time me run, me get fifty lashes again and he cut off me toe. Yes, backra evil, real evil…

"Fredric, me boy," he continued, "me long fuh de day when we be free again. When backra don' own we body, just like he don' own we mind."

Braima closed his eyes and gently rocked backward and forward.

"When dat day come?" Fredric questioned.

"We mus' use we mind fuh plan dat day. Massa must neva know when dat day gon come, or we neva, neva be free," Braima whispered.

"We body belong to backra in de daytime when he 'wake, but we mind belong to we in de nighttime when backra sleep. Dat when we plan fuh freedom. You wid me, boy?"

Fredric saw the cold, serious look in his uncle's eyes.

"Yes, me wid you," Fredric replied.

The pair spent every free moment in each other's company for the next few weeks. Darting glances and whispers filled the spaces between them.

CHAPTER 41

SENSES

July 1812

"You must dust and change the linens today, Meg," Jane Matilda instructed. "The dust is becoming unbearable. I hope to get you help as soon as the grinding season is over."

She watched as Meg struggled upstairs to the bedroom of the great house with a freshly folded load of laundry.

"Me tek it one day, one day, Missus. Me do what me can. Me change de sheet today and me dust too."

She reached the top of the stairs, lowered the basket onto the floor and wiped the salty sweat dripping from her forehead with the back of her hand. Meg was exhausted. She was the only house slave and had been working as hard as the field slaves. Up before the break of dawn, she never finished a day's work until late at night.

"The dusting is important. Do it now, and leave the rest for later," Jane Matilda scolded, impatience clear in her voice.

Meg meandered off to find clean dusting and polishing rags.

"I swear I don't know which is worse, the dust, the heat, or the putrid air," Jane Matilda said to herself.

On most days the great house benefited remarkably from the steady northeasterly trade winds that blew fresh sea air from the Atlantic across the fields and in the open windows. Sometimes the wind died and barely a leaf stirred on the high branches of the trees that lined the roadway. On those still mornings, the house slaves had to rush to carry out the night soil from the bedrooms and privies before the heat of the day released the pungent odor of human excrement into the atmosphere. There was also a standing order to refresh and place strategically the potpourri vases with their aromatic blends of dried flowers and citrus peel throughout the residence. The owners were very picky and concerned about breathing "noxious vapors" and preferred a sweet-smelling house. Given the prevailing winds, this was not a problem on most days. The sea breeze would sweep in, having collected scents of lily and lilac on its way over the bush and river banks and then mingle these with a delightful last ingredient: Damask roses from Jane Matilda's garden. These had been brought from England and added a last note of subtle fragrance to the bouquet that drifted in from the windows. Visitors remarked on the heady floral mix of scents that suffused the rooms, especially those with access to the breeze.

Occasionally, however, through some perverse quirk of nature, the wind shifted and blew over the cesspits on its way to the great house. This occurred periodically and in defiance of attempts to relocate these pits to prevent their exposure to the trade winds. Nevertheless, it seemed that at least once a season a formal dinner service was ruined by foul excremental air gusting in through the windows and destroying the appetites of those at the table. Every plantation on the coast experienced this phenomenon, including Mon Paix et Repos. The special irony of these occurrences did not register with the owners or their guests, but was much appreciated by the enslaved workforce.

Jane Matilda picked up her glass of ice-cold lemonade and moved to the wicker rocking chair in the shaded area on the house's front porch. As she sipped and swallowed the tart yet sweet, refreshing liquid, she thought about Ben and Conrad. The three of them had spent many happy afternoons on this porch. She thought about the dreaded disease that had taken them away and the last time she had laid eyes on her beloved boys.

The plain wooden pine box that held their bodies was deep and slim enough to ensure they would hold each other for eternity. Conrad's little body lay stretched out on Ben's tall slender frame as the father's arms encircled the child's shoulders. The box was adorned with prized roses and ferns from Jane Matilda's garden neatly tucked around their lifeless bodies, to enfold them with the love she knew would never end. After the box was lowered into the mossy ground of the Moravian churchyard, Jane laid mounds of roses to mark the spot until she could place the headstone later, which simply read, *Ben and Conrad — sleeping safely in the arms of Jesus.*

"Oh, how I miss you both!" she whispered, as she gazed in the direction of the churchyard. Warm, salty tears left wet tracks on her full, rosy cheeks and dripped from her chin. This tender moment was abruptly interrupted by Meg's squealing.

"Missus, Massa Henri at de side door!"

Jane Matilda could not allow anyone, especially her workers, to see her in this weak state. She quickly scurried into the study, closed the door, wiped her face and pinched her cheeks to bring some colour back in them.

"Let him in — I'll be there in a minute," she called back.

She composed herself for a moment and then casually walked into the parlour where Henri was waiting.

"Hello, Henri. Is there a problem?" she asked with what she hoped was her usual businesslike manner.

"No problem, Mrs. Hoggsworth. I just needed to let you know that I will be making a quick trip into Stabroek for about two hours. Tobias will be in charge until I am back. I want to look over the shipment of copper sheeting that just came in before it's all gone. I will come by late this afternoon and let you know if it is worth the purchase."

As he looked at Jane Matilda, Henri noticed that she seemed somehow softer than usual in her appearance. The streamer on her blouse was undone, and he could see the exposed cleavage and the rounded edge of her full breast. He felt his face flush and his body harden with excitement. He hoped she could not sense his reaction.

Jane Matilda tried to maintain her appearance of composure, but she was still raw from the recent tears shed for the loss of her husband and child. She felt helpless and, for the first time, uncomfortably aware of Henri's appraising eyes on her body.

Jane Matilda cleared her throat.

"Thanks for letting me know, Henri. Is everything else in order?"

But Henri Rymes barely heard her as his mind flooded with strong desire for the woman before him, suddenly so vulnerable and fragile.

"Yes, all is well," he managed, his throat tight with feeling.

He turned and walked out of the house into the bright sunlight.

Henri took the carriage into town. His thoughts were dominated by the scene in the parlour with Jane Matilda. He had never seen her look so womanly, her eyes so gentle and lips so kissable, and those breasts such an invitation to pleasure. Henri thought about every moment of the encounter until his imagination ran wild. He fantasized about moving in closer to her until he could feel her breath on his face, their bodies touching, his fingertips caressing her full, rounded breasts. He imagined her looking up into his face, and closing her eyes to savour his hands caressing her yielding body, responding with growing passion to his touch. This could be the beginning of something special between them.

He was glad he had a reason to go back to see her — maybe he could also bring a small gift from one of the fine shops. This would give him an opportunity to show that he was the man she needed, a man who could attend to her desires of every kind in many delightful ways.

Back at the plantation house Jane Matilda realized that something had happened between her and Henri. He had looked at her differently, his eyes first fixing on hers and then travelling down to her chest, where he obviously liked what he saw.

Fiddling with her slightly undone blouse, she realized with a gasp that he must have seen a part of her exposed breast. She had loosened the blouse to let some air in and then forgotten it was unfastened. Had he thought she was flirting with him?

Jane Matilda felt confused at first. This gave way to a growing delight at the thought of him wanting her; but she was conflicted because he was a common working man, her employee. How could he think she would entertain that type of feeling for him? She blushed with embarrassment as her armpits dampened with perspiration. She must fix this misunderstanding, and she must do it soon.

CHAPTER 42

REVENGE

December 1812

It was the middle of harvesting season. Grimes's crew were fully immersed in work on Jane Matilda's plantation. They spent their time between Grimes's homestead and the sugar cane fields of Mon Paix et Repos.

The morning was already muggy and airless. The birds were too lazy to flit from branch to branch and sat in clusters wherever there was shade. Braima could not afford to be lazy but walked slowly towards the side entrance of the main house on Liefde to collect new cutlasses for the crew. The other men had taken their places on the dray cart in preparation for the day's trip to the fields. Grimes had warned the workers not to come within twenty feet of the main house unless he called them.

"Massa Grimes, Massa Grimes, you say fuh remind you 'bout de cutlass, sar," Braima called out, standing far aw ay enough to keep his distance from the main house.

A few minutes later the door opened and Louisa leaned out and placed four new shiny cutlasses on the landing. Braima's heart skipped a beat. He had heard the girl's stifled distressed screams at night but had not seen her since Grimes had moved her into the house.

Louisa didn't look at him but focused her dull gaze on the tools. Braima eyeballed her, quietly willing those eyes to look at him. They didn't. She just turned and walked back into the house. As she did, Braima saw it — she was with child. Judging from the size of her belly, she would be a mother very soon. Braima's excitement slowly turned to anger. *This backra has done it again*, he thought. Clenching his jaw, he quickly walked to the house, picked up the tools and joined the others on the dray cart. The ride to Plantation Mon Paix et Repos allowed Braima some much-needed time to think.

***

Mahaad noticed Braima's sullen mood, which lasted most of the morning. During their meal break he walked over and sat with his friend. He hoped to find out what was bothering him and to share in the plantain, maize, and boiled fish Mariama had prepared. Braima had boasted about what a good cook she was, and how she often shared her meals with him.

"You don' like de food Braima — you face got no smile." Mahaad mocked, with a grin.

"Every scream dat come from Louisa mouth crush me head," Braima confided. "Even when me shut me eye, me still can see how dat backra tek she just like he tek nuff-nuff woman. Dis backra evil and he mus' pay. Mahaad, backra tek me family honour and backra tek me sista. 'Cause o' backra me got no mama and no fadda. Backra bruk up me family. And, he tek Louisa, and now she wid pickney — backra pickney. Backra mus' pay."

"She wid pickney?" Mahaad was caught off guard. "How you know, Braima — how you know she wid pickney?"

"Me see she big like pygmy hippo ready fuh drop. No smile, no dimple, all gone. Backra do dat." He closed his eyes and shook his head fiercely. "Backra mek dat — he tek 'way she smile Mahaad."

Seeing Louisa earlier had been a cruel reminder of what he had learned from his sister about Grimes. Now Braima was recounting those horrors and rage was building like an unstoppable wave that threatened never to recede. Louisa had been taken against her will, just like his sister, and not by just any backra, but the backra who owned him and mistreated him every day. That night, he sat in his corner of the hut for hours and looked vacantly through the broken wooden window into the blackness.

He slept very little.

***

The next morning, Mariama noticed that Braima was preoccupied when he arrived in the cane fields. He had walked past her without his usual cheerful wink. She decided to check in with him during their midday break. Mariama sat behind the rubber tree and faced the little shallow stream, where he and Mahaad regularly took their lunch and waited. She soon heard them arrive on the other side fully immersed in conversation and unaware that she was in the vicinity.

"Me got fuh find a way fuh mek backra pay, Mahaad. But how?"

"Backra own all o' we, Braima," his friend replied. "We can't mek he pay again. He done own we."

Mahaad had grown accustomed to listening to Braima's complaints about his mistreatment, but this time he felt it was different.

"Me don' know how, but me gon' find a way. Me owe it to me fadda, me mama, and me sista. Me owe it to Chief Kenei and me village elders. Me owe it to Louisa. And me, Mahaad, me owe it to me. He tek de woman me want, and who want me. Backra got fuh pay."

Her brother's vengeful rant caught Mariama's attention. She could feel the intensity of Braima's rage in the pit of her stomach. He had told her about Louisa's captivity in Grimes's main house. As she listened now, the memories of her own violation and suffering at the hands of this cruel man rose like sudden flames from a smoldering fire.

"Pray to Allah, Braima. Pray fuh strength," Mahaad urged his friend.

"Me pray, Mahaad, but me got no strength, me jus' got rage."

"Pray fuh strength, Braima. Allah give strength fuh help you trew," Mahaad persisted.

"Yes, strength fuh beat backra down, Mahaad, dat de strength me need. Me mus' find a way."

"You can't find a way Braima — fighting backra not gon' wuk. He got gun and you got none. Prayer help me, Braima. Me tell you how: many moons ago, when me was boy, me send me small brudda fuh help me mama collect wild fruit and maize fuh feed de family. It shoulda be me, but me was lazy, so me stay in de tree and watch de birds. Later, when me go back to de village, me find no fruit or maize, no mama, and no brudda. Village people say lion eat dem, but me know dat somebady tief dem. Braima, me hang me head in shame and neva face me fadda again. Me lef' me village fuh search fuh dem — dat is when dem tief me and sell me to backra. So every day, me pray to Allah fuh strength fuh face de shame. Not backra tek me honour, me Mahaad give it up — me give up me mama and me brudda. Now everyday me live, me try fuh get me honour back. Every day me hope fuh find dem, just like you find Mariama. And every day me pray to Allah fuh me fadda fuh forgive me. Braima, me trus' Allah, he all me got — you should trus' Allah too."

Braima listened intently to his friend, appreciating the sadness of the story, but then returned to his anger, which began to change into cold calculation — a plan was beginning to form. As he worked the rest of the day, different scenarios played out in his head, and he finally settled on an idea for his revenge. Now he just had to follow through. He would need Fredric's help.

Mahaad's support for her brother and the role that Allah played in his life were like a balm for Mariama's troubled soul. A warm glow was ignited in her heart at the thought that her brother had such a generous friend. Mariama hoped to get to know him better.

"Come, boy. Me teach you fuh mek ball. Me see backra play dis game when me live 'pon St. Kitts."

Fredric's eyes lit up. "Game? Wha' game?"

"Ball game. Backra call um cricket," Braima answered nonchalantly.

"We mek de ball from cane leaf. When you chop down de cane, cut off de leaf and keep um. Every night we roll de leaf up and mek a ball, and we do de same ting over and over till de ball get big enough. Me teach you de game. You wan' learn?"

Fredric smiled and nodded his head. "Yes, yes. Me wan' learn."

"A' right, tomorrow we start fuh collect cane leaf."

Braima had hatched the first part of his plan to pay back the backra.

CHAPTER 43

LOVE OR LUST

February 1813

Henri sat on his porch seething with envy. He had just watched Ed Grimes enter the front door of the plantation house to spend the evening with Jane Matilda. Henri had spent the afternoon rehearsing the words he would say to Jane when he arrived at the great house that evening and present her with the delicate lace-trimmed handkerchief he had purchased in town. She had opened the door to his hopes ever so slightly earlier that day — and now he felt ready to proceed. But then Grimes had beat him to it and gotten there first.

"How dare the bloody scab! He just keeps getting in the way," he growled. "I have waited for this day for so long and now he has interjected himself at the time when the stars have finally aligned for me."

His mood deepened as he recalled the loyalty and dedication he had shown to Ben and Jane Matilda. He imagined an ardent speech to her: "I helped to build this business, during Ben's life and after his demise. I've always shown you great respect. How could you choose that lying jackass over me? He is nothing more than a bounder, falsely attentive to women, a drinker of rum and gin, not tea. He acts high and mighty and pretends to be whatever he thinks you want him to be, and mark my words, dear lady, as soon as he has won your heart, he will treat you no better than the slaves in his charge. You deserve more — you deserve me. I will treat you like the lady that you are, just like Ben used to. Please, Jane Matilda, do not fall for his treachery — choose me."

Soon Henri began to pace up and down the porch, casting sporadic glances at the door of the great house. He hoped to see the imposter leave the premises.

Grimes had become a constant visitor to the plantation house, and Jane Matilda was enamoured with his charm. The first gift he had given her was free labour, then the male slave Mahaad to replace the dead Watson. Grimes had praised Mahaad's work and promised to take him back if Jane Matilda didn't need the extra hands anymore. She had been touched by Grimes's generosity.

When he arrived that evening, he brought packages of tea and biscuits, small jars of jams and a wheel of Edam cheese purchased from a recently arrived British shipment. Jane Matilda was delighted and invited Grimes to stay for a light supper. He accepted, and the two retired to the parlour to await service from Meg, the cook. Jane Matilda walked over to the brandy cabinet to pour an aperitif. Grimes joined her and offered his assistance.

"Let me pour the drink for you, madam," he offered.

"Thank you, and you can call me Jane Matilda. 'Madam' is so very formal. I would like to think we've become friends. May I call you Ed?"

Jane Matilda smiled as she reached to take the amber-coloured aperitif goblet from Grimes's hands. His fingers touched hers and a tingle of excitement ran down her spine. She moved over to the richly upholstered sofa and gestured for him to join her.

Her eyes shining, she announced "Ed, would you please join me in toasting the success of our sugar cane harvest? This has been one of the most plentiful years since we ... since I have owned Mon Paix et Repos." She raised her glass proudly in a toast but felt awkward to have included Ben.

Sensing her slight discomfort, Grimes seized the opportunity to reach in and kiss Jane Matilda gently on her lips. Caught off guard, she giggled from embarrassment.

Suddenly there was a thudding sound from the front hallway of the house. Leaping to her feet, Jane Matilda was horrified to see two fast-moving balls of fire rolling along the parlour floor. She screamed, and then they heard the door slam shut. Grimes jumped up and ran to the door. He tugged frantically on the handle, but it was locked. There were no windows; the parlour was in the middle of the house.

The fire leapt quickly onto the silk Venetian rug in the centre of the room and then caught the fabric-covered, well-oiled wooden furniture. As Grimes slapped at the flames, Jane Matilda banged on the door, her screams increasing when there was no response. She broke into fits of coughing as clouds of smoke billowed around her, making it difficult to breathe. Grimes launched himself desperately at the heavy greenheart door, but it held against his efforts. This gave the fire more time to take hold, which it did, engulfing the bookcase, catching the wallpaper and turning the room into a throbbing cauldron of flame, heat, and smoke. Now the two were on their knees, Jane Matilda coughing and whimpering and Grimes gagging, while raging against a situation he was unable to master. Then they slowly succumbed and their cries ceased, with only the sound of the inferno to mark the sudden and unexpected end of their lives.

Meg looked up, puzzled, at the sound of footsteps running along the hallway on the main floor. She dried her hands on her apron and scurried up the few steps leading to the main hall just in time to see a figure leaping over the porch railing. She smelled something burning and followed the scent, which led her back into the front hall. Seeing tendrils of smoke seeping out from under the closed parlour door and hearing shouts from within, she ran over and twisted the latch only to find it locked and with the key missing.

She pounded the solid wood with the palms of her hands. But it was pointless and she stepped back shouting for help.

"Fire, Missus! Fire, Missus!" She banged as hard as she could again. There was no answer. The smoke was thicker now and she could hardly breathe. The five-foot-tall Meg gathered her skirt and raced out the front door coughing and blinking.

"Fire! Fire in de house! Fire!"

She ran down the front steps, still shouting, and turned to see plumes of smoke billowing out of windows and flames shooting from different parts of the house. The heat was intense, so she backed away, coughing, her eyes burning from the smoke. Slaves ran towards the house now, shouting and pointing; some carried buckets of water, but the heat drove them back. The plantation house was a cauldron of flames.

Juma ran to Mariama's hut, shouting, "Come out de hut and see de fire — big fire! De house 'pon fire!"

"Fire?" Mariama jumped up from her mat and the two women raced down the lane together and then stopped, stunned, at the edge of the lawn. Enormous sheets of flame lit up the sky where the plantation house had once stood in all its glory. Screams and the roar of the inferno filled the evening air. More than a dozen slaves, both male and female, led by Henri, were attempting to douse the fire with water from buckets and other available containers. Their small brigade, however, was no match for the blaze, and the heat soon drove them back.

Mariama looked around for Fredric but could not see him in the crowd. He was probably with Braima, she thought, and turned her attention back to the flames.

After a few minutes the constable, the fiscal, and some of the other planters arrived, and Henri began to push the slaves over to a corner of the lawn to do a roll call.

Everyone was accounted for except for Fredric.

The constable approached the group now and took Meg aside.

"They said that you called the alarm. Do you know how this happened?"

"Somebody run 'pon de porch, sar. When me run up de stairs, sar, he run 'way, sar. Den me see de smoke and me run, sar."

"Where is your Missus, Mrs. Hoggsworth?" the constable asked.

"She in de fire, sar. She and Massa Ed, sar."

Overcome by the nearness of death and the enormity of the destruction, Meg began to weep uncontrollably.

"Did you set the fire by mistake, Meg?" the constable asked, eying her closely.

"No, sar. Fire start in de parlour, sar," Meg said through sobs. "Dat where me see de smoke come from under de door, sar."

"Was anybody else at the Plantation House with your Missus?"

"Yes, sar. Massa Ed, sar."

"Edward Grimes? And apart from him?"

"Me don' know, sar."

"Did you see anyone else leaving the plantation house around the time of the fire?"

"No, sar, me hear footstep, but me don' see who. Somebody jump over de porch, sar, but smoke too tick and me run, sar."

"Would you say it was one set of footsteps or more than one?"

"What you mean, sar?"

"Do you think it was more than one person on the porch?"

"Me don' know, sar," Meg replied.

The constable grunted and frowned. Turning to Henri, he said, "Let's keep this one around for more questioning."

"Meg, go and stay in Juma's hut and don't leave," Henri ordered.

Still visibly shaken, Meg walked off down the path towards the women's huts.

"Did anyone else see anything?" the constable said, raising his voice to the entire group, as he walked through the crowd.

Philippe, one of the field hands, glanced around to ensure the overseer was out of earshot, and then he whispered, "Massa Ed and Massa Henri argue nuff. Massa Ed come and tek de Missus. Dat mek Massa Henri mad. So maybe dat mek he bu'n down de house, sar."

"Did you see Mr. Henri at the plantation house earlier?" the constable asked Philippe.

"No sar, me see he 'pon he porch, but he walk roun' in circle like he worry 'bout someting," Philippe responded.

"How do you know that he was worried about something?" the constable probed.

"'Cause he walk roun' and roun' and he hold he chin and talk to heself — dat how me know. Me watch he from me hut."

"Did you see anyone go to the main house?"

"No, sar."

The constable turned his attention to Henri.

"What is your full name?" the constable asked.

"Henri Rymes. That's Rymes without an H," Henri answered.

"Where were you earlier this evening, Mr. Rymes?"

"I was in the overseer's quarters, where I live."

"When was the last time you saw Mrs. Jane Matilda Hoggsworth?" the constable continued.

"Late this afternoon; I was returning from town. She was tending her garden," Henri replied.

"When was the last time you saw Mr. Grimes?"

"I saw him earlier this evening. He was making his way to the plantation house, I believe," Henri replied.

"You believe, or you know that he went to the house?" the constable asked.

"I saw him walk up to the front door of the estate house. I was sitting on my porch and have ... had a clear view of the front door," Henri answered.

"Did you see him enter the house?"

"I did."

"Did you and Mr. Grimes get along?"

"Somewhat. I've never worked with him directly, but we were cordial to each other."

"I will want to speak with you further, Mr. Rymes. Will you remain here on the plantation?"

"Yes, I will be here until Jane's ... I mean, Mrs. Hoggsworth's Demerary solicitors have concluded their business."

"Do you know where the slave Fredric is? He is the only one missing from the list you have provided. A search party of plantation owners and the fiscal with a few dogs are out to find him," the constable added.

"No, I do not know his whereabouts. He should be on the grounds like the rest of the men," Henri replied, as he scanned the crowded grounds looking for the young man. Then he walked in the direction of the front gate.

The fire continued to burn, but the flames had abated somewhat.

Suddenly there was a commotion as the fiscal and two other white men arrived in the laneway. The constable walked over and they began to talk in lowered voices. Nevertheless, Mariama was close enough to hear most of the conversation.

"We found the two slave scums who set the fire," one of the men said.

"Where did you find them?" the constable asked.

"They were hiding in some bushes. One of the other chimney chops saw them scale the porch to escape, just like the maid said. Our dogs led us straight to them."

"Rymes, the overseer, identified them as Fredric and Braima," he continued.

Mariama's ears perked up at the mention of those names, and a ball of icy dread began to form in her stomach.

"We will make a good example of them. We'll show the terrible price a slave must pay for murdering white people. Let's be sure they suffer long and slow before the release of death, which, no doubt, they will crave in short order. What an abomination, to take the lives of Mrs. Jane Matilda Hoggsworth and Mr. Edward Grimes."

Mariama cringed as tears welled in her eyes and the ball of ice grew larger.

"We will see to it now," the taller white man said, as they turned around and left the lane in unison.

Mariama clasped her hands over her mouth, stifling a scream, and dropped to the ash-strewn ground. The ice in her chest had

now overtaken the rest of her body and frozen every part of it. Juma
saw Mariama collapse and rushed over to her friend.

"Wha' happen Miz Mari, tell me, tell me ... talk to me,
somebady, anybady, help ... someting happen!" Juma was frantic.
Mariama lay still.

Juma's scream brought Mahaad running over to where Mariama
lay. He was still holding a half-filled bucket of water from the nearby
pond used to help douse the fire. He joined Juma on the ground, and
they both tried to get Mariama to respond. Mahaad scooped both
hands into the bucket and splashed the cool water on Mariama's face,
to which she moved her head and a slow low sound escaped her lips.

"Mariama, Mariama," it was Mahaad's gentle quiet voice
whispering in her ear. "Wake up, Mariama," he continued. He then
turned to Juma, "Help me lif' she head up slow, den mek she sit up."
Juma did as he requested. Together they brought her into a sitting
position, rinsed her face, and offered her water to drink. A few minutes
later they accompanied a teary-eyed Mariama back to her hut.

"Dey gat Braima and Fredric," she said softly. "Dey say dat dem
set de fire."

"Oh lawd, Juma, you tink dey wrong?"

But in her heart, Mariama knew, and so did Mahaad.

"Yes, wrong, wrong, wrong. Me stay wid you tonight Miz Mari.
Me stay till we see dem." Juma said to her friend.

Ten minutes after she had made the promise, Juma began to
snore softly; her head leaned against the wooden wall of the hut.
Mariama gently lowered Juma's body onto her mat and let the
young woman sleep.

Mahaad sat on the floor next to Mariama. He wanted to hold
her, to comfort her, but he was nervous, so he fidgeted and twisted
his hands instead.

As he walked back to his hut later, he wondered if he had done
enough to mollify his friend's desire for revenge.

For the rest of the night, Mariama paced around the small hut.
She imagined what the punishment for Braima and Fredric could
be. She hoped for the best but feared the worst.

CHAPTER 44

MY BROTHER, MY SON

February 1813

Just before dawn, Mariama left her hut and walked towards the blackened shell of the still-smoldering great house. In the distance she saw them. As she drew closer, her breath caught in her throat and her knees buckled. Two severed heads were fastened on fence posts at the side of the road and across from the gate — for all to see.

She saw the smoky greyish-white of Braima's eyes behind his partially closed lids. His jaw was still clenched as if in some final refusal to submit to the will of his attackers. Even death could not deny him this resolve, and it showed. Next to Braima's lifeless head was Fredric's, whose face was still frozen in a scream.

Mariama knelt between them on the soggy earth, still soaked with their blood.

"Braima, my brother, my friend — brave son of Yele, a Mende warrior until the end — the backra has got you now!" she cried out. "And you, Fredric, the look on your face! You're not a warrior, you're a follower my son, but a brave one. With your lizard skin and blue-green eyes, Hessie could have been your mother. Oh son, my son, I wanted to call you Kamal like my KeKe, to honour him and to feel that you belong to me. But you don't look like him: not your colour, not your face, not your hair. Miz Blumefield named you Fredric and I felt that you only came through me and were never mine. But you were mine, my only son, though they owned you, just like they own me. Braima, take him, my beautiful son, to the ancestors. Oh Fredric, oh Braima, oh KeKe, oh Maa, oh Allah, oh God! Help me, help me, please help me — I can't do this anymore, I can't, I can't ..."

Grief rose like a sudden river in the rainy season. It grew into a torrent without depth or dimension. The love for her son that had eluded her during his short life she found now in his death.

Mariama clung to the blood-streaked posts that bore the two heads and wept convulsively until she had no more tears. The air, thick and muggy, smelled of metal and ammonia. She scanned the pasture for evidence of their bodies and found none. Above, the sun had hidden its warm face as if in mourning. In its place the blue-grey sky was like a shadow, cold and dark, cast across the sombre scene as half a dozen carrion crows circled overhead. But she had work to do, and finally struggled to her feet and straightened her shoulders.

Mariama covered Braima's lifeless head with her smock. She rocked it back and forth to dislodge it from its post anchor, while his blood seeped through the cotton garment. She gently laid it on a tuft of grass nearby, symbolic of an earthly pedestal. She repeated the action, only this time keeping Fredric's head in the smock. Cradling her terrible, precious bundle, she set off down the path.

Suddenly she heard footsteps. She turned to see Mahaad hurrying after her.

"Where you goin', Mariama?" he said, his voice gentle.

"Fuh bury dem. Me bury dem so backra can't hurt..."

Her voice trailed off as tears choked her once more.

"Me help you. You can't do dis alone," Mahaad said as he picked up Braima's severed head, his voice gentle but shaky, his eyes weepy. "Rest me friend, now rest."

Together they walked into the bush placed the heads in a small alcove and quickly began to dig into the damp earth with their bare hands. Sensing the grim task at hand, Mahaad grabbed pieces of a broken tree limb that lay nearby and gave one to Mariama. Together they dug as quickly as they could then quietly, buried the heads of Braima and Fredric in the same shallow grave.

Suddenly, they heard the sound of raised voices.

"Quick — split up! Massa Henri mustn't see we togedda!" hissed Mahaad, and he dashed away through the bushes.

Mariama stepped out onto the path in the other direction. A minute later she turned a corner, and Henri and a group, including two other white men and three slaves blocked her way. She stood still and looked away.

"Where did you hide those traitors' heads?" said Henri, glaring at Mariama, her blood-stained smock and dirt covered arms tauntingly visible. "You'll speak up or risk some lashes."

Mariama lowered her head, bit down on her bottom lip and stared adamantly at the sun-scorched grass beneath her feet.

Henri turned to his posse.

"Those blackamoors don't deserve a burial. They broke the law and killed white people. They are forever damned and must not rest in peace."

He turned back to Mariama. "Speak!" he yelled, but still Mariama continued to look down without a response. His anger intensifying, Henri removed his pith helmet and smacked her sharply across the head with it once, twice. Mariama's knees buckled. She lost her balance, stumbled forward and fell to the ground.

"Strip her," Henri ordered, and the three male slaves moved forward and ripped off Mariama's blood-stained clothing. She lay naked against the hard earth.

"Answer me!" Henri screamed as he landed a kick to her stomach.

Then, slowly and meticulously, he drew his foot back and kicked her in the forehead. She cried out in pain, and he landed half a dozen more kicks at her head and torso.

Mariama tucked her head into her chest and held her arms up to shield it from the constant blows, as warm, briny blood filled her mouth and seeped past her bruised and swollen lips. But still she said nothing. Braima and Fredric deserved a resting place, and she was going to ensure that neither Henri Rymes nor any other backra would take that away from them. She only wished she could find the rest of their bodies so they could have a full burial. Now, from the corner of her half-closed left eye, she saw the brown boot swing through the air and felt it connect to her temple. Then, everything went black.

"She's out," Henri said. "Leave her alone and let's continue the search. We have to find those heads. Hurry. Maybe she didn't move them far."

Henri Rymes and his search party left the pasture and headed east — the wrong direction. They planned to question every person in the vicinity.

CHAPTER 45

HEALING LIGHT

February 1813

Mariama lay curled up, naked, and unconscious at the side of the path.

"Mari, can you hear me? It's me. I have Fredric here, too. Wake up, Mari! You can't come here yet. Wake her up, Maa." It was Braima's voice.

"Soon child, soon," her grandmother said soothingly.

Mariama could hear the voices, but in the hazy, foggy surroundings, she couldn't see anyone. Then slowly, in the distance, a dim, flickering ball of light appeared and began to move slowly towards her. With each flicker, it grew in size. When it was about twelve feet away from where she was lying, she saw the ball of light separate into three smaller balls. Each ball floated in the air, bouncing softly. The smallest ball floated towards Mariama, while the other two remained in the background.

"Mama, Mama, dere's no backra heah." It was Fredric's voice, coming from the ball of light in the foreground. "We is free heah, Mama. We is free." Mariama peered into the ball's centre. As she did, she could see her young son's head and face take shape. A warm, gentle feeling flooded through Mariama. The other balls came into the foreground to join the first one. Mariama realized that they were all together now.

Then she heard her maa's voice: "My little wise one, you are good and you are love. At your birth you shared that goodness and love to heal the land, the animals, and the people of the village. Allah blessed you with the gift of healing, and you must know that nothing and no one could ever erase the blessing you have been given. This blessing lies deep within you in a hidden place where Allah has placed it and where He protects it. Your offspring will inherit this gift, and like you they will be able to heal all things, people, land, and animals around them. No one else can reach this part of your being. Only you can go there to find love and peace, to be healed, and to heal. Only you can reach that special place.

"Be aware that evil comes in many forms, and it is usually done onto us. You must keep it on the outside and not let it seep into you, for then it will become a poison and, like a parasite, spread throughout your whole being. You keep evil out by thinking and doing good. Evil will touch your body, but it must not touch your soul. My little one, to shake off the pangs that evil brings, you must go to your innermost secret place to dip yourself in the well of true healing. There you will find the warmth of peace and love to restore your broken body and spirit.

"When you get to this innermost place, be still. Let your tears flow if they must. Just like at your birth, when the rain you brought healed the land and quenched the animals' thirst, your tears will begin the healing. Then pause and wrap your arms around yourself. Cover yourself with big, warm, gentle hugs until you feel great love come from within and wash over you.

"Spend as much time as you need in this secret place. And when you leave this refuge, you must take the love, peace, and healing you have found there to share with someone else — even if it is the one that brought you evil. To complete the healing cycle, you must do two good deeds, no matter how small, that will make life for others around you better. In other words, for every wrong that is done to you, you must do two rights. Soon good will outdo evil. It is the only way to begin your true healing. My little wise one, those are the steps to take when evil tries to bring you down.

"Go there right now, my child. Feel the presence of good, the presence of love, and the presence of healing. This is your Sande. Use it, and it will take you through the rest of your days."

Suddenly, the three balls of light blended back into one and disappeared. Then, as if nature were participating in her vision, the heavens turned dark and released an onslaught of silvery sheets of rain. The freshening wind breathed courage into Mariama's battered body as the warm, healing raindrops washed over her.

Mariama awoke and watched as bands of rain blew across the pasture. The sounds of the downpour reassured her that she was alive. She reached for her soggy wet skirt and blouse and slowly dressed herself. She thought calmly about the visitation from her maa, her brother, and her son, and found an inner voice rising up in reply to her grandmother.

All this time I worried that everything that happened was my fault because of something I've done or not done. But now, Maa, you show me that it isn't my fault. An evil was done to me, but I am more than what has happened to me, much more. At first all I could think was "poor me, I am nothing now, my body stolen and ravaged, my family gone." But then Fredric came to me, and then Braima came back. Fredric came to show me that love can come from evil. Now I have to forgive myself for being so blind, as all I could see in his face was a white man looking back at me. I could not see the gentle true soul that was my beloved son. Thank you, Maa, for helping me see life and love again, even through the pain. I will let the hurt be washed away and learn to live and love again. That is the message of the rain, and whenever I feel its touch and hear its sound, I will remember this healing message of goodness and love.

***

Later on that day, Mariama and the other slaves watched quietly as the constable and a few other white men lifted the small, white bundled remains of Jane Matilda Hoggsworth and Edward Grimes onto a waiting dray cart and headed towards Stabroek.

CHAPTER 46

REACHING BACK

March 1813

The Mon Paix et Repos great house fire site had several visitors over the next week including a solicitor and the local constable. One notable caller arrived in a carriage that pulled up in the laneway beside Henri Rymes's house on a Tuesday afternoon. A tall, light-skinned black man, dressed in breeches and a long-sleeved cotton shirt with lace trim at the neck and around the cuffs climbed down from the driver's seat. The large brass buckles on his shoes caught the tropical sun as he moved. His sandy-brown hair was slicked back and pulled into a neat ponytail. Watching him from a distance, Mariama thought he could be a freed black who chauffeured around other freed blacks who didn't own carriages.

The carriage driver held his right hand out to assist the passenger. A tall, buxom woman stood up from her seat, took the offered hand and gracefully stepped down. Holding a parasol as protection from the early afternoon sun, she walked directly to the entrance of the overseer's house. The parasol was tilted at an angle that obscured the woman's face. Mariama saw the front door of the house open and the woman enter.

Massa Henri was in charge until the solicitors wrapped up the sale of the estate and its slave holdings. Juma had already been sold with a few other slaves, and Mariama wondered where Allah would take her next. She speculated about how soon she would know her own fate. It couldn't be long now. As Mariama pondered her destiny, the visitor to Massa Henri's house was offering to purchase two female slaves.

"Me would like two women, but me tek whateva you got," Hessie said to the solicitor.

"We only have one woman slave available, but could give you a strong, quiet male as well. Would that work?"

"It wuk. Me need two, so me tek he."

Hessie had inside information that Mariama was the only female slave left on Plantation Mon Paix et Repos and had come especially for her friend. She kept this preference hidden. She hoped that the male slave would be Mahaad but was willing to bargain for his purchase. As it turned out, she did not have to.

Mariama was summoned to come to Rymes's house and was petrified to find out where she would be sent next. Upon arrival, she saw Mahaad waiting outside. Her heart skipped a beat; she hoped that he was going to share her fate. She had increasingly thought about him, with feelings of warmth she'd never experienced before. She wanted to be wherever he was, especially now that she was alone. For the time being, it would be her little secret.

Then the door opened, and with her lowered eyes she saw a pair of legs that were surprisingly familiar. As her gaze travelled up, her heart beat faster and she dared and hoped but doubted that what she saw was real. Mariama had been suffering severe headaches and spells of fogginess since she'd received the kicks to her head from Henri Rymes. So she squeezed her eyes repeatedly to clear any fuzziness or confusion and to focus. It was her — those knowing green eyes met hers at last, dancing with quiet joy. Mariama was dumbfounded and could barely hide her excitement. *Hessie*, she called out in her mind — *it's Hessie!*

Her transaction complete, Hessie, now a free black woman, left the property with her human purchase as promptly as she had arrived. The carriage turned out of the property and onto the main public road, Hessie looked over at Mariama and she broke into raucous laughter. Mariama was still too stunned to join in Hessie's euphoria — she barely gazed at her friend and shook her head. "How you … how you do dis, Hessie?" was all she could muster.

"Me buy you, and now you free," Hessie chortled, happy tears rolling down her cheeks.

Mahaad sat next to Mariama, wide-eyed and overwhelmed with what he was witnessing.

"And you buy Mahaad too … but he…" Hessie cut Mariama off.

"He come … 'cause he help you… Bush gat ears, Mari, bush gat ears."

Just like she had learned that Mariama was the only female left on the plantation, Hessie had heard that Mahaad was the only young male slave left. She also learned about his ongoing support of her friend.

"We guh to Stabroek and you live wid me," Hessie said with a big smile. She was delighted to have kept the promise made to herself on leaving Plantation Victory. She was reunited with Mariama.

CHAPTER 47

FINE THINGS

March 1813

As Hessie had walked to Stabroek after her release from bondage several years before, she had reflected on her daydreams while still a slave to the Blumefields.

"Me want fuh sell fine tings. Dat's what Missus used to say, 'fine tings.'" Hessie smiled. She had come up with an idea to sell lace products. She had figured out that adding lace to clothing, linens, and certain household items enhanced their quality and refinement. Lacework was a skill Hessie had developed. She trimmed ready-made curtains and tablecloths, bedding, shirts, dresses, and even handkerchiefs with delicate and elaborate tracery. She turned them into fine things coveted by the local gentry and would-be gentry.

In Stabroek, she could not find a small storefront to get started. None of the white property owners would rent one to a recently manumitted slave. So Hessie did the next best thing: she created a stall in the open-air marketplace and started her business. "Massa use me fuh nuff, nuff years. Now is time fuh use me fuh me."

She smiled as she recounted the shillings and the few rare pound notes she had saved. After all, it hadn't cost much to buy her freedom from Missus Henrietta. She thought back to the time a few nights after Joseph Blumefield had been sent to his ancestors by Millie, helped by the herbs that Josie had selected. That night Henrietta had taken Hessie to bed and made her experience the caresses of a woman starved for affection.

"Lie down," Henrietta had ordered. "Take off all your clothes and lie down." Hessie was bewildered but did as she was told. She watched in further confusion as Henrietta got undressed, climbed onto the bed beside her, and pulled Hessie's face towards her own. Then, to add to Hessie's confusion, Henrietta leaned in and kissed her squarely on her lips. Hessie kept her eyes shut and pressed her lips together firmly in resistance. She could smell liquor on Henrietta's breath.

"Open! Open!" Henrietta demanded in between hungry kisses, her tongue probing at Hessie's sealed lips. As Henrietta's mouth continued to suck and pry, Hessie slowly did as she was told and parted her lips. Henrietta immediately thrust her liquor-infused tongue into Hessie's dry mouth. Her hands reached for Hessie's exposed breasts as, moaning softly, she straddled her head housekeeper's body.

Hessie had never felt a woman's mouth on hers. But this was not just any woman; this was Henrietta Blumefield, her mistress and owner. After her initial feeling of alarm, Hessie could feel her body begin to relax. As Henrietta's tongue moved from her lips to her breasts, she felt her nipples harden. All her resistance crumbled, and Hessie lay in her mistress's bed and did as she was told, not reluctantly but willingly. Henrietta touched and stroked Hessie in places she had not been caressed before, never roughly but always with a strange tenderness and urgency. Hessie could sense how hungry Henrietta was for closeness.

For the rest of that night, with Henrietta's guidance, Hessie received a pleasure she had never experienced from any other human being. There was no talking, just a silent guiding of hands and heads, as the long night of passion unfolded.

Henrietta awoke before Hessie and watched the beautiful creature she had admired from a distance lying snuggly in her bed. She wanted to wake up to her every morning and go to bed with her every night. These feelings, immoral though they were, stirred strong sensations in her. Thoughts of how to bring this musing to fruition ruminated in her mind. How could this even be possible? Hessie was a slave, and if she brought her to Britain, she would have to be her servant, as it was not legal to own slaves there. Could she conceal a sexual relationship with her black female servant from the new wealthy friends she would make — after all, she was now a rich widow. Would Hessie even want to be with her if she was free in Britain, much less be her lover? Henrietta felt torn. She could sell Hessie, but felt a surprising surge of generosity and, yes, affection, for her slave lover. Should she free her? Henrietta decided that she would let Hessie make her wishes known when she awoke. With lustful desire, she gently patted the sleeping beauty's buttocks and softly kissed her naked nipples.

After a few hours, Hessie opened her eyes. As they lay together in the big four-poster bed, Hessie broke the soft tension between them and offered to pay Henrietta the full price for her freedom.

"Me want buy me, Missus. How much you wan' fuh me?"

The request didn't catch Henrietta off guard. In fact, she was tickled by it and fully expected Hessie to want her freedom. After all, she had served her and Joseph well.

"You've worked hard and you've been loyal, Hessie. One shilling is all I will take from you," Henrietta replied.

Then she rolled over and playfully gave Hessie's right nipple a gentle squeeze as she kissed her on her lips.

Later that morning Hessie went down to her room to retrieve the shilling she needed. After completing her manumission transaction with Henrietta, she said her goodbyes to Millie and Mariama and then gleefully skipped over to the huts.

"Where Josie?" she asked Buck, who was sitting outside.

"She wuk for Massa McDuff today."

"When she come back?" Hessie asked.

"Not till nightfall."

"Tell Josie me buy meself from de Missus. Tell she me gon stay in Stabroek till me find me own place. Tell she me thank she, and me see she 'pon Sunday at de market."

That morning she had walked out of Plantation Victory a free woman, proud but alone.

CHAPTER 48

THE SUN

August 1815

As a free woman, Hessie enjoyed sitting in her market stall on Saturday mornings, observing the steady movement of people and the noisy chatter and laughter of the crowds. And on this morning, as on many others, a familiar movement in the periphery of her vision revealed the presence of Hadali watching her as he always did.

She had seen him many times in the market trading his cassava products but had never paid any attention until one day he set up his stall nearby. Two long black braids framed his firm jawline, and his deep-set, kind brown eyes were tucked under prominently arched eyebrows. His neck was slender but flowed into powerful shoulders and muscular arms. He gently and confidently moved around his wares, making deals with blacks and whites alike.

Hessie also noticed that his eyes followed her every move. He was not like the backra or the other slave men, though — his eyes didn't travel up and down her body. He mostly looked at her face, and he smiled at her shyly, appearing timid whenever their eyes met. His gaze was soft. Hessie liked the attention. She smiled back at him.

"Hadali, that is what they call me," the bronze-skinned Amerindian man had said, smiling at Hessie. "Hadali means sun. I am Wapishana."

Hadali always wove colourful feathers into the end of each braid — bright blues, yellows, reds, and sometimes greens.

"Why you put bird feather in you hair, Mr. Sun?" Hessie asked, encouraging a conversation.

"Birds protect from evil," he explained. "Feathers bond you to ancestors. Maybe you wear feathers too, then you be tied to your ancestors," he said with his gentle smile, revealing perfect white teeth.

Hadali's cassareep and cassava bread always sold quickly. He was usually out of his wares within an hour of arriving at the market and would spend the rest of the time visiting with other traders. There was some bread left now, however, and Hessie reached into her pocket for coins.

"What they call you?" Hadali asked Hessie, although he already knew. He wanted to hear it from her own lips.

"Hessie, dat's what. And how much you wan' fuh dat bread, Mr. Sun?"

She flashed a big smile and batted her green eyes, just like she had seen Henrietta Blumefield do when she wanted something from her husband. This gesture caused Hadali's heartbeat to quicken and his cheeks to flush.

"Two pence usually, but for you, one pence … Hessie," he replied, smiling and playfully holding up three round discs of the cassava bread.

Hessie handed Hadali the money and accepted her purchase.

"Maybe me get me some of de cassareep nex' time," she said, smiling mischievously.

Over the next few weeks, Hadali's trips to the market grew more frequent, and his products became more varied. He added items for Hessie's interest: a variety of foods, colourful feathers, and soft, tan leather shoes adorned with fringes and colourful beads.

Hessie began to realize that Hadali was different from the other men she had known. He liked her and didn't just hunger for her body. And he looked happy just to be near her. On market days Hessie began to take extra care with her grooming. She braided her hair the day before and wore clean lace-trimmed smocks and skirts to attend her stall.

One morning she bought a pair of his intricately tooled shoes — moccasins, they were called. "You look like the Amazon moon," Hadali had teased, grinning with delight.

When the market rush ended that morning and most of their wares had been sold, Hessie and Hadali walked over to the riverbank together. There they sat and talked, sharing sweet cassava bread and dried meat he had brought with him. She told him many things about her life, such as her childhood without parents and her slave family at Plantation Victory. Hadali told her about his village upriver, his people and some of their customs.

"I must tell you," he said reluctantly, "some in my family catch slaves. My father was postholder for the Dutch people. He watched over the Rupununi. I am proud of my people and live by their customs. As a young boy, though, I ran away when I saw with my own eyes the taking of life. Two young runaways killed, a boy and a girl."

His words sent chills down Hessie's spine.

"You a killer, Hadali?" Her eyes widened as she spoke.

"No, no, not me. The older men fight with the runaways. One child was choked to death, the other shot by a musket," Hadali said sombrely. "For many nights I lay in my hammock but could not sleep. I could not put people in chains no more. My people's way is to live free to roam across Mother Earth, under the watchful eye of Father Sky. That is why I left. I must follow my heart and let my mind grow."

Hessie reached over and touched Hadali's hand. He looked over at her with tear-filled eyes.

As the sun began to set, Hessie bathed her tired feet in the river, put on her moccasins, and bid Hadali goodbye. After she had left,

Hadali lay on the riverbank next to his canoe and reflected on his growing friendship with Hessie.

He had long watched her from afar when she came to the market and hoped that one day she would notice him. She stood tall and clever, picking the right produce while leaving the rest behind. He had watched and hoped she would look his way.

There had once been a long stretch during which Hessie had stopped visiting the market. Hadali had waited and watched, but there was no sighting of her for many, many moons. The white men's heads always snapped around when she walked by, but they watched only her curves and did not see her cunning. Hadali loved watching her negotiate with the merchants. She always got her way, that tall, clever, confident, beautiful being. He longed to see her.

And then one day she returned to market. She had looked to the east, in his direction, and he had felt her gaze even before seeing her searching eyes. Was it the warmth of the sun, or was he blushing? He hoped she could not see what he was feeling. Her beautiful eyes, circled by the light of the bright morning sun, brought memories of the rich emerald greens of the Mazaruni at sunrise.

Hessie, Moon of the Amazon. What a perfect fulfilment to his many wishes. She had noticed him — yes, finally, she noticed him.

Hadali's mind went quiet and he looked up at the sky. The stars were brighter than ever as they glowed in their scattered brilliance across the heavens. He watched them for a while from his spot on the riverbank, and before long he fell asleep.

He opened his eyes to the early morning sun. His face lit up with a smile as he remembered talking with Hessie the day before, sharing bread and meat and time with her. Now that she knew he existed, he would do his best to make certain she never forgot.

CHAPTER 49

COMING FROM THE HEART

October 1815

A few months later, in a tiny rooming house on America Street, preparations for a prospective lover's visit were in the works. Hessie felt anticipation and fear building. After serving him tea, she would ask Hadali to stay the night. Her heart beat with pleasure and excitement, but there were bursts of dread in the pit of her stomach. She was thrilled and anxious about the prospect of spending the night with him and hoped he would accept her invitation.

"Look, Mari. Look how good dem drops turn out. Mmmm. Me proud, real proud o' me coconut drops."

Hessie backed up from the makeshift oven of rocks and coals. She smiled as she admired the irregularly shaped baked cassava and coconut drops splayed out on the square metal sheet.

"Dem look good," Mariama said with a smile.

"You mama was a good cook, and you a good cook too." Hessie teased Mariama.

The drops' light-brown colour was close to Hessie's complexion. With Mariama's help, she had made them to share with Hadali.

"Me gon' go to de shop fuh get some tea, just like Missus Blumefield. Me gon mek some fuh Hadali when he come after market."

She rubbed her hands together in glee. That man made her heart race.

"Oh, Hessie, you like Hadali. Me know you do," Mariama said, giggling.

"And you like Mahaad," she grinned. "Yes, Hadali a fine man, Mari." Hessie smiled but said no more on the subject. "De shop close soon, so me go now."

Hessie picked up a few shillings and left her three-room house on America Street. She quickened her steps so she could reach the tea shop on Water Street before it closed for the day.

Mrs. Faulkner knew Hessie only as Henrietta's girl. When Hessie arrived in the shop on a Friday afternoon, the owner was taken aback.

"Hessie, it's Friday, not Saturday. Where's Henrietta?" she asked.

"Me not Henrietta's gal no mo', Miz Faulkner. Me is free now. Miz Henrietta gone to Englan' long time now," Hessie replied pleasantly. She had given Mrs. Faulkner the same explanation many times over for the last six years. Mrs. Faulkner seemed to forget each time she saw Hessie in Stabroek.

"Oh, then what can I get you?"

Mrs. Faulkner was unruffled by Hessie's response.

"Black tea. One shilling worth."

Mrs. Faulkner went into the old wooden chest and scooped a small handful of loose-leaf tea. She weighed it on the cast iron scale and then emptied the tea leaves into an old piece of English newsprint.

Turning to Hessie, she said, "Here, one shilling's worth."

Hessie looked at the small package. She had purchased tea at this shop before and recognized that the amount was insufficient. She looked at Mrs. Faulkner questioningly. The proprieter looked back at her without expression. Hessie knew not to raise any fuss.

She paid her for the tea, picked up the small package, and left the shop. As she strolled along Water Street, she felt the frustration well up inside her. Mrs. Faulkner had cheated her, and there was nothing she could do about it. She muttered to herself, "Ain't nutten right 'bout dat. Ain't nutten."

She continued her walk back to the hut and her thoughts drifted back to Hadali. "I will take your hand and place it on my chest, and you will know my heart," he had said to her on his last trip to Stabroek. Hessie had studied Hadali in puzzlement as he gently lifted her right hand and placed it on his chest. She had felt the rapid rising and falling, the rhythm of his heart meeting her palm and then her fingertips. When she lifted her eyes to meet his, they were closed, but the smile on his lips was unmistakable. "Now you feel how my heart beats just for you, Hessie, Moon of the Amazon," Hadali had whispered with his eyes still closed.

Hessie smiled as she strolled towards home. The sun was now setting, and her frustration from the encounter with Mrs. Faulkner slipped away with it.

***

Mariama waited for Hessie to come back from the shop. It was near midnight and she still hadn't returned. She went down to Mahaad, who lived in the room on the ground floor.

"Hessie go to de shop fuh tea and she don' come back. Me real worry, Mahaad."

"De shop close long time, Mari. You sure she gone to de shop?" Mahaad looked at Mariama with concern. "Maybe she gone wid Mr. Hadali." He winked and smiled at Mariama.

"Nah, Mr. Hadali not in Stabroek. He come tomorrow fuh market. She gon surprise he wid tea and biscuit, just like de British — like Miz Blumefield do," she said.

Mahaad's brow furrowed. "When she go to de shop?"

"Long befo' dark, befo' shop close. She should come back long time," Mariama said as she paced the little hallway and glanced at the door.

"A' right, we go look fuh she, but we mus' wait till daybreak in case backra tek we fuh runaway." Mahaad said with a worried look.

As the dawn broke through the morning skies, the two of them set out along America Street and turned onto Water Street. They walked up to the store, tracing what would have been Hessie's route to get there. They were on their way back when they saw her pink headscarf lying on the side of the pavement. Mariama reached down to pick it up and scanned the surroundings. Her fear was confirmed. She saw Hessie lying in the alleyway nearby.

Mariama and Mahaad dashed over to where she lay. They reached out to touch her, but they already knew. Hessie lay peaceful and alone, a small package of loose-leaf tea at her side. Mariana's eyes filled with tears as she looked down at her *ngor* — her big sister. For the first time since Mariama had known her, Hessie's face wore a look of surrender.

"Why, sista? Why now? Why you give up?" Mariama wailed. "Now you free. Now you really, really free."

Mariama knelt down at Hessie's shoulder and touched her face. Her once-dancing green eyes were lifeless and fixed. Her big braids were still neatly pinned in an upsweep on her head. If not for the dried blood caked on her face and neck, she would have looked peaceful.

Mariama stood up and dried her tears. Walking silently side by side, she and Mahaad went to fetch the constable and returned with him a few minutes later.

"Who does she belong to?" he asked as he stood looking down at Hessie.

"She is free, sar. She buy she from Miz Blumefield long time ago," Mariama said. "We is free too, sar. She buy we from the solic … solicitor." She struggled to get the word out.

"I need to see the papers. Where do you live?" the constable asked.

"We live 'pon America Street at Miz Hessie house," Mariama said.

"I will be there tomorrow to check the papers. Now you can go ahead and bury her."

Without another word he walked away. Mariama looked over at Mahaad.

"Me don' gat de papers," she said, terror in her eyes. "Me don' know where Hessie keep dem or if she get dem from de solicitor. We be in trouble when de constable come back. We got fuh run, Mahaad, or dey gon sell we back to backra."

CHAPTER 50

TO STABROEK WITH LOVE

October 1815

In a small Amerindian village up the Demerary River, the afternoon rain had eased as Hadali climbed into the weather-beaten dugout canoe. He glanced up at the pinkish-gold streaks of the dusky sunset. He must leave soon, he thought, to reach Stabroek in time for market the following morning.

His journey through the night on the dark-brown water with its orange tinge would last twelve hours. He lowered his eyes to observe the Demerary's gentle ebb and flow. Pockets of rich, creamy foam were building in crevices beneath overhanging corkwood trees, their sprawling, exposed roots hugging the riverbank.

Hadali checked his food and water supply one more time before launching his canoe. His produce was intact. He looked forward to paddling through the tropical forest and hearing the cacophony of wildlife that sheltered within it — crickets, bullfrogs, bats, great lumbering howler monkeys, tiny sakiwinkis, and the various night birds that called in the dark.

He pushed off from the riverbank, and the canoe slipped along the centre of the inlet, gliding past arched mangroves, far enough away from the edge to avoid the venomous labarias and bushmasters and the camoodie constrictors that lurked among the reeds. As he paddled in silence on the beautiful moonlit river, his mind wandered to more pressing matters. Now that he had decided to ask Hessie to be his wife, he began to rehearse the things he would say to her when he saw her. This was harder than he had thought it would be. It had taken him many, many moons to gather the courage to ask her to marry him. Now he worried that he wouldn't be able to find the right words. And what if she said no? Hessie was a free woman, free to make up her mind about him too. Hadali loved her strength; he wanted a strong partner who would be good in business as well as in life. Over the years he had watched Hessie, and she had shown him all these qualities. And of course she was beautiful, and other men admired her too, although he hadn't seen her take to any man over the time he had observed her. He would be happy if she chose him, and he hoped he could make her happy, if he was the lucky man. His mind was made up; he was going to ask her on this trip. He just had to figure out what to say.

In his pocket was a precious stone. Hadali had bartered for it with the pork-knockers, near his village in the Rupunini some time ago. He had given them rations of cassava bread and cassareep, and in turn they had given him this tiny, beautiful, clear precious stone. He patted his pocket now, his heart leaping as he imagined seeing the colour of Hessie's eyes reflected in it when he offered it to her. Then he would profess how much he wanted her to be a part of his life. Maybe he would say something like, "My heart has caring, admiration, and love for you, my Hessie, Queen of the Amazon. Will you be my wife?" Yes, that might do…

After many hours of quiet paddling, Hadali welcomed the dawn. Colourful orange and blue parrots, scarlet ibises, flamingos, and brilliant orange cocks-of-the-rock darted across the skies. Others perched on overhanging tree branches. Despite the pleasure he took in the exuberant display around him, he felt a perplexing undertone of sadness. As the canoe moved out of the inlet into the river mouth, the multi-coloured birds coalesced and crowded back into the mangroves. Their part of the journey was over. Hadali guided the canoe into the open river and began the final ninety-minute glide towards the small dock in Stabroek.

At the market Hadali stretched his back, stiff from paddling, and began to unpack his wares. Today he had cassareep, cassava bread, smoked fish, and cured meats. When he had arranged the goods to his satisfaction, he donned his long ceremonial coat and a new pair of brown moccasins. His hair was freshly braided, with beautiful bright green feathers woven into the ends.

Seeing two familiar figures approaching, he shaded his eyes with his hand. It was Mariama, with Mahaad following closely behind her.

Hadali grinned and held his arms wide to welcome them.

"Hello! The great spirit greets you, daughter of the Earth," he said to Mariama, and then his face fell as he saw the grim look on Mariama's face. "What is it?" he asked, his heart beginning to race.

"It's Hessie, Mr. Hadali," Mariama said softly.

"Where is…" Hadali did not finish his sentence.

"Hessie gone…" Mariama choked on her words. "Gone to she ancestors."

"What ancestors?" Hadali managed. His mouth was suddenly dry.

"Me don' know dem," Mariama answered.

Hadali looked at Mahaad, who said quietly, "She dead, she dead."

Hadali stood in place for a moment, clutching his chest and thinking this couldn't be happening, as Mariama sobbed.

The marketplace was beginning to get busy as other vendors gathered around. Hadali stepped away from the crowd and walked towards the river, blinded by tears. He heard footsteps behind him and turned to see Mariama and Mahaad following him, keeping a respectful distance. He stopped and let them catch up, and the three walked together to his canoe to talk.

"When … how?" he began, when they were away from the crowd.

Her voice breaking, Mariama told him about finding Hessie's lifeless body, and about their talk with the constable.

When she had finished, Hadali closed his eyes, his face contorted in agony.

"I must see her," he said, his voice tight.

Hessie lay where Mariama and Mahaad had moved her, in a shady spot behind the alleyway in a small ravine. Hadali knelt beside her and gently touched her face. Even in death her beauty shone through. To him, she looked as though she was asleep, and her lips were pursed with the strength of character he had seen so many times before. Her cheekbones were prominent, and her eyelashes still held their curl. She looked so peaceful. Hadali longed to see her green eyes — the eyes that would match the feathers in his braids, the ones that would reflect the brilliance of the tiny stone in his pocket.

How he wished he had told Hessie that he had fallen in love with her. He had hinted at his feelings but never found the courage to say the actual words. Now it was too late.

"Give me a moment with her. Let me be alone with her, please," Hadali pleaded, his voice breaking.

"Yes, Mr. Hadali. We wait over dere," Mariama said, pointing to a clump of trees nearby. She gently clasped Mahaad's hand and led him away from Hadali and Hessie.

Hadali leaned in closer and stroked Hessie's cheek once more.

"My beautiful Amazon Moon, today was the day I was going to tell you. Today was the day I was going to ask you, and now that time is stolen from me. I hope you know my heart. It beats for you, only you, and now it breaks. I do love you and will sorely miss you, my beautiful Hessie, oh, my beautiful Moon."

He bent his head and gently placed a soft kiss on her forehead. Wiping his eyes with the back of his hand, he stood and walked to where Mariama and Mahaad waited.

"We must help send her back to her ancestors now," he said.

"Yes, and me get some o' she favourite tings from de house and send wid she," Mariama said.

Hadali nodded and turned to Mahaad.

"Mahaad, you help me find a place with a break in the trees, so the moon can watch over her from above. It will be peaceful there." He turned back to Mariama. "Go now. We must work fast," Hadali said. "You are not safe here anymore."

Mariama set off towards the house as Hadali and Mahaad began searching for a final resting place for Hessie.

CHAPTER 51

IT IS WITHIN

October 1815

At the door of Hessie's house, Mariama paused, a lump forming in her throat. There were signs of Hessie everywhere: the coconut drops they had baked the day before, the spools of lace, folded clothing waiting to be trimmed with different widths of French lace. The house seemed empty now; the light had gone out of it.

Swallowing down her sorrow and her anger, she remembered the instructions of her maa: "To release the pain that evil brings, go to your innermost secret place to dip yourself in the deep, true healing. Tears will begin the healing. Then pause, get quiet, and embrace yourself with big, warm hugs until great peace and love come over you to help heal your broken body and spirit."

Mariama sat on the floor near the door and quieted herself. She could feel the wooden planks of the floor pressed against her legs and buttocks as her breath entered and left her body. Tears welled up in her eyes and then very gently began to flow down her cheeks. They were not angry tears but tears of release, a blessed release that brought with it the knowledge that she had come through so much violence and pain, and that these had altered her way of seeing the world but had not changed her. Her maa had told her, "You are good, you are loved," and in spite of the evil present all around her, Mariama knew that she was still a worthy person. She just needed to remember this and reconnect with the pure spirit buried deep within her soul.

Mariama wrapped her arms around herself. At first it felt awkward. She fumbled until she had swathed herself tightly in her own warmth. Wanting to fully experience her connection with her inner goodness, Mariama paid close attention. She inhaled and exhaled purposefully, each time a little bit deeper, counting her breaths.

She repeated this purposeful deep breathing, all the while embracing herself and gently rocking her body forward and backward, inhaling on the backward sway and exhaling as she leaned forward. Soon, everything in the space felt lighter and a little brighter. The tighter she hugged herself, the lighter and less troubled she felt. After a while her shoulders, arms, and chest relaxed fully, and a warm and peaceful feeling encircled her.

Mariama had found her reservoir of love and was now ready to let go of the hurt and slowly open her heart to receiving and giving love. Her maa had reassured her that she had enough love and good within to sustain herself and still share with the world, and she could feel its spark.

She noticed that in this state of mind she was no longer dwelling on all the losses she had experienced but rather was mindful of what she still possessed. She was more focused on simple things, like breathing, and smelling — though faintly — the salty odour of the Demerary River flowing nearby; like visualizing all the cheerful colours in the countryside, the flowers and birds and the teeming green presence of the natural world around her. These were some of the simple blessings that surrounded her, which she would draw upon to perform the acts of kindness her maa had proposed.

At length Mariama opened her eyes and realized that she felt calm. She had only ever experienced this kind of peace as a young girl sitting under the baobab tree in her village. She gently pulled herself up from the floor and walked into Hessie's room, where she gathered up two white, lace-trimmed sheets. She bundled them up and then selected a smaller sheet, and finally a large jug of water and a small knife. With a quick glance behind her, she quietly closed the door to Hessie's house and walked back through the streets to meet Hadali and Mahaad. As she walked, thoughts of the good deeds she was going to perform filled her mind.

At the alleyway she paused and looked around to ensure that no one was in sight before quickly disappearing down the tiny path that led to an alcove near a small pond where Hadali and Mahaad were waiting. There was a mound of earth beside a freshly dug hole.

Almost reverently, the two men moved away to allow Mariama to prepare the body. She knelt beside Hessie and opened her bundle. Lovingly she washed Hessie's feet and face and wrapped her body in the two sheets. Using the smaller sheet, she created a lace-trimmed bonnet around Hessie's head.

"You look fine, Hessie, real fine," Mariama whispered. "Now me must send you with some ration — some of Mr. Hadali cassava bread, some sugar, and some good rum fuh you journey home to you ancestors. Tek it and go safe." Mariama set the items to the right and left of Hessie's arms, then she rose up and walked over to where Hadali and Mahaad waited.

As soon as the sun had set, the three of them lowered Hessie's body along with her care packages into the ground. Then, standing together, they said their farewells.

"Goodbye, Hessie. Me thank you fuh set me free," said Mahaad.

"Goodbye, me sista, me beautiful, brave friend," said Mariama, her voice unfaltering.

Hadali gazed for a long moment at the earth that now covered Hessie's body. Then he began to speak, his voice clear and steady: "You are in the air and the water and in the moon and in the sun. You are now everywhere. Farewell, Hessie, my moonbeam over the Amazon," he said solemnly and then turned and walked away.

Mariama and Mahaad covered the grave with leaves and branches and a few wild flowers. Then, reaching for each other's hand, they too walked away.

Hadali was waiting for them by the road.

"We must hurry," he said. "You have everything you need, Mariama?"

"Yes," Mariama said.

She looked at Mahaad and then glanced questioningly back at Hadali.

"Yes, Mahaad can come too," Hadali said, "but we must hurry. We run from the law now. Every minute counts."

Mariama and Mahaad hurried back to Hessie's house to collect a few belongings and Hadali went down to the water to prepare his boat. They agreed to meet at the dock in half an hour.

At the waterfront, Mahaad eyed the canoe uneasily.

"We all gon' fit?" he asked.

"Yes, we'll be fine," Hadali answered. Then he glanced questioningly at Mariama's small bundle.

"Is me fine tings Hessie mek fuh me. Me tek dem wid me. Dey ain't gon tek much space, Mr. Hadali. Me mus' tek dem. Dey 'mind me o' she," Mariama pleaded.

"It's fine," Hadali said.

He had already placed his unsold inventory back in his canoe, and now he helped Mariama and Mahaad settle in among the wares.

"Mahaad, you sit in the middle, and Mariama, you sit close to him. It will keep the weight balanced so we won't tip."

With his two passengers secured, Hadali climbed in, pushed the boat off and slowly steered the canoe out into the dark, slick waters of the Demerary.

CHAPTER 52

WHAT NOW?

October 1815 – August 1816

As the canoe edged into the current, Mariama thought back to that first voyage she had taken, so very long ago, and the horrors she had seen and experienced then. She was still hurting from the recent loss of Hessie, but right now she needed to focus on survival. She didn't know where they were headed, but she trusted Hadali.

Suddenly Hadali stopped paddling and leaned forward.

"Lie down and take cover under the tarp. I will tell you when to get up," he whispered urgently, pointing towards the middle of the boat.

Mariama and Mahaad did as they were told. Hadali slowly resumed paddling, trying not to draw attention to himself or his hidden cargo. The gentle lapping of the water against the sides of the canoe lulled Mariama into a quiet comfort. She was relieved to be leaving Stabroek and the fear of losing their freedom again behind. She looked over at Mahaad, beside her, and wondered what he was thinking. He hadn't said much since their journey had begun.

Huddled among the sacks of produce, Mahaad was having similar thoughts. Like Mariama, he was sure he didn't want to be owned by any backra again. He wondered also if Mariama had noticed the times he had touched her. He thought about her quiet and thoughtful manners and how she looked out for people she loved, like her brother, her son, and Hessie. And now she was looking after him, too. She didn't have to ask Hadali to bring him along, but she had. He wondered if she cared for him. He hoped she did.

Hadali's whisper interrupted their thoughts: "You can relax now and sit up." His voice was sad but more assured than earlier in the day. "This part of the river is safe. We will travel for one more hour and then take a tributary to the right. It will take us about five more hours to get to the hideout. You can stay in the little village there as long as you like. When we get there, don't tell anyone where you've come from. If anyone asks, just answer 'from upriver.' It is all you need to say."

Mariama listened intently and stole a look at Mahaad. He reached over and gave Mariama's hand a squeeze. She immediately felt her shoulders relax and returned the gesture.

Mariama felt safe with Mahaad. Whenever he was around, a joyousness enveloped her, and she missed him when he was absent. She recalled how Hessie had told her that he was a good man and could one day make her a fine husband. But thinking of Hessie brought back a wave of sadness. With her other arm, she squeezed the small bundle she had brought with her. Most of the things in it had either been owned by Hessie or had been given to Mariama by her sister-friend. As she sat, one hand on the small bundle and the other in Mahaad's, tears slid down her cheeks. She held tightly to his hand and grasped the parcel more firmly, afraid of losing these precious links to people — one living, one dead — who loved and supported her. Mahaad moved closer to Mariama and gently wiped away her tears with his free hand. Then he softly kissed her on her right cheek, and she rested her head on his shoulder.

Hadali watched quietly from the back of the canoe, ambivalence creeping over him. He was happy for them but sad for himself. How he longed to be with Hessie and touch her once more. The pressure on his eyeballs grew as tears gathered in his tired brown eyes. He brushed a hand across his cheek and paddled harder, hastening the canoe away from the pain he wished to leave behind.

As the canoe traversed the quiet glassy inlet of the Demerary, Mahaad saw the mottled body of a labaria sunning itself under a corkwood tree on the riverbank. Not long ago Braima had taught him that this serpent's strike was precise and deadly. Mahaad pursed his lips and gently snuggled up to Mariama. She had fallen soundly asleep against his shoulder.

The two of them remained nestled together as the canoe slipped across the dark waters. Even the crickets and howler monkeys were quiet that night. The odd bat darted from overhanging bushy trees. The moon was hidden behind clouds, and the sky was as gloomy as the mood in the canoe.

Several hours later Hadali beached the canoe so they could rest and have food and water. Mariama awoke and she and Mahaad helped pull the boat onto the riverbank. Hadali shared his cassava bread, maize, and strips of dried labba meat with his guests. They drank from a clear stream near a large tamarind tree.

When they finished eating, Mariama dug in her bundle and held out a small blue package to Hadali. Tiny sparks of excitement filled her body and caused her hands to shake.

"Dis fuh you, Mr. Hadali," she whispered.

Hadali looked at her questioningly.

"What is it?"

"It belong to Hessie," said Mariama, her hand still outstretched. "Now it belong to you."

Slowly Hadali reached out and took the package. He opened it carefully. Then his eyes widened. Arrayed on the blue cloth were silver coins, shilling pieces and pound sterling notes. "I can't … I can't take it," he murmured. "I can't, Mariama. It's too much."

"Tek it, Mr. Hadali," Mariama insisted. "I know she want you to tek it. I got some for me and Mahaad. Now dis fuh you."

Hadali continued to stare.

"Where did Hessie get so much money?"

Mariama ignored his question. "Me got one more ting for you, Mr. Hadali."

She reached back into her bundle and gently pulled out a white lace-trimmed handkerchief. It was one of Hessie's most recent creations.

"Hessie mek dis fuh you," Mariama said with a shy smile. "She was gon give you when you come dis trip. Sometin' special inside fuh you, Mr. Hadali. Open it."

As Mariama watched, Hadali opened the beautiful cotton handkerchief and let out a gasp. Curled up inside was a lock of Hessie's spirally, shiny hair. Overcome, he ran his fingers along its thick wavy coils.

"Now you always got Hessie wid you, Mr. Hadali," Mariama said shyly. She was pleased to see the look on Hadali's face.

"Oh, Mariama, this is even better than the money," Hadali said, his voice thick with tears. "It's a piece of my Hessie that I will keep with me. I will wear it close to me, and she will be with me always. You have done a good deed and given me back some of the joy I lost yesterday. Thank you for this wonderful gift."

As he paddled, he continued to observe the two lovebirds. In the midst of his sadness, the thought of Hessie's precious memento brought Hadali comfort.

Rising to his feet, he said, "Mahaad, come with me. Help me gather some wild plums." He held out a hand to Mahaad. "Mariama, you stay with the boat and the supplies. We come back very soon," Hadali added as he and Mahaad disappeared into the bushes.

As soon as they were out of her sight, Hadali stopped and looked at Mahaad.

"I see you look at Mariama with caring. Do you feel love for her?" he asked.

Mahaad blushed. "Yes. When me with Mariama, me heart sing, just like de yella kiskadee in de tree. Me, Mahaad of Dar Banda, very happy fuh Mari fuh be me wife."

"Why don't you tell her how you feel?"

"Me have no gifs fuh Mari. Me have no bride price, you see, Mr. Hadali. In Dar Banda de man mus' give gifs to de fadda o' de woman he want — me gat no gifs fuh she or she fadda, even doh me know he gone back to de ancestor."

Hadali smiled and reached into his coat pocket. He withdrew his hand and offered Mahaad a tiny packet. It was so small that Mahaad had to peer into Hadali's hand to see it.

"This is a gift that you can give to her. It was to be my gift to Hessie when I asked her to be my wife. As you know, that chance was taken from me.

"Here," he said, pressing it into Mahaad's hand and closing the young man's fingers around it. "You take it and use it. Give it to Mariama and ask her the question. I think she might say yes."

Mahaad opened his hand and gasped. In his palm was the most beautiful stone he had ever seen. As a boy, Mahaad had seen a similar stone in the ring worn by a village chief. This stone was slightly larger and brighter. Mahaad gazed at Hadali with disbelief.

"You give me..." Mahaad's voice cracked. "You give Mahaad dis gif, Mr. Hadali? You good man."

"You should ask her now," said Hadali, smiling broadly. "Go ahead — ask her." He gave Mahaad a little push in the centre of his back to start him walking. Hadali drew his tense shoulders up and the two men walked back to where Mariama was sitting. Mahaad's heart raced as he wiped small beads of sweat from his shiny sunbeaten forehead. Suddenly he froze.

Hadali gave him another gentle nudge, and Mahaad raised his chin and walked over to Mariama. He sat down next to her and reached for her hand. Then, before he could lose his nerve, he blurted out: "Me ... Mahaad like — love Mariama. Can Mariama be Mahaad ... be me wife?"

Mariama smiled, squeezed his hand and nodded.

Mahaad threw his arms around her. Then, he leapt into the air like a little boy. "She say yes! Mari say yes!" He danced crazily around in the path, all the while clutching Hadali's stone in his palm.

"Give the gift to her. Give it to her!" Hadali shouted, helpless with laughter.

He stepped over to Mahaad and tried to open his hand, but Mahaad grabbed him by the arms and swung him around. Mariama smiled as she watched the two men, and just for a moment she was transported back to happier times in her village when she had sat with her back against a tree watching a celebratory dance.

Mahaad ran over to Mariama now, knelt at her feet and offered her the precious stone.

"It fuh me wife," he sang. "It fuh me wife."

Her mouth agape, Mariama gawked at Mahaad, then at Hadali and then back at the stone.

"Where you get dis? Oh, Mahaad, it beau … tiful," she whispered.

"Tek it and keep it. It's you own now," he said.

Then he ran into the bush and came back with a broken branch, which he threw on the path just ahead of them. He grabbed Mariama's hand, pulled her up on her feet and whispered something in her ear.

Mariama smiled at him, ran over to the boat, lifted Khadi's cowrie shells and glass bead necklace from her small bundle and placed them around her neck. Then she came back to join Mahaad. With a big grin, she nudged him and together they jumped over the branch — a sign of jumping over the sorrows of the past and into the beginning of their new life together. They both laughed out loud, and Mahaad planted a kiss on Mariama's lips. She giggled some more.

"And now we is married," Mahaad announced and kissed her again.

Hadali came forward and put his arms around the shoulders of the newlyweds.

"Come now," he said warmly, "we must get you two to a safe place to start your new life. Out of respect, I must quickly discuss your arrival with Onuk, our village leader. Stay here until I return with his approval for you to join us."

Hadali disappeared into the bushes and Mariama and Mahaad held hands and waited. A few minutes later, he emerged from the reeds, walked several steps along the path, raised his fingers to his lips and let out a piercing whistle. Mahaad and Mariama observed uneasily.

"Don't be scared. My people live inland," Hadali said calmly.

There was a rustling sound. Suddenly the bushes parted and the clearing began to fill with people. Some greeted Hadali, and others observed the strangers in his company. There were men and women, young and old, children and babies.

When everyone had gathered, Hadali placed his arms around Mahaad's and Mariama's shoulders once more. "They are friends to me," he said to the group, "good friends. Take care of them, and let them join the community."

Mariama looked shyly around at the people in the clearing. Most of them had Hadali's complexion. Some of them were of mixed race, and others had darker, glossy skin like her. She immediately felt at home.

Hadali squeezed their shoulders once more and then strode to the canoe. There he gathered some of the food supplies and the small bundle that Mariama had brought with her.

"You will be safe here," Hadali said as he handed the items over to them both. "Be happy. I will return to see you sometimes." Then he waved goodbye, launched his canoe and left.

Mariama and Mahaad followed Onuk and the villagers towards their new home. There was just over a hundred members, a blend of Indigenous and African peoples. They walked along a beautiful sun-dappled winding path, overhung by lush, shady trees. Out of the corner of her eyes she saw something that looked vaguely familiar. A partially wilted white flower with crusted brown edges lay at the periphery of the path, its stamens limp, deprived of lifegiving water. Mariama paused and gazed first at the trunk, its girth and smoothness, of the young baobab tree nearby. A sudden warmth and a slow smile spread over her face. She had not seen a baobab in Demerara before. The path continued down into a hollow, and tucked away on the other side of the moss-covered rocks was a neatly manicured village of small mud-daubed huts with thatched roofs, similar to the ones in Mariama's village back in Yele. For a brief moment she was catapulted back in time. She half-expected to hear drums and see merriment in the clearing. Instead, the rest of the villagers carried on with their activities, pausing only momentarily to observe the newcomers.

Onuk led them to a hut and told them it was to be their own. It was simple, but somehow it felt like home.

**

Before long, Mariama became absorbed into the life of the village and participated in every aspect of its daily activities. Her favourite chore was looking after the children and teaching them to count and add. Mahaad joined in the men's activities — farming, fishing, hunting, and taking care of the compound. Both he and Mariama felt strangely connected now to their new home, a part of something bigger than themselves. They had found the village life they had left behind so many years ago.

One year later Mariama and Mahaad welcomed twins into their family. First came their daughter, Khadija, (who Mariama nicknamed Freedom). Right behind Freedom came their son, Kamal.

EPILOGUE

July 2018

"See girls, at eighty years old, I can still bend down and touch my toes." Queen Livingston was in great shape and showed off her fitness. She was tall and slim and had taken good care of herself over the years.

"Wow, Auntie Q, you're pretty good you know. I'm turning sixty, and I can't do that without falling flat on my face." Her niece Cynthia beamed as she praised the family matriarch.

A young woman entered the door of the church basement. With her palm over her heart, she smilingly and almost rhythmically announced, "Greetings cousins, one and all."

Queen looked up, returned the heart gesture and beckoned her over.

"Come over here and tell me … whose child are you?"

"I am Olivia, and my parents are Wendell O. and Wauneta Livingston. There are sixteen of us Livingston children from three mothers. We're scattered around the world: some in England, Barbados, across the U.S. — from New York to California — and some right here in Canada. I am number twelve and the only one in Quebec. We're a very diverse and mostly successful brood, but some of us have never met!"

"Wow, Wendell was a busy man in his youth, wasn't he?" Queen chuckled with a twinkle in her deep brown eyes. "But," she continued, her voice gaining volume so that heads turned in her direction, "you know, there is something serious here that I want all of you to know because it's important, so listen. For centuries our Mende ancestors in Africa had many, many children and men often had more than one wife. Yes, it's true! The Mende loved children because they were precious and brought joy and wealth to life. Then the bad times came and many of us were dragged across the ocean into the hell of slavery and we stopped having children. Yes, we stopped because we could not bring them into a life without hope and freedom. The bad, bad times ended and we were freed, but into hardship. Still, things were better and we began to have babies again! Imagine, Uncle Cedric from Pomeroon had twenty-two children with three women, and his two brothers William and Geronimo, or Gerry as he is known, each had sixteen and eighteen. Many of their children farm or work the Guyana hinterland. So your father is in good company, Olivia. My grandmother used to say 'children are a blessing.' And she was so right. We are a blessed family and have regained what was once taken from us."

The door swung open again and seven people entered amidst chatter, laughter, and hugs.

"Look who just walked in — it's Stella and her tribe. Come girl. Come give your old great aunt a hug." Queen held her arms opened jubilantly.

Stella Tait gave the same greeting that her cousin Olivia had earlier, and Queen reciprocated, smiling all the while.

"Auntie Queen, you do look well. It is wonderful to see everybody. I bring greetings from everyone in Georgetown, Linden, West Demerara, and Essequibo. Let me look at you; you haven't aged a bit since I saw you last." Stella hugged her aunt enthusiastically amid giggles.

"Well girl, as they say in Guyana, *if yuh plant plantain yuh can't reap cassava*, or as you young people would say, 'you reap what you sow.' I've always taken good care of myself. I eat right and keep active, but most of all I put God first, I don't hold grudges, and I'm grateful for every day. It's nice that the results are evident." Queen threw her head back and laughed loudly. She was in great spirits. She delighted in seeing the multitude of generations congregate for these important festivities.

"How are your parents, Clothilde and Emmet? Did they come with you?"

"No, they didn't, and here's why: *Yuh can't drink mauby and belch beer,*" Stella replied with a grin. She loved playing the Guyanese proverbs game with her great aunt. "They're not like you; they got lots of aches and pains, so they've cut back on travel. In fact they aren't doing much these days, except going to church," she added, glancing over her right shoulder.

Everything was nicely laid out for the *Meet and Greet.* The drink choices at the bar ranged from mauby, guava, and sorrel fruit drinks to Eldorado, 25 year old aged rum, to accommodate multiple tastes. A small table to the left of the bar held glass dishes with inch-sized pieces of savoury blood pudding and zesty mango achar, next to a tray of pickled onions held together with cubed gouda cheese. It was the perfect accompaniment — what Auntie Q always called a "cutter" — for the alcohol service.

On the other side of the room, three-foot-long rectangular tables draped in the colours of *The Golden Arrowhead* held up to three dozen warming trays of decadent deliciousness. Fare included rice and pigeon peas with stew beef in a spicy, garlicky, brown sauce; four-cheese creamy macaroni and cheese pies; cook-up rice with salt beef and pig tails boiled in coconut milk, seasoned with thyme, onions, bouillon, and sprinkled with wiri wiri for the perfect pop of heat. Chicken chow mein, colourfully accentuated with corn, sweet peas, shredded green cabbage, and lots of scallion topped off the main dishes.

The dessert table was simple, except for the velvety smooth, rich, dark, and buttery rum cake covered in blue and white royal icing, the outline of a lush green baobab tree in its centre. The colours of the cake decoration mimicked those of the Sierra Leone national colours. It was a great feast displayed for the first night of three days of festivities.

Young Sanatha Livingston sat in a corner of the room and observed the throngs of people and the joyful revelry around her. She bundled the black reunion T-shirt and the colourful celebration program into a nylon gold-coloured bag. Name tags complete, she waited for folks to wander over to the reception table. One hundred and twenty people had signed up and paid to attend.

I am glad I don't have to remember them all, she thought, as she scanned each new face bursting with excitement that entered the room.

"Go over to Cynthia and get your package. The weekend program is full — I hope you all enjoy what we have planned." Auntie Queen announced in all her splendour.

The room designed to accommodate one hundred was full, but the door kept on swinging open. Having reached capacity, people were spilling into the choir room.

"We might have to move up to the sanctuary, if it continues like this." Cynthia snickered as she watched another swarm of people enter, and their voices rise in a joyful cacophony.

"Well, Auntie Queen, it is said that *when Mumma dead, family done*. This family ain't done yet; in fact they are just beginning to connect. We had better get started." Cynthia was conscious of the time. She had checked her cell phone a few times to ensure that she had not missed a text message from anyone having difficulty finding the church.

Auntie Queen took to the platform at the front of the room, microphone in hand. She cleared her throat and began to speak.

"Welcome my dear family to the first Livingston/Tait/Carter Family Reunion here in beautiful Waldorf, Ontario, Canada. I am extremely honoured to be matriarch of this family and living up to my name, Queen. I am grateful for this day. There are one hundred and twenty of us in this place — all limbs or branches of the same tree. Take a moment to locate yourself on the family tree on the far wall, and place a little gold star next to your name.

Each and every one of you is special because you come from goodness. What do I mean by that, you ask? Well, there's an old Guyanese proverb that states *Good gubby nah ah float ah top.* The interpretation is that goodness isn't always easily found on the surface. One must go deep within to find it. For you young ones noticing the hand on heart gesture made by the older members of the family, know that is a reminder that our goodness lies within. It's a birthright handed down from an ancestor, a message that each of us need to know to help to take care of ourselves and each other. Another Guyanese proverb says *wha' hurt eye does mek nose run water.* Now the interpretation of this one is, 'when one member of the family is hurt all others feel it.'

"So in a nutshell, I need you all to cherish your goodness, remembering that it lies deep within, and always, always take care of each other. Never, ever believe you can walk this road called life alone; we all need each other.

"Do take this opportunity to connect and remain a part of each other's lives. And, for the naysayers who think differently, I will leave you with one last proverb: *Nah every big head get sense.* This one might be self-explanatory, but I will give you the interpretation anyway. It means that a person might have a big head, but it doesn't mean that he or she is necessarily brainy or smart. So, be smart, take my advice, and enjoy this time together."

She placed her palm over her heart, then gestured an extension of that goodness with an open palm to the crowd. They responded in kind. She then left the platform and continued to mingle with the crowds.

Thirteen-year-old Sanatha had listened intently to the welcome greeting from her great, great aunt Queen. She watched her socialize with the people in the room. As soon as she returned to the back of the room, Sanatha walked over to her and asked, "Auntie Queen, would you explain what you meant by we come from goodness that is deep inside? And who is the ancestor that gave us this birthright?"

Queen was pleased that Sanatha had asked these questions. She smiled and offered the story, the way it had been told to her. "Well," she said. "Just over two hundred years ago, in the village of Yele, in the southern province of Sierra Leone, a young girl your age named Mariama was kidnapped on her thirteenth birthday. She is the ancestor I referred to in my greeting. Here is the story of her life, which is also a part of the story of our family."

CPSIA information can be obtained
at www.ICGtesting.com
Printed in the USA
LVHW090759280821
696342LV00005B/412